EARTH CRY

BOOK 2 IN THE EARTH SONG SERIES

NICK COOK

ABOUT THE AUTHOR

Somewhere back in the mists of time, Nick was born in the great sprawling metropolis of London. He grew up in a family where art was always a huge influence. Tapping into this, Nick finished college with a fine art degree tucked into his back pocket. Faced with the prospect of actually trying to make a living from his talents, he plunged into the emerging video game industry back in the eighties. It was the start of a long career and he produced graphics for many of the top-selling games on the early home computers, including *Aliens* and *Enduro Racer*. Those pioneering games may look crude now, but back then they were considered to be cutting edge. As the industry exploded into the one we know today, Nick's career went supernova. He worked on titles such as *X-Com*, and set up two studios, which produced

Warzone 2100 and the *Conflict: Desert Storm* series. He has around forty published titles to his name.

As great as the video game industry is, a little voice kept nagging inside Nick's head, and at the end of 2006 he was finally ready to pursue his other passion as a full-time career: writing. Many years later, he completed his first trilogy, *Cloud Riders*. And the rest, as they say, is history.

Nick has many interests, from space exploration and astronomy to travelling the world. He has flown light aircraft and microlights, an experience he used as research for *Cloud Riders*. He's always loved to cook, but then you'd expect it with his surname. His writing in many ways reflects his own curiosity about the world around him. He loves to let his imagination run riot to pose the question: *What if?*

ALSO BY NICK COOK

Prequel to the Multiverse Chronicles

The Earth Song Series (The Multiverse Chronicles)

The Fractured Light Trilogy (The Multiverse Chronicles)

In memory of Tommy Donbavand, a wonderful author, friend and a true inspiration to me and so many others.

CHAPTER ONE

MY LIFE WAS MADE up of a tapestry of memories, yet some shone far brighter than others. Like when my Aunt Lucy had taken me on a surprise holiday to Disney World Florida. We'd ridden a simulator, sitting on a hydraulic rig that moved according to the action happening on the huge IMAX screen in front of us. I could so clearly remember how we'd followed the flight of a bird as it had soared through the air, pitching in our seats. Every moment had thrilled me. It had felt like the closest thing to flying – certainly every journey in passenger jets had paled in comparison. Until now. That magical experience was being totally eclipsed by what I was experiencing in this XA101.

I sat with Jack, Mike and Tom in this experimental electric-powered stealth aircraft owned by Sky Dreamer Corp. It wasn't the almost silent propulsion system that made this trip so exceptional, although that was impressive in its own right.

A moment ago, a very calming view of a sunset had filled the screens mounted into the cockpit walls of the XA101 – the computer equivalent of a screensaver. That serene view had been negated over the last thirty minutes by the booming crackle of thunder outside the craft and turbulence that bounced us around in our seats like stones in a can.

Then Tom had said, 'Delphi, show live external view,' to the XA101's AI system and our cosy cabin had been instantly transformed.

Now Jack, Mike and I stared around us, slack-jawed at the almost seamless 360-degree view of the towering thunderstorm we were flying within. My mind scrambled to absorb the almost perfect illusion of our seats hanging in mid-air as the towering clouds slipped past, lit by internal flashes of sheet lightning. I had to fight the temptation to squeal like I'd done as a ten-year-old on that Disney ride all those years ago. This really did feel as if I was flying like a bird.

In contrast to my elation, Mike had paled and squeezed his eyes shut as he clutched a sick bag to his mouth. It was his third one since we'd fled Orkney.

It had been a long trip. The Learjet we'd left Scotland in had deposited us ten hours later at some secret runway in a desert in searing heat. From there we'd boarded this second XA101 – to wherever it was we were going.

Mike groaned. 'You could have bloody warned us before you toggled the outside view on, Tom.'

'Sorry, I didn't mean to upset you,' Tom replied.

'Maybe you should blank the walls again for Mike's sake,' I said.

'But he's got his eyes shut now anyway,' Jack said. 'And this is all pretty neat. Besides, if we get torn apart by the storm, I'd rather see my end coming.'

'You're so not helping me here, mate,' Mike muttered.

'There's really nothing to worry about,' Tom replied. 'This craft is made of Kevlar and carbon fibre – combined with some incredibly strong experimental alloys. An XA101 can take a whole lot more than this storm.'

The muscles in Mike's face cabled as he clenched his jaw together even harder. 'Right...'

I sat forward in my seat towards Mike opposite me. 'Keep your eyes closed and try breathing into your bag. That should help a bit.'

Mike screwed his eyes tighter and his sick bag started to inflate and deflate as he breathed into it.

'I'm sorry that you're suffering, Mike,' I added, 'but I wish Tom had turned on the external cameras before now. This is seriously epic.'

'That would have been impossible, I'm afraid,' Tom replied. 'I'm only allowed to turn on the external view since we are so near to our destination – all part of the security systems.'

'Why's that?' Jack asked.

'Even I'm not allowed to know the exact location of this Sky Dreamer secret facility.'

'Why Sky Dreamer Corp's paranoia?' I asked.

'It carries out critical research and if the Overseers ever learnt of this facility, it would make life exceptionally difficult for everyone concerned. Plus, what you don't know can't be tortured out of you.'

And there it was again: yet another reality check of this crazy-serious situation. I'd managed to drop not only myself into this, but also Jack Harper, an archaeologist and former military trauma surgeon, and Mike Palmer, geologist and theoretical physicist.

The XA101 shook again with another rattle of turbulence.

I noticed the beads of sweat blossoming on Mike's forehead. With the scent of body odour mixed into the lovely hint of sick floating around the cabin, I made a mental note to bring some air freshener the next time we flew together.

I leant forward and patted Mike's arm. 'Hang in there.'

'Doing my best.'

Tom tipped his head towards the ceiling. 'Delphi, turn on HUD instrumentation.'

Instantly the forward section of the cabin displayed flight-instrumentation graphics over the images of the storm clouds rolling past us.

'Oh, that's neat,' Jack said.

I quickly took in all the new information in front of me. We were currently travelling at an altitude of 20,000 feet with 'four miles to target' counting down on the display.

'Aha,' Jack said, pointing at what should have been the floor of cockpit but was instead the images of clouds. Through the gaps in the storm I saw glimpses of a jungle landscape far below.

'So wherever the secret destination is,' I said, 'it has to be somewhere tropical – near the equator?'

'Yes, but that's as much as I know,' Tom replied. 'Let's not speculate any further.'

A chime came from a hidden speaker and Delphi's synthesised female voice rang out. 'Attention, severe turbulence ahead.' Tom had selected her calming tones in preference to the male version we'd had earlier in the flight, thinking it would help Mike to relax.

'Prepare for engagement of safety restraints,' Delphi said.

Before I could ask what that meant, a metal hoop rose from the back of our seats, curving over our shoulders and clamping us into our seats like harnesses for an extreme rollercoaster.

Mike's eyes snapped open as he took in what had grabbed him, then widened at the view still around us. 'Shit!' He squeezed his eyes shut again.

'No need for concern, everyone,' Tom said. 'Just relax and let the XA101 take the strain. It was built to handle this sort of thing in its stride.'

Jack leant towards me. 'But what about us humans, hey?' he whispered.

'Damn you, I heard that,' Mike said.

'Sorry, buddy,' Jack replied, winking at me.

A huge fist of wind slapped the XA101 and we bucked in the sky.

It was just as well Mike didn't have his eyes open. Despite his reassuring words, for the first time Tom looked concerned too.

'OK, everyone, as the weather is so severe, we'll have to make a very rapid descent,' he said. 'Delphi, engage Zeta approach pattern.'

'Affirmative,' the craft's AI replied.

On the cockpit screens either side of us, the wings of the craft started to rotate to a forty-five-degree angle. The nose of the XA101 immediately dropped and we began to descend fast, rushing towards an opening in the clouds. As we streaked through the gap, the cabin vibrated and shook us within our harnesses as the airframe creaked and groaned around us.

'Is this too late to become religious?' Mike said through his clenched jaw.

'It's never too late,' Jack replied.

'Two miles to target,' Delphi announced as we dropped like a meteorite towards the jungle.

'Shouldn't you take the controls or something, Tom?' I asked.

'Trust me, the AI running this craft reacts at least four times faster than the best pilot could manage in these difficult conditions.'

'So trust the damned programme with our lives?' Jack asked.

'Uh-huh,' Tom replied with a forced smile.

The thunder clouds blazed over our heads as rain swirled past, drumming on the outside of the XA101 like thousands of ball bearings. Beneath us an endless tree-green expanse became visible and a green rectangular box appeared on the front screen that framed an area of the jungle canopy.

'What does that green indicator mean?' I asked.

'That's our destination marker – not long to go now,' Tom replied.

'But there's nothing there except trees,' Jack said.

Tom raised his eyebrows at him. 'Wouldn't that be embarrassing if I'd managed to programme the wrong destination and we were about to become a smouldering crater in the ground?'

'Seriously not helping now,' Mike said, his eyes still closed.

A bolt of lightning lanced down from the clouds, striking a tree that towered over its neighbours. It burst instantly into flames.

'Thunder and lightning, very, very frightening,' Jack sang badly to the tune of the old Queen song.

'Bastard,' Mike muttered.

The sheets of rain thickened for a moment, obscuring the view. We heard the electric motors whining for the first time as the cockpit shuddered violently and the nose tipped almost vertically towards the ground. The rectangular destination marker was now almost the size of the front screen, yet still filled with nothing but jungle.

Jack traded a frown with me and I had to resist the urge to grab his hand.

Tom caught our expressions. 'Trust the tech.'

'Fuck that,' Mike said, grinding his words out between clenched teeth.

The XA101 rocketed down, raindrops streaming past the external cameras that fed the view.

'Altitude two thousand feet,' Delphi said with an infuriating calmness.

The wings pivoted again until they pointed straight up from the main fuselage, the motors screaming as hurricane-force winds buffeted the craft.

'Altitude one thousand feet...'

Slowly, way too slowly it seemed to me, the nose of the

XA101 started to rise and at last the velocity of our aircraft began to drop, yet the jungle was still rushing up to meet us.

'Altitude five hundred feet...'

'Oh crap,' Jack whispered.

And then it happened. We hit the tree canopy and branches whipped past the cockpit. My stomach rose to my throat, bile bitter in the back of my mouth.

'Fuck!' Mike shouted as his eyes sprang open and he stared at what was happening around us. His hands clawed at the seat arms so hard I was surprised he didn't break them right off.

But then the branches disappeared.

'Altitude two hundred feet...' the computer voice said.

'Just how tall are these damned trees?' Jack said.

Tom gave us a ridiculously calm look.

I glanced down and saw a gaping hole of nothingness below. We dropped inside and the lights on the nose of the XA101 turned on.

Jack, Mike and I stared at the strata of rock sliding past the virtual surroundings.

'We're in some sort of tunnel, Tom?' I asked.

He smiled at me. 'Absolutely. I did promise you that we weren't going to crash.'

'You could have bloody well explained yourself a bit better,' Mike replied as he wiped fresh vomit from the corner of his mouth.

'Yes, sorry, maybe I should have. It's certainly quite the rush the first time you are introduced to Eden.'

'Eden?' I asked.

'Oh, you'll see it for yourselves shortly.' Tom smiled. 'Then you'll understand the choice of name.'

The sound of the storm muted as we descended into the vertical shaft. On the HUD of the XA101 our air speed fell to ten knots and then five.

We dropped out of the tunnel into a large dark cavern and the XA101's light beams skimmed over the walls. A moment later dozens of huge spotlights blazed into life from the rocky ceiling and the view was transformed.

We were in a natural cavern at least a hundred metres wide with no other obvious tunnels leading out of it apart from the shaft down which we'd descended. Beneath us was an aqua-blue lake ringed by a narrow shoreline that sloped up to meet the walls.

Mike's eyes widened. 'This is a sinkhole, right?'

'Indeed it is,' Tom replied. 'Natural erosion formed this cavern from the rainfall that has seeped through the ground.'

Two large white round cylinders started to descend from the belly of the XA101.

'Floats,' Tom said, answering the silent questions in our eyes. 'Among the XA101's many other remarkable capabilities, it's also an amphibious craft.'

'Is there anything this ship can't do?' Jack asked.

'Not much, although a coffee machine would be nice.'

With a soft whine the XA101 settled on to the surface of the lake, sending out gentle ripples over the mirrored surface. Its stubby wings rotated in opposite directions, turning the XA101 on the spot. Then the wings returned to level, engines pointing forward, and the aircraft surged gently towards the shore.

My mind was still scrambling to process what I'd thought was us plummeting to our deaths, together with this new surreal experience, when we stepped out through the open cockpit door on to the rocky shore. Directly overhead, I could see a framed round view of the jungle canopy high overhead through the shaft above. Flashes of lightning illuminated the brooding storm sky.

'Home, sweet home,' Tom said.

'This is Eden?' I asked, looking around at the otherwise empty cavern.

'Not quite – but soon,' Tom replied.

He stepped forward and placed his hand on a slightly extruding lump on the wall. A faint red glowed beneath his palm from the rock.

'Agent Tom Hester identified,' a female synthesised voice said, echoing around the chamber like some sort of omnipotent AI god.

Tom took a half step back as a gentle vibration passed through the chamber, sending further ripples across the surface of the lake. And then a whole section of the rock face before us started to slide upwards to reveal a huge highly polished steel door. It looked like something straight out of a bank vault. Massive clamps holding it closed hissed open and the door swung out towards us.

Jack, Mike and I gawped at the brightly lit corridor sloping down the other side of it.

'This is like a Bond villain's lair,' I said.

'Oh, it's quite the opposite,' Tom replied. 'Let's just say that when one of the world's richest corporations creates a special project with a visionary leader at the helm, it goes all in. So if you'd like to please follow me.'

I traded *what the hell* looks with the others as we followed Tom into the sloping corridor. We'd only taken a few steps when a loud noise came from behind us. I turned to see the vault-like door swing shut with the unmistakable hiss of a vacuum, making my ears pop.

'Now be prepared to have your minds well and truly blown,' Tom said with a grin.

CHAPTER TWO

AFTER A GOOD FIVE minutes of walking, our boots squeaking over the polished white stone floor, we reached a door – though not your common office variety, more like the sort pressurised door that you would find on a submarine.

'Is this some sort of bunker complex, Tom?' Jack asked, voicing what the three of us were no doubt thinking.

'If by bunker you mean somewhere that could resist a direct nuclear strike overhead, an earthquake or any other sort of natural disaster, then yes, that's a pretty accurate description.'

'And what's so important down here it needs this level of protection?' I asked.

'For now all I'll say is that the work going on here will one day hopefully save humanity from its own destructive tendencies.'

'What's that meant to mean?' Mike asked.

'I promise you will have all the answers you will need and more soon enough – just have a bit more patience. And I really don't want to spoil the big reveal.' Tom waved his hand over a metal pad mounted to one side of the door. With a series of clanks, locking bolts disengaged from the frame and the door swung outwards with a hiss of air.

I gestured to the pad he hadn't actually touched. 'How did you just unlock this door?'

'The doors in Eden use a number of biometric measures, and this one can only be opened if triggered by a special ID chip – placed beneath the skin of my palm.'

'Bloody hell, that's all very cyborg,' Mike said.

'Maybe. However, it's a secure and convenient form of security, which is the key thing,' Tom replied. 'Anyway...' He gestured for us to step through into the circular room beyond the doorway.

As soon as we'd passed into the next room, the door closed behind us with a clunk. The sound reminded me of those prison movies where the new guy enters and hears the iconic slamming of a door, signalling their loss of freedom. I prayed that this wouldn't turn out to be that in any way, shape or form.

Built into the walls of the circular room ahead of us were three metallic tubes, each a metre wide, intersecting the room's walls floor to ceiling.

'Now to begin this tour properly,' Tom said.

'It's already been pretty damned impressive,' Jack said.

'Not compared to what's beyond these doors.'

He approached the middle tube and, as it began to rotate automatically, I heard the thunder of rushing water. The tube slid into position and an archway cutting through the middle of it was revealed.

'If you follow me you'll see how we generate all the power that we need for this facility,' Tom said, again answering the question in all our eyes.

It was becoming more and more obvious with every passing moment that some seriously big money had been thrown at this place. I'd once caught a YouTube video on luxury bunkers, but this underground complex seemed to be on a whole other scale.

We followed Tom through the doorway into an enormous underground cavern and the source of the thundering water was revealed. At the far end, a waterfall from a wide cave mouth poured into a boiling river that flowed across the bottom of chamber. Mist floated up and filled the room with a fine haze, causing the large lights on the ceiling to cast multiple rainbows through the spray.

Tom handed us each a waterproof poncho from a locker next to the door. 'You're definitely going to want to wear these.'

As Mike slipped his on, he pointed at the ceiling and the large hanging columns of tapering rock. 'Will you look at the size of those limestone stalactites? They must each be twenty metres long at least.'

'Actually, we've measured them, and they're more like twenty-five,' Tom said.

'You could charge good money for people to see a cave like this,' I said.

'Yes, we probably could, but making money isn't what Eden is about.'

'What is it about then?' Jack asked.

'About ensuring the long-term survival of our species – hence the name Eden.'

Tom headed out over the gantry crossing high above the river. Within moments our ponchos and faces were glistening with moisture thanks to the huge cloud of spray rising up from the river. It was deafening, reminding me of a visit to Niagara Falls with Aunt Lucy, but even louder because this was contained in the chamber that echoed and seemed to amplify the sound. And like Niagara Falls, this was just as exhilarating, maybe even more so since the experience was intensified by being underground.

We reached the middle of the gantry and Tom turned to face us. He pointed towards the opposite end of the cavern, indicating the churning river. It disappeared through a huge round grate over which the letters 'H1' had been stencilled on to the rock face. Beyond the grill, the tops of large rotors spun at high speed.

'That's one of the ten hydrological generators that power this complex,' Tom shouted over the roar of the water. 'Between them they supply over three hundred gigawatts of power.'

'That's a hell of a lot,' I said. 'Are you running some sort of heavy industry down here?'

'That and all sorts of everything,' Tom replied. 'Sky Dreamer lives up to its name down here, building the visions of this planet's brightest minds. It takes a lot of power. Let me show you some of that now.'

We headed to the far side of the gantry and placed our ponchos in another locker. We stepped through another door tube and entered a cavern that made the last one seem tiny. In this vast space, with a roof so large it needed huge metal pillars to support it, the roar of water was replaced by the hissing of pneumatic machines. Hundreds of robotic arms swung and danced their way through their work across the production floor in an automated industrial dance of creation.

In one corner I recognised the stubby profile of an XA101 wing being worked on by three articulating robotic arms equipped with different tools. Then I spotted the people. There were hundreds throughout the factory wearing either blue coveralls or lab coats. Some hurried across walkways raised on metal stilts crisscrossing the production floor, vaguely reminding me of a scene from Fritz Lang's film *Metropolis*. The scale of what was going on down here was breathtaking.

'Impressive,' Jack said. It had to be the understatement of the century.

'I hope so. This room alone cost ten billion to construct,' Tom said. 'As you may have guessed, this is our main production facility and where we assemble our prototypes, many of which are at the bleeding edge of science.'

Mike blinked, his eyes wide like a kid at a funfair. 'I can't believe all this is down here.'

'There's plenty more to see yet,' Tom replied.

We followed him along one of the walkways and passed over a giant cube device. Inside, a section of a XA101 cockpit was being built, layer by layer, using a black viscous substance flowing from fine metal nozzles moving on motorised gantries.

Tom pointed to it. 'That's a giant-scale 3D printer that uses carbon fibre for its construction material.'

'You really do have the best toys down here,' I said.

'The best that money can buy. Those it can't, Sky Dreamer manufactures.'

We followed Tom to the far end of the factory and exited through another silver tube door. As the tube rotated closed behind us, the sounds of factory were shut away and I took in this new smaller room.

Men and women dressed casually in jeans and T-shirts were operating control consoles lining one wall. But it was the huge ten-metre-wide monitor on the wall that grabbed my attention. It showed a video feed of what appeared to be a rocket engine with a spiderweb of pipes mounted in the middle of another large rocky chamber.

Tom crossed to one of the women working at a console and they had a whispered conversation. Then he turned back to us with a wide smile. 'We're in luck. Julie here, the head of the test control team, has just told me that they are about to begin a test run of our latest orbital-lift Starbright KL303 rocket engine.'

Julie beamed at us. 'You couldn't have timed it better,' she said in an Australian accent. 'But please wear some ear protection. The rocket engine on that screen is in a chamber five hundred metres of solid rock below us, but, trust me, you'll need it.'

Tom crossed to a locker and took out four pairs of ear protec-

tors, sliding the first pair over his ears and then handing the rest
out to us.

The hum of the equipment around us was suddenly muted to
a background whisper.

Julie pressed a button on her computer and a large numeric
display on the wall above the large screen started to count down
from ten.

The men and women remained relaxed as if this happened
every day – for them it probably did. But Jack, Mike and I all
stared at the screen, our expressions expectant as if we were at
Cape Canaveral for lift-off.

My heart thumped in my chest as the countdown flashed.
Three, two, one...

With a distant rumble audible even through the ear protectors, the rocket engine blossomed into life with a lance of burning
jet fire. I quickly realised there was something very different
about this design compared to others. To start with, rather than a
round flame shooting out of the back, this was producing a
ribbon-shaped one from a thin rectangular aperture.

'As you can probably see for yourselves, Starbright doesn't
use the standard bell-shaped engine nozzle that's been used for
years in rocket design,' Tom shouted over the roaring noise filling
the control room. 'This is actually a vectoring design that NASA
experimented with but decided was too expensive. The design is
much more efficient than a bell engine, particularly in the upper
atmosphere. And it's also great for doing this...'

Tom nodded to Julie. She placed her hand on the lever and
pushed it all the way forward. The rocket plume tripled in size,
its flames now playing across the surface of the chamber wall
opposite.

The ground began to shake beneath my feet and the deep
rumbling bass note became so intense that my abdomen seemed
to vibrate in time to it.

'Maximum thrust achieved,' a male technician called out.

'Commence vectoring tests,' Julie replied. She spun a calibrated knob in her console to the right.

At once the engine nozzle pivoted upwards, directing the jet flame towards the ceiling, already scorched black. Then she turned the knob in the opposite direction and the jet nozzle rotated towards the floor.

'That's just all a bit amazing then,' I said.

'It most certainly is,' Tom replied with a smile.

'Attitude test successful; shutting engine down now,' Julie called out. She slammed her hand down on a red button and the rocket spluttered into silence, followed by billowing smoke rapidly filling the chamber. Everyone took their ear protectors off.

'Start the extractors,' Julie said.

One of the men near her flicked a switch and large fans set into the ceiling whirred into action. Within moments they'd sucked the smoke out of the chamber, leaving it clear.

Julie spun in her chair to face us. 'What you've just witnessed is an early test of our vectoring system for Starbright. With this technology, not only will we have a more efficient way of getting our probes into orbit, it is also a huge step towards changing the economics of mining asteroids for ever.'

'No wonder you're keeping this under wraps from your competition,' Mike said.

'Oh, this is just the tip of the iceberg,' Julie replied.

'Our founder is a truly remarkable visionary,' Tom said.

'I'm really looking forward to meeting this Jefferson guy,' Jack said.

Tom traded a smile with Julie. 'And you will very shortly.'

He led the way to another door tube at the far end of the room and we entered a small amphitheatre. Tom crossed to a lectern. He pressed a button on the back and a large panel slid down to reveal what I thought was another large screen. Then I noticed the rivets round the edge – this was actually a huge window. But it was what was through it that stole the air from my lungs.

It seemed to be a small base complete with faceted geodesic habitation modules built on a red rocky landscape. In the centre was a far bigger glass dome with large shrubs visible through its glass walls. Around the complex were a collection of extensive solar arrays and people in environment suits taking soil samples from the ground. But it was the outer surroundings that were mind-blowing. The base appeared to be sitting under a pale orange Martian sky.

'No fucking way,' Mike said as he stared through the giant window.

Tom smiled. 'Yes, it's very disorientating when you see Eden for the first time.'

'Isn't Eden the name of this whole facility?' I asked.

'Yes, it is, but it also takes its name from the science research project you're looking at,' Tom replied.

'And what *are* we looking at exactly?' Jack asked.

'All our work here comes down to one thing – ensuring the survival of the human species. This long-term simulation is a key part of that. The atmosphere within that chamber is as close to the one found on Mars as our terraformation scientists can achieve. The trainee astronauts have been locked in there for over three hundred days, doing a test run of our planned first expedition to Mars. We have already learnt so much, all of which will be applied to the real mission we're planning to launch in five years' time. We have even built a seed vault that will be transferred once a sustainable colony has been established. We have also been actively researching technologies to reverse global warming.'

'Bloody hell, seriously impressive,' I said.

'Oh, even this isn't everything.'

I exchanged *how can he top that?* stares with Jack and Mike as we followed Tom out through yet another door tube into every fantasy of a pimped-out science lab I'd ever had.

We found ourselves in another large cavern. Running along each of the four walls had to be at least a hundred labs that had been dug out of the rock face, with glass at the front of the chambers and a door in each. The scene reminded me of leafcutter ants scurrying between different tanks carrying their foliage loads. Here, rather than ants, people in white coats worked at benches with every piece of complex-looking lab equipment imaginable, every room with its own 3D printer. In one lab towards the corner lasers bounced around a series of mirrors. I had no idea what any of it did, but it was science geek heaven to me.

Much to my disappointment, I realised we weren't making for any of the labs but headed towards a featureless cylindrical room in the middle of the chamber.

Tom gestured towards it. 'That's Jefferson's private office, the Citadel.'

So here came the big moment – we were about to meet a living legend. We hadn't stopped since fleeing Orkney and I hoped I looked halfway decent. I certainly hadn't had a shower in a very long time. I had to strongly fight the urge to breathe into my palm for a fresh breath test.

Tom approached a cylinder door and stood before a domed lens sticking out of the wall. A beam of light danced over his face before fading away.

Tom turned to us and once again caught the question in our eyes. 'It's a full-facial 3D scanner with retina identification built in.'

'Your bio chip isn't good enough security by itself?' Jack asked.

'Not when it comes to direct access to Citadel and Jefferson it's not.'

Jack crinkled his brow at us as the door tube rotated.

The contrast of this room to the utilitarian labs outside couldn't have been starker. We appeared to have entered a library with walnut bookshelves built to the curve of the walls. Beneath a rectangular window with a view of the chamber outside sat a brunette woman in a wheelchair working at a computer, maybe in her late thirties or early forties. In the middle of the room a man in an expensive-looking grey suit sat at a large desk. An old-fashioned anglepoise lamp with a green glass shade illuminated a stack of papers in front of him. The guy was using a fountain pen to write numbers down in a blue A4 leather-bound notebook.

I headed towards the desk, my hand outstretched to avoid any body or breath odour embarrassment, my gaze taking in this mysterious Jefferson guy. For a living legend he looked quite ordinary. Probably in his fifties, with a thin face, grey hair, hawkish nose and brown eyes. Not that his appearance mattered – here was someone who could make a vast difference to our mission of saving our world.

'Mr Jefferson, it is a real honour to finally get to meet you,' I said.

The guy gave me a slightly bemused look.

Tom coughed and jutted his chin towards the woman who had angled her wheelchair towards us.

'Lauren Stelleck, I presume,' she said in a drawling American accent.

The woman's blue eyes seemed to probe straight to the centre of my being.

'You're Jefferson?' I blurted out.

She sighed. 'It's a sad reflection of our time that people still naturally assume that someone very successful in this field has to be a man. So very perplexing.'

I mentally cringed. 'I'm so sorry, Ms Jefferson. I'm a paid-up feminist too.'

She laughed and raised her hands. 'Lauren, please relax, and do call me Alice. If I'd been behind that desk when you came in, maybe you would have put two and two together sooner. Casper,' she said to the man at the desk, 'you'd better introduce yourself.'

'Hi, everyone, I'm head of the legal team, hence the uniform. I was just running through some of the supplier contracts with Alice.'

'Casper is rather old school, as you can see. I wouldn't mind if he turned up in a Hawaiian shirt and cargo shorts, but some things can't be changed.'

'Old habits, Alice,' Casper said with a smile. 'Anyway, I must be going. I need to chase through these contracts.' With a wave to us he disappeared from the room.

Mike stepped towards Alice and pointed at the window to the labs. 'What you've done down here is utterly incredible.'

Alice shook his offered hand and tilted her head to one side. 'You're Mike Palmer, am I right?'

'Yes, that's me.'

'When we have some time I'd love to pick your brains about your E8 theories. I'm something of an amateur fan myself.'

'You are?'

'As with most areas of science, yes. I find cutting-edge theories wildly stimulating.'

'In that case, I'd love to talk it through with you.'

'Then we shall.'

Jack stepped forward. 'It's great to finally meet you at last, ma'am.'

'Please, not so formal. Just call me Alice. You must be the famous Jack Harper. I'm so sorry about what happened to Skara Brae and your dig site.'

'Not as sorry as Colonel Alvarez will be if I ever get my hands on him again.'

'Just so, Jack, just so...' Alice gazed at all of us in turn with that spotlight gaze of hers. 'Tom's told me a great deal about all of you.'

'All good, I hope,' Mike said.

'I can assure you that my report has been glowing,' Tom replied.

At that moment the door opened again and an old dark-eyed, grey-bearded guy wearing green coveralls walked in.

'Everyone, meet Niki Lindén, our head of security and my right-arm man when it comes to intelligence gathering,' Tom said.

'So these are the new recruits?' Niki said in a Nordic accent – Icelandic, maybe.

'We'll have to see about that, but so far the welcome tour has been pretty impressive,' Jack said.

'It's like that for everyone the first time they see it,' Niki replied. 'Tom, I'm glad you're back – I have an urgent matter I need to discuss with you.'

'Which is?'

Niki's eyes travelled to Jack, Mike and me.

Alice waved her hand at him. 'You can relax, Niki. We have no secrets when it comes to our very special guests.'

Niki nodded. 'In that case, we have had a significant cluster of TR-3B sightings over Illinois that we need to follow up on.'

'A what?' Jack asked.

But I'd come across that name hundreds of times across the UFO forums. 'You're talking about Astra, aren't you?'

Tom nodded. 'I am indeed.'

'We're not talking about a crappy old car here, are we?' Mike said.

'No. The Astra is something of a legend in UFO circles,' I replied. 'It's basically a US military craft that uses an antigravity drive, which is rumoured to have been reverse-engineered from recovered alien craft.'

'You're shitting me?' Jack said.

'I'm not, although I can't swear it's true either.'

'Well, I can,' Tom said. 'I've seen this craft with my own eyes – it's something so secret that even the US president knows nothing about it. The Overseers have as much money as they need for their secret projects like Astra, thanks to their penetration into our world's governments and militaries, and their direct control over the US black budget. Worryingly, there the sightings of Astra craft have significantly increased recently.'

'Why's that worrying?' Mike asked.

'When I was working undercover infiltrating the Overseers organisation,' Tom explained, 'I discovered their master plan that they have been working towards for many years now. Astra is a key part of it. Unfortunately, I was unable to learn exactly what that plan was before my cover was blown.'

I sighed. 'Because of us.'

Tom held up his palm towards me. 'I can put your mind to rest there, Lauren. Whatever that secret is, it's buried so deep within that organisation that it's only known by people at the highest level.'

'The same secret oligarchy who run our world,' Jack said.

Alice nodded. 'I can assure you that this secret organisation is just as great a concern to us as it is to you. Whatever their motivation for developing Astras, you can guarantee it won't be in the general public's interest. And that is why Tom is continuing his investigation into their activities.'

'Talking of which, I'd better go and get briefed by Niki,' Tom said.

'Do please let me know if there are any developments,' Alice told him.

He nodded and turned towards us. 'I'll see you all later for the traditional welcome drink in the Rock Garden.'

'The what?'

'The Rock Garden's a bar here in Eden – and something of an institution.'

'You'll all love it,' Niki said.

'Perhaps that will have to wait for tomorrow,' Alice said. 'I imagine our guests will desperately need to catch up on some rest once I finish the final part of the tour with them.'

A smile filled Tom's face. 'Then I hope you're all ready to have your minds blown.' He winked at us as he stepped out through the door with Niki, which rotated closed behind them.

I turned back to Alice. 'I can't wait for whatever is coming next, but first there's something I'm dying to know.'

'Which is?' Alice asked.

'This place is beyond incredible, but why build it under-ground? I realise advanced rocketry like your Starbright engine is something you don't want your competitors to know about yet. And your Eden project lends itself to being constructed in a large natural cavern, especially if you want to simulate the Martian atmosphere. But you could have saved yourself a ton of cash by building it all on the surface inside huge buildings, which would have been just as effective.'

'Lauren Stelleck, you are very perceptive,' Alice said. 'You'll soon discover the reason for the extra level of secrecy.' She pressed one of the buttons on the arm of her wheelchair.

The view of the labs through the window started to slide upwards as the room descended into a shaft lined with polished rock – without so much as a gentle tremor.

I stared at Alice. 'This room is actually a lift?'

'Oh, it most certainly is.'

'And what's at the bottom of wherever we're headed now?' Jack asked.

'The stuff of dreams,' Alice replied with a wide smile.

CHAPTER THREE

MIKE GAZED out at the rainbow strata colours in the polished rock moving past the windows. 'This is a geologist's idea of heaven.'

Alice nodded. 'But please don't go chipping out lumps of my beautiful stone walls.'

Mike chuckled. 'I'll try to restrain myself.'

Jack peered down at the two-centimetre gap between the window and the walls of the shaft outside this round lift room. 'So how far are we going down? I wouldn't be all that surprised if you took us to the centre of Earth.'

Alice chuckled. 'Not quite that deep.'

I was already building up a mental picture of Alice, a true visionary who was prepared to go to incredible lengths to make her dreams a reality. And if what we'd seen already was anything to go by, what awaited us at the bottom of this ride promised to be something truly exceptional.

The lift room began to slow and another laboratory slid into view as we exited the shaft. Through the window I saw a young woman with blonde shoulder-length hair jumping up from her laptop.

'Welcome to my private lab,' Alice said.

The young woman, who had an elfish face with large eyes, bounded over towards us as the door tube opened into the lab.

'This is my lab assistant, Jodie Elliott,' Alice said.

Jodie thrust out her hand to shake ours. 'Great to meet you all,' she said in a similar accent to Niki's although her surname suggested maybe a different country.

I noticed Mike hanging on to her hand a fraction longer than was polite with a slightly goofy smile on his face.

'Good to meet you too,' he said.

We stepped out into a huge lab that put the others we'd seen to shame. Built into another cavern, the room was filled with lab benches and banks of 3D printers. But it was what was at the other end of the room that really caught my attention.

A metal doughnut ring about two metres wide wrapped in an intricate latticework of fine metal pipes had been mounted on metal rods over the floor. The only time I'd seen anything like this was on a visit to the experimental fusion plant at Culham in Oxfordshire with Steve, who'd been my boss at Jodrell Bank. Although that torus ring reactor had been larger than this one.

I gestured towards it. 'Are you dabbling in fusion power down here?'

Alice shook her head. 'We leave the development of fusion power to others. However, once we iron out the kinks, the device before you will have just as big an impact as fusion power.' She turned towards Jodie. 'I think it's time for a demonstration to our visitors, don't you?'

Jodie's cheerful expression evaporated like someone had just doused her with ice water after a hot sauna. 'But the energy field is nowhere near stable enough yet, Alice.'

'That doesn't matter. I just want to give our guests a taste of what we are trying to achieve here.'

'In that case, of course,' Jodie replied. She bobbed back to her desk and began tapping at her laptop. A moment later a humming sound came from the torus ring and I felt the tingle of static wash over my skin.

'This looks as though it's going to be interesting,' Jack said.

'Oh, it's most certainly that,' Alice said.

'Torus core temperature is now one hundred and twenty Celsius,' Jodie called out while looking at her laptop screen.

'Things are about to get interesting...' Alice said.

As we approached the torus ring I immediately felt the heat radiating off it.

'OK, apart from being a fancy space heater, what else does it do?' Jack asked.

'What you're looking at is a mini accelerator ring,' Alice replied.

'As in a particle accelerator, like CERN?' I asked.

'Not quite. This accelerator contains liquid mercury that is now being spun at high speed using a magnetic field within the ring.' Alice glanced at Jodie. 'Could you demonstrate the next step?'

'Sure.' Jodie jumped up and came back to join us. 'I need a volunteer for this.'

Mike's hand quickly flapped in the air like he was trying to get picked for a football match. 'I am so your guy.'

Jodie flashed him a dazzling smile. 'Maybe you are...'

Jack raised his eyebrows and I managed to suppress a smile. There was an obvious spark between these two and it seemed I wasn't the only one who'd noticed it.

Jodie took Mike by the arm and led him up a short set of stairs to the end of a small wooden chute, which sloped downwards and finished about three metres above the centre of the accelerator ring. She picked up a bowling ball from a number sitting a rack and handed it to Mike.

'You need to roll this down the chute,' she said.

'Sounds easy enough,' Mike replied.

He placed the bowling ball on the chute and gave it a gentle nudge. As the heavy ball rolled it gathered speed rapidly. I braced myself for the inevitable thud when it struck the floor.

'Get ready for the magic part,' Alice said. The ball reached the end of the chute and plummeted straight downwards, but then...

I gasped as the bowling ball slowed as though the air round it had turned to treacle.

Mike stared at Alice. 'Some sort of magnetic effect? The bowling ball has a metal core and is charged with an opposite polar field?'

'I can assure you that there is no metal in that bowling ball,' Alice replied. 'It's just pure plastic resin, nothing else.'

My mind reeled as Jack gawped at it. Could this be what I thought it was?

'And just to prove this isn't a trick...' Alice said. She headed over to a nearby lab bench and took a banana from a plastic box.

'Hey, that's my lunch,' Jodie said.

'I need it as a prop for our little demonstration,' Alice replied. 'Besides, you can help yourself to a whole year's worth of fruit from one of the canteens.'

Jodie grinned. 'True.'

Alice aimed the banana at the ring as if about to shoot a basketball hoop from her wheelchair. She lobbed the banana forward and it arched upwards and then down towards the middle of the torus ring – where the bowling ball was still slowly heading for the floor. As the banana approached, it moved in a crawl and began tumbling end over end in slow motion.

'What the hell sort of magic are you weaving down here?' Jack asked.

But I was grinning like a mad thing.

Alice rotated her wheelchair towards me. 'Lauren, you look as though you might have an idea what this is?'

'I think so. It's something that comes up on the UFO forums all the time. This is a magnetic accelerator, rumoured to be the same device that powers the TR-3Bs. A device that reduces the effects of gravity by seventy-five per cent.'

Jack gave me a shocked look. 'You're seriously telling me that this machine generates antigravity?'

'You can see that for yourself, Jack,' Alice said, gesturing towards the slowly descending banana and bowling ball.

'And of course we've seen the Angelus micro mind use some sort of antigravity drive, so we already know this is technically possible,' Mike said.

'But that's alien sci-fi tech and...' Jack flapped a hand at the torus ring. 'This is tech that someone on Earth built. For me that makes it much more real.'

'Not the stuff of magic in other words?' I said.

'That,' Jack replied.

A warbling alarm came from the laptop and Jodie rushed back to it. '*Perkele!*'

'That's a Finnish swear word, I believe,' Alice said.

Jodie groaned as she stared at the screen. 'Just as I feared. The energy field is becoming unstable.'

Sparks flew out of a wiring conduit connected to the accelerator ring as the acrid smell of burning filled my nose. A split second later the bowling ball and banana came crashing down to the floor.

'That's one of the kinks I mentioned,' Alice said. 'Unfortunately, we're still a long way from an operational and reliable drive.'

'A drive?' I asked.

'Ah yes. Follow me and I'll show you.' Alice spun her wheel-chair round and headed for a door tube behind the accelerator as Jodie unhooked a fire extinguisher and directed it towards the flames playing over the wiring conduit.

The door revolved and we stepped into the bottom of a huge vertical shaft, which had to be at least three hundred metres wide. Sitting at the bottom of the shaft on one of four landing pads was every fantasy I'd ever had about seeing a UFO come true. A smooth silver saucer – not a rivet to be seen anywhere – stood on three articulated tripod legs, a ramp with steps lowering from the middle of it.

'Holy crap, it looks like you snagged yourselves an alien UFO,' Jack said.

Alice shook her head. 'I can assure you this is all our own work. She's called *Ariel*. This craft is a full-scale 3D-printed prototype just waiting for us to crack the antigravity drive unit you just saw. Once we have, *Ariel* will form the backbone of our efforts to fulfil the mission statement of Sky Dreamer Corp: to colonise Mars. An antigravity drive will also of course spark a revolution for our species.'

'With spaceships you mean?' Mike asked.

'Not only those,' Alice replied.

I already knew what she was getting at. This technology was the holy grail for UFO hunters.

'Do you mind if I answer this, Alice?' I asked.

She smiled and nodded.

'A working antigravity drive has huge implications for our world. It could be used in all forms of transport, including people's cars. Once we have a way to negate the effects of gravity, transport costs will tumble. We could even have flywheel power generators spinning for ever – if gravity wasn't a factor. Can you imagine the impact that alone would have on fossil-fuel industries such as oil?'

'The oil companies would be out of business in a matter of years,' Jack said.

'At least when it comes to producing fuel,' Alice replied. 'And that's why the Overseers, who make a good deal of their money from oil and the associated energy industries, have suppressed the knowledge of this technology since the recovery of the saucer from the Roswell UFO crash in the 1950s.'

'You're saying that Roswell actually happened?' Mike asked.

'I most certainly am,' Alice replied. 'Of course, the truth was quickly buried, but since then the Overseers have had the US military reverse-engineer that and other downed UFOs. Over the years they have perfected this technology, as we have seen with the Astra craft.' Her expression grew fierce. 'For all these years the Overseers have had a way to tackle global warming, but instead they have continued to line their pockets.'

So there it was. The Overseers had risked the future of our world for their own financial gain. It was the worst evil I could think of. A few had prospered at the expense of everyone else.

'I'd like to show you one other thing in here,' Alice said. She manoeuvred her wheelchair over to the curving stone walls of the shaft. The bottom three metres of the rough stone had been polished like the walls of the lift room. Along the entire circumference small spotlights illuminated its surface. But it was only as we neared the walls that I started to make out the hundreds of names engraved into the stone.

'Are these the names of employees?' Mike asked.

'Some of them, yes...' Alice's expression became drawn. 'This is a memorial for all the people who have lost their lives at the hands of the Overseers. The ones who worked for me were trying to secure information about the antigravity drive system.'

I shook my head. 'And all the other names?'

'Some are the people who tried to reveal the truth about UFOs and were killed for their efforts by Overseers agents. Others were scientists getting close to breakthroughs that would have threatened the Overseers' grip on the energy industries.'

We turned to look at the names stretching away round the circumference of the tunnel and an icy feeling crawled over my skin.

'But there must be thousands of names in here,' Mike said.

'Actually, there's just over ten thousand. Some of the names might shock you. Follow me.' Alice wheeled her chair along the curving wall, stopped and scanned down the list of names in front of her.

She pointed to one and the air caught in my throat as I read the inscription. 'J. F. Kennedy.'

Jack stared at Alice. 'You have to be shitting me. You're telling us that the Overseers were behind President Kennedy's assassination?'

'Indeed they were, Jack. Kennedy was determined to reveal the truth about aliens to the general public. His efforts eventually came to the attention of the Overseers. We all know the rest. And it wasn't just Kennedy...' She pointed to the name below the American president.

Goosebumps rippled over my skin as I read the name.

Marilyn Monroe.

'No way!' I said.

'I'm afraid so,' Alice replied. 'The rumour was that Kennedy was having an affair with Monroe. And thanks to Kennedy she saw evidence about the existence of aliens and their craft retrieved by our military. When she threatened to go to the press and blow the story wide open, the Overseers stepped in again, but in her case they made it look like suicide.'

'This is all too much,' Jack said.

'I know how you feel,' Alice replied. 'But there's a final name I would like to show you all.'

We followed her round the curving wall and stopped next to a door opposite the one through which we'd entered. Here the list of names ended and Alice pointed to the one of the very final ones.

As I read it, I had to bite back a sob as tears filled my eyes.

Lucy Jacobs.

Alice reached up and squeezed my shoulder. 'I'm so sorry for the loss of your aunt, Lauren.'

I nodded, wiping away my tears.

Jack gave me such a broken look that it lanced my soul. I could see the echo of the loss of his wife written in his eyes.

Mike patted my shoulder.

'Sorry, everyone,' I managed to say. 'My aunt's death is still really painful for me.'

'Never be sorry for loving someone,' Jack said.

I slowly nodded as my heart seemed to pull me towards him. Here was someone who really understood.

Alice pointed to the names after my aunt. 'And these are all people who have died since at the hands of the Overseers – including the victims who were killed in the hospital on Orkney and the people who helped you on the rig.'

My gaze snagged on Greg's name, followed by Calum and Jim at the bottom. It felt like a slice of ice was being pushed into my heart.

'So many lives,' Mike whispered.

'Too many,' Alice replied. 'And that's why I wanted you to see this memorial. I know how committed you all are to bringing the Overseers down and locating the other micro minds. However, if anything underlines just how dangerous that could be, it's this long list of victims.'

I wiped my eyes again and looked at her. 'Alice, I can only

talk for myself, but I intend to do whatever it takes to bring those bastards down.'

Mike nodded. 'Yep, me too. Somebody has to stop them, especially when they're risking the survival of our world.'

I felt strong arms wrap round my shoulders and turned into Jack's hug. 'We're in this together, Lauren. Always.'

I nodded, feeling my love for these guys so damned much that I wanted to cry even more. 'You two really are the best.'

'You'd better believe it,' Mike said.

'And I promise you all right here, right now, that I will give you every support resource I can to help make this happen,' Alice said. 'We'll combine our efforts to take this fight to the Overseers. What do you say?'

Jack released me and stepped forward. 'Alice, I think I can speak for all of us and say that the moment we stepped on to your XA101 from the oil rig, we were already on board in more ways than one. So a big fat yes to helping you kick the Overseers' asses in any way we can.'

She gave him a small smile. 'In that case, we need to discuss how we can work together – specifically what I can do to help you discover the whereabouts of the next Angelus micro mind as it comes online. But first you need some good food and drink in your stomachs, not to mention some well-needed sleep.'

'Yes to all of the above. I'm shattered,' Mike said.

Alice wheeled her chair to the second door, which rotated open and Jack and Mike followed her through. But I hung back.

I traced my fingertip over Lucy's name. For her, for all those others who had died, and for the sake of our world, we had to win this.

In that moment I felt a clarity and sense of purpose that maybe I hadn't had in a long time. With a fresh determination to see this through to the end, I followed the others through the doorway.

CHAPTER FOUR

AFTER THE SUCCESSION of wonders we'd seen, what was before us still managed to steal my breath away.

Mountains were silhouetted in the distance and bright star constellations shone in the night sky overhead. Golden light streamed from the windows of a large log mansion, I would have been prepared for anything. But as I stepped through into the next area to join Jack, Mike and Alice, my mind whirled at the sight a few hundred metres away, nestled in among some pine trees. To the right of it lay a beautiful lake, reflecting the stars overhead and surrounded by willows.

Beautiful by any measure.

Yet we still had to be far below ground level. And wasn't it still daytime?

'Whoa there,' Jack said, summing up exactly how I was feeling.

Alice spun her wheelchair to look at us. 'It's quite the head rush the first time you see it.'

'Some sort of projection?' Mike asked.

'Some, but not all of it,' Alice replied. She tapped a few keys in the arm of her wheelchair. Instantly the star consolations were replaced by a bright blue sky with the sun shining down on us, transforming the scene to a summer's day.

At last the spinning sensation, not too different to the feeling of stepping off an intense rollercoaster, began to calm in my mind. I could now see what was really going on to create this illusion.

We were standing in the largest chamber yet, in which the natural stone dome had been transformed by huge display panels mounted on to the walls. The sky and mountains were projected on to these displays, but the house and lake were different.

'That house looks real enough for someone to live in,' Mike said.

'That's because someone does – me,' Alice replied. 'That building is actually my old family home from Wisconsin. I had it transported here and rebuilt, log by log. I realise it's a huge indulgence, but it's a connection to my old life that I hated to leave behind. This is my home from home and also my sanctuary.'

'Going by the name Citadel for your office above, I was expecting some sort of fortified bunker down here,' Mike said.

'Trust me, it's that too. Right now we're standing a good three hundred metres beneath the surface. As bunkers go, this one could give the American military's NORAD mountain base a good run for its money. I don't get out much these days, so I've tried to make this as comfortable as I can down here. And living in my old family home gives me all the memories I could wish for.'

I caught the edge to her words, realising there was a whole history behind this mysterious woman about which I had no idea. And why had she shut herself away from the world down here? A broken heart maybe? Or possibly something more prosaic – perhaps she had some autoimmune disease that made her susceptible to infection? But then surely we would have had to pass through some sterilisation process before meeting her. Whatever the answer, I was certain it would be interesting, because Alice was, without doubt, a complex and fascinating woman.

I gestured around us. 'This is truly and once again astonishing, Alice.'

'Why, thank you, Lauren. I invite very few people into my inner sanctum. But for you I'm going to make an exception. I'd like you to stay with me whilst you're with us. I have more than enough guest rooms for you all.'

'Are you sure that wouldn't be putting you out?' Jack asked. 'You must have lots of sleeping quarters elsewhere in Eden.'

'We do, Jack, but I see kindred spirits in all of you. Besides, I want to be a good host, especially after everything you've been through. Tom tells me that you were all tortured by the Overseers?'

'We were,' Jack replied. 'And Lauren got herself shot rescuing Mike and me.'

Alice gave me a concerned frown. 'And how is your injury now, Lauren?'

It was a good question. With everything that had happened over the last few days I hadn't really given much thought to my physical well-being since we'd fled the oil platform on board the XA101. I started to do a physical inventory and immediately noticed a dull throbbing ache in my arm where Alvarez's bullet had luckily passed straight through.

'Don't worry, Jack did a great job of fixing me up in the field.'

'But we should check your dressings,' Jack said. 'Not to mention get some more antibiotics pumped into your system.'

'You can talk, mate. What about all those scalpel wounds in your chest?' I turned to Alice. 'This poor guy was cut to ribbons by that bastard Overseers colonel, Alvarez.'

Jack shrugged. 'Ignore her, I'm fine. I don't need anyone fussing over me.'

'Typical doctor in other words,' Alice said. 'Even if their arm was hanging off they'd say it was just a flesh wound. We have an excellent infirmary here with state-of-the-art medical facilities. So if you don't mind, if only to humour me, please let my medics check each of you over.'

'Not necessary for me,' Mike said. 'I got off lightly compared to these two. Just some bruised muscles.'

Alice smiled at Mike. 'Please don't try to argue with me. Mike, I realise you're too old to be my son, but please think of me as an overprotective mother looking out for your well-being. I just want to make sure you're OK after what you've been through, both physically and emotionally.'

'You're talking about psychiatric help too?' I asked.

'Post-traumatic stress disorder wouldn't be unexpected with everything that you've recently experienced. I'm not suggesting that you have it, but offering help if you want to take me up on it.'

I was probably more messed up than I cared to think, especially after the amount of death I'd seen recently. And then, of course, there was what had happened to Aunt Lucy. I probably did need someone to talk things through with, but I didn't want to admit that. Maybe I just needed to catch my breath first after the whirlwind ride from Orkney, debrief with the guys and kick back before confessing I might need the help of a shrink. I guessed I wasn't alone. Instinct told me Mike was OK, not least because he'd taken the moral high road of choosing not to kill anyone, a luxury I envied. But who knew how recent events had messed with Jack's head, a guy who was still deeply screwed up over the death of his wife. Yet his face was relaxed as he shook his head at Alice.

'I've had my fair share of therapy so I'll take a rain check on that,' Jack said. 'And with regards to my physical injuries, you do know that doctors make the worst patients, don't you?'

'Of course I do,' Alice replied. 'But that won't stop me

ensuring you get some help. Whether you want it or not, you'll at least have a physical check-up. I insist.'

It was like watching an unstoppable force meet an immovable mountain as they stared at each other.

But then a smile filled Jack's face and he slapped a mock salute. 'Yes, ma'am.'

'Good, I'm glad we understand each other,' Alice replied, also smiling. 'In a moment I'll get Jodie to escort you all up to the infirmary. Then afterwards you'll come back here to join me for dinner. People tell me I'm quite the cook and my New Orleans-inspired gumbo always seems to snare hearts and minds.'

'That sounds great and everything,' I said, 'but we also need to sit down and have a serious talk about the Kimprak threat that Lucy, the Angelus AI, told us about. After all, they're on their way to harvest this world for resources.'

Alice's expression became drawn. 'And we will, Lauren, I promise, as a matter of priority. But that can wait until tomorrow – after you've had a decent night's sleep.'

The following morning I woke up after probably the best night's sleep I'd had in years. The room wasn't too hot or too cold, the mattress was ridiculously comfortable and the eiderdown duvet as cosseting as any bedding I'd ever known. My idea of heaven in bed linen form.

I stretched my arm against the fresh bandages that one of the Eden doctors, Mary, had administered. She'd given me a thorough check-over and seemed very impressed by Jack's handiwork in the field in dealing with my bullet wound. Thanks to that, I was set to make a full recovery, Mary had told me. Though I might be left with some lingering stiffness that could play up in extremely cold weather. She'd wrapped my arm with a fresh bandage and started me on a fresh course of antibiotics, just like Jack had suggested. The dull throb of pain from my left arm was noticeably easing this morning.

Mary was much less impressed with Jack's care of himself, who had protested every step of the way in the neighbouring cubicle to mine as she'd redressed his chest wounds. Jack hadn't been exaggerating that doctors made the worst patients.

I breathed in the almost sweet air wafting in from my open bedroom window. I swung my legs out of the bed and padded across to look at the view. I pulled the curtains back to see the sunrise kissing the lawns with golden light. Ducks paddled on the lake, ducking their heads for underwater morsels. The shadows of fish, trout maybe, were visible in the crystal-clear water beneath the white flowering lily pads floating on the surface. An arching footbridge crossed the lake, which seemed so familiar I was sure I'd seen it somewhere before. Nearer to the house, chickens in a large coop pecked at the ground. Three robotic lawn mowers trundled over well-tended lawns. And in the meadows beyond, two black and white cows munched their way through the lush grass.

OK, so this place was fake, but that didn't stop it being wonderful. It was certainly testament to Alice's vision of achieving the impossible, a vision that she seemed to apply to everything she did. She was my sort of woman.

I pulled a white fleece dressing gown on and tied the belt round my waist, enjoying its silk-soft touch.

Now for some coffee to kick-start my brain...

I headed downstairs into the large kitchen. Thanks to all the family photos and portraits lining the walls, it had a very homely feel to it, with several old-fashioned dressers housing patterned plates, cups and saucers. I could easily imagine Alice's grandparents living here.

The scent of fresh coffee snagged my senses and I spotted a

half-full cafetière on the side. So I wasn't the only one up with the sunrise. As I walked over to the counter, one of the larger photos caught my eye – a younger version of Alice, probably in her early twenties, sitting at the controls of a light aeroplane on the tarmac. The door was open and she held up her thumb and beamed out at whoever was taking the photo.

Beneath the photo someone had written *Alice's first solo flight.*

So she'd been a pilot once. That probably explained a big part of her fascination with all things flying and the Sky Dreamer's rocket programme. Alice was one of those people destined to do great things with her life because she was simply extraordinary.

I helped myself to a mug from a cupboard and filled it to the brim with black coffee. I breathed in the scent of freshly ground beans, possibly Java, and in a dreamy happy state gazed out of the window at the ducks paddling across the lake. This place really was a little slice of heaven.

The murmur of distant voices came through an open doorway. I headed out on to a veranda and spotted Jack and Alice sitting at a table facing the lake, gazing out at the virtual mountain range. Alice's head bent slightly towards Jack and he extended his hand to squeeze her shoulder, a tenderness in the gesture. I couldn't hear their conversation, but their body language made it obvious they were talking about something painful for Alice, especially going by the way she was now staring at the ground. Whatever this conversation was, it was a private one.

But just as I was about to turn round and head back inside, Alice's sixth sense must have kicked in because she glanced up and saw me. She raised a hand and beckoned for me to join them.

I padded over the lawn, the soft grass like velvet under my feet.

'And I thought I was an early riser,' I said as I reached them.

'I like to be up at the dawn, even if it is a virtual one,' Alice said.

'And I found it hard to sleep,' Jack said with a waver in his voice.

I couldn't help but notice that he didn't turn round to look at me. What was that about? There was a bottle of pills next to his coffee too. Probably antibiotics like those Mary had prescribed me...but what if they weren't?

'So how did you sleep, Lauren?' Alice asked.

'Like a proverbial baby. That bed is incredibly comfortable.'

'Oh, don't I know it. I've stayed at the finest hotels around the world, but I never sleep as well as I do in the beds here.'

I nodded and turned to Jack. 'So have you been bringing Alice up to speed about everything that happened back at Orkney?'

He finally looked up at me and I saw the redness round his eyes. He'd been crying – and crying hard. The feeling that I was intruding ramped up tenfold. But I was here now and couldn't exactly turn and run away – although part of me wanted to do just that.

He coughed, clearing his throat. 'Not yet. I thought it would be better if we brief her together. I didn't want her to think I was crazy.'

Before I could stop myself, the question was out of my mouth. 'So what have you guys been talking about?' I could have groaned at myself for being so tactless.

'Chewing the fat, that's all,' Jack replied, avoiding my eyes.

The hell they'd been. I glanced down at Alice's left hand and saw a distinct lack of a wedding band.

Oh fuck... I thought, and then immediately berated myself. Where the hell had that come from? What Jack did was his business; I knew better than to react like this. But how was it that this woman had got Jack to open up when he'd been so evasive with me about anything emotional?

If Alice picked up on my discomfort, she didn't say. She simply finished the last of her coffee and smiled at me. 'Right, let's get some serious breakfast going to feed our brains for the day ahead. It's going to be a significantly long one for all of us.' She turned her wheelchair to me. 'Lauren, could you give me a hand in the kitchen?'

I nodded, looking to Jack but he was already staring off into the distance. I stepped towards him but felt a gentle touch on my wrist. Alice had reached out to me from her wheelchair as she passed and held her eyes to mine. She gave me a slight headshake, saying, 'We'll leave you to finish your coffee, Jack. Come and join us when you're ready.'

Jack didn't so much as turn as we headed for the house.

'Any chance you can tell me what's going on with Jack?' I asked once we were out of earshot.

Alice gave me an apologetic smile. 'It's not my place, Lauren. I'm really sorry. I hope you can understand?'

'Yes, of course,' I replied, but really I didn't. As much as I hated to admit it, I felt jealous. I knew I was being petty and should rise above it, but it was hard not to feel like a young girl again who had been abandoned by a close friend for a shinier and prettier version of me...especially when that new *friend* was a billionaire and brilliant at everything she did.

Stop it, Lauren, you're better than this.

I needed to get a hold of myself. Besides, who Jack opened up to was his business. But as we walked back towards the veranda a sense of heaviness weighed my steps down, the lightness I'd felt when I'd woken already stolen away.

CHAPTER FIVE

JACK, Mike and I sat on the veranda with Alice and Jodie, the remains of a suitably large American breakfast in front of us. It had included a seemingly endless supply of pancakes and a huge pile of fresh fruit that I'd pigged out on.

Over breakfast, we'd brought Alice up to speed with the finer details of what had happened on Orkney that Tom hadn't included in his report. We'd explained at length about how I'd managed to pitch us into what we'd nicknamed the twilight zone, a reality between our world and the eighth dimension, using the Empyrean Key from Skara Brae. Alice had listened intently as we'd explained how Lucy had constructed temporal physical locations in the E8 realm for us to exist within and through which she could communicate with us. And when we'd confirmed what Tom had already told her – that the Kimprak were heading towards Earth in a solar-sail-powered asteroid craft – she visibly paled.

I sipped my third coffee of the morning and spotted Tom heading along the path towards the house.

He raised a hand in greeting. 'I see Alice has treated you to one of her famous breakfasts.'

Jack patted his stomach and smiled at her. 'You, Alice, are the queen of pancakes. Possibly the best I've ever tasted.'

She beamed at him. 'Why, thank you, kind sir.'

At least Jack was brighter after his tears earlier, but it was hard to ignore the growing spark between him and Alice.

Tom helped himself to a mug of coffee and sat down in a weathered rocking chair. 'So are we all set for the big conversation about what happens next?'

'I don't know about anyone else, but I'm certainly thinking more clearly after a good night's sleep,' Mike said.

Jodie smiled at him and Mike grinned in return. The two of them had been flirting like teenagers since she'd joined us for breakfast, but it was good to see someone happy after what we'd all gone through back on Orkney.

'We'd better make a start.' Alice cradled her hands together in her lap. 'After everything you've told me about this AI you've called Lucy, it's become increasingly obvious that it's an absolute priority to help you locate her other micro minds as quickly as possible.'

'I couldn't agree more,' I replied.

'I still think we should blow this whole thing open and get the public on our side about the Kimprak threat,' Mike said.

'I understand your view,' Alice said, 'but the Overseers control most of the world's media. You can imagine the spin they'd put on such a revelation if we tried to do that.'

Jack rested his elbows on the table with his hands interlocked. 'Then one priority will be drawing up a list of likely archaeological sites where we may find the other micro minds. I could put together a shortlist, but that's going to require some serious research on my part.' He turned to Alice. 'Could you sort me out with a laptop with internet access?'

'Oh, I can do better than that. You can use Delphi – if you'd like.'

I gave Alice a confused look. 'The XA101 AI?'

Alice laughed and nodded at Jodie. 'You're our computer expert, among many other things, so it's probably best if you explain it.'

'No problem,' Jodie said. 'Delphi is actually the name for our cloud-based computer AI. The system runs every aspect of Sky Dreamer Corp, including this whole facility. Delphi is obviously nowhere near as sophisticated as your Lucy, but still very powerful in her own way. For example, you could set up an automatic alert if Delphi detects any news online possibly indicating another micro mind is waking up.'

'That sounds incredibly useful,' I said.

Jodie nodded. 'And, Jack, Delphi's AI algorithms will be ideal to assist you with your research into Neolithic sites constructed within the same era as Skara Brae. Here, let me demonstrate.' She turned her head to a speaker mounted on one of the veranda's posts. 'Delphi, please display archaeological sites constructed within five hundred years of Skara Brae.'

'Commencing search using stated parameters,' Delphi's voice replied from the speaker.

A pulse of light spread through the gentle scudding clouds displayed in the cavern monitors overhead. A huge computer-style window opened over the sky image, displaying Earth as a globe and a steady green dot marking the position of what I knew was Skara Brae on Orkney. Flashing red dots began to appear all over Earth together with photographs of Neolithic standing-stone sites showing over the cavern's sky dome, some linked together with green lines.

'Holy crap, that's impressive,' Jack said.

I instantly recognised Stonehenge among the many images.

'You're telling us this whole ceiling can be used as one giant computer screen?' Mike asked.

'Absolutely,' Jodie replied. 'It's basically a huge interactive whiteboard.'

'And it's very useful,' Alice added. 'I often use it for brainstorming new ideas, and for little things too.'

'Like your grocery list, huh?' Jack asked with a smile.

Alice laughed. 'Not quite.'

I tried to ignore my stomach twisting at how easy it was between these two.

'The technology you have down here is mind-boggling,' I said.

'As far as human technology goes, that may be true, but it's like a child's toy compared to what you've told us about Lucy,' Alice replied.

'Talking of Lucy, there's one thing I don't understand about her,' Jodie said.

'What's that?' Mike asked.

'Why not keep all her micro minds in one place? Why would the Angelus scatter them across the planet and hide them?'

'To be honest that's been bugging me too,' I said.

Tom's eyes narrowed as he gazed off into space. 'My instinct is that it's related to security concerns.'

I sat up. 'How so?'

'It may be something to do with making the Angelus micro minds more difficult to either destroy or capture.'

'Well, that didn't work out as intended, seeing as something managed to shut her down and give her the AI equivalent of Alzheimer's.'

'Lucy has no idea about who attacked her then?' Alice asked.

'None at all, so the sooner we start recovering these other micro minds to get to the bottom of that, the better,' I replied.

Tom took a sip of his coffee. 'Is there anything we can do to help speed up that process? Time is obviously of the essence here.'

Jodie patted Mike's arm. 'Go on, tell them your stupendous idea.'

Mike smiled at her before returning his attention to the rest of us. 'As you know, I was able to locate Lucy's micro mind in Skara Brae by tracing the origin of the monowave earthquakes rippling out across the planet. But it took me quite some time to pinpoint the exact epicentre through my own sensor readings. As the other micro minds wake up they will send out the same monowave pulse, acting as the equivalent of a fingerprint. We can tap into the existing global earthquake warning system, which uses a network of accelerometers, seismometers and alarms to detect when a substantial earthquake is in progress.'

'This feels like a great first step, but monowaves aren't the only way to detect a micro mind becoming active,' I said. 'The Overseers were able to locate Lucy when one of their military satellites spotted the neutrino burst activity. I contacted an old colleague of mine at Jodrell Bank, Steve Andrews, who reached out to the team running the IceCube Neutrino Observatory in Antarctica. They confirmed the activity within the atmosphere. My hunch is another ground-based neutrino burst will give us the earliest warning about another micro mind coming online.'

'You're a step ahead of me, Lauren,' Mike said. 'And you're right, we need a two-pronged approach to crack this. The problem is that the IceCube detector can pick up a neutrino burst somewhere on the planet but has no way of detecting where exactly. So we could combine the two approaches and, Alice, as you're in the space business, I was wondering...'

'Go on?' she said with a smile.

'Would it be possible to build our own network of neutrino-detecting satellites to mimic what the Overseers are doing? If so, between those and our monowave detection, we should be able to locate the waking micro mind with reasonable precision.'

Alice nodded. 'It all sounds very expensive, but –' a wide smile filled her face – 'money is no object when it comes to this. Besides, we can launch a fleet of CubeSat micro-satellites that piggyback on to our commercial satellite launches. It will take some time, but within a year I'm sure we can have a rudimentary space-based neutrino-detector network in place.'

Tom held up his hands. 'I realise you science types love your toys, but there is another obvious way to detect them – keeping an eye out for any reports of new crystal runes appearing.'

I shook my head. 'That was the last element of the phenomenon to appear, Tom. If we wait for it, I can guarantee the Overseers will beat us to the waking micro minds.'

'OK, but having to wait a year isn't ideal,' Jack said. 'After all, according to what we've learnt from Lucy, we've only six years left until the Kimprak arrive.'

'So in the meantime we can use reports of neutrino activity from IceCube to alert us and combine it with any monowaves picked up by the earthquake warning system,' I said. 'It just means it won't be so fast for us to locate them.'

Jack nodded. 'It's not ideal, but I guess it will have to do.'

'So what happens when we get a bead on one of these waking micro minds?' Tom asked. 'Do we send in a squad of highly trained soldiers to secure the site?'

I shook my head. 'That's way too heavy-handed and will draw attention, especially if it's at another major archaeological site. We'd be better off sending in a small reconnaissance team...'

Tom's eyes narrowed on me. 'And I'm sure you can guess who I'm going to suggest.'

My eyes travelled to Jack and then Mike. 'What do you say, guys?'

'Damned right. This is our gig,' Jack said.

Mike nodded. 'Hell, yes. I've come too far to hand over the reins to somebody else.'

Tom nodded. 'In that case you'll need an intensive training regime. That is, if you're really serious about going back out into the field again.'

'Of course we are,' I replied.

'Hang on – would this intensive training involve guns?' Mike asked. 'If so, you can count me out.'

Tom held up his hands. 'I use a tranquilliser gun in the field for that very reason, Mike. It might not be as effective in all situations, but it allows me to sleep with an easy conscience at night.'

'Yeah, I'd prefer that,' Mike said without looking anywhere near Jack and me.

Jack gave me the barest shrug, then turned to the others. 'Look, I don't know whether to be flattered or insulted that you have Lauren and me pegged as two gun-wielding fanatics. We just did what was needed when the shit hit the fan. But please don't forget I'm a trauma surgeon with minimal combat experience beyond my basic training. And Lauren had no other choice but to pick up a weapon.'

'No one is judging either of you, especially me,' Alice said. 'I realise that it's not your area of experience, however by all accounts you seem to have acquitted yourself very well at Skara Brae.'

I couldn't help but notice that Mike was staring at his feet. We were definitely being judged by at least one person round this table.

I decided to ignore it. 'Whatever the moral arguments, I could certainly do with some training,' I said.

'Me too – special ops isn't exactly my core skill set,' Jack said.

'And you, Mike?' Tom asked.

'Give me a tranquilliser gun and I'm cool with that.'

Jodie reached out and squeezed his arm.

'Then starting tomorrow I'm going to turn you into a three-person squad,' Tom said, 'but you'll need someone in charge. It's better to have a clear chain of command, when, as Jack says, "the shit hits the fan".'

'In that case I nominate Lauren as team leader,' Jack said.

'Seriously?' I said.

Mike was nodding too. 'Yeah, I agree with Jack. You are cucumber cool in a crisis, Lauren, and I won't forget how you single-handedly rescued Jack and me from the Overseers. I'd certainly trust you with my life again.'

I sighed. 'Then I accept.'

Alice sat back in her wheelchair. 'Then it sounds like we have a plan. Is there anything else we need to discuss right now?'

'Actually, there is,' Jodie said. 'If it's OK with you, Lauren, I'd like to run a battery of acoustic tests on your Empyrean Key. I'm keen to discover if we can learn how it functions – if you don't mind helping out with your synaesthetic ability?'

'I'm more than happy to.'

Jodie beamed at me. 'Great. The more we know about how Angelus technology works, the more that may help us in the future.'

'Then I just need to get it from the bag in my room. But please be gentle.'

'Hey, it's made from stone and has survived for five thousand years, so I doubt there's a lot Jodie can do to damage it,' Mike said with a smile.

'Don't you worry, Lauren. I'll treat it as though it were fragile glass.'

I gazed up at the photos of the prehistoric sites still superimposed on the sky above like a surrealist painting. Maybe one of those would contain the next micro mind to awaken. I for one couldn't wait to recover it.

CHAPTER SIX

THE NEXT FOUR weeks were a whirlwind of constant activity. Everyone had been working flat out as we tried to locate the next waking micro mind – in my case helping Jodie with her testing of the Empyrean Key. When not doing that, Tom and Niki's intensive training regime kept me – and Mike and Jack – busy. We'd had only moments to explore the rest of Eden properly in our rare downtime.

Tom's initial tour had barely scratched the surface. There was everything from a full-blown IMAX cinema to a huge laundry and several amazing canteens that could easily seat a hundred each. Yet they were more like top-class restaurants thanks to the incredibly skilled chefs who served up meals to suit every palate. And that was just as well, since the people working in Eden seemed to have come from every corner of the globe, all exceptional and gifted in their own specific area. The best of the best. Alice had told us she wasn't concerned about academic qualifications, but raw natural talent and aptitude that could be moulded if necessary – something that made me warm to her even more.

I could certainly feel the common sense of purpose in the air as I walked through Eden. And when Alice turned up in a room to check on the progress of a project, it was like a rock god had just walked in.

I'd discovered this place had extensive sports facilities, including an Olympic-sized pool and several gyms kitted out with all the latest equipment. There was an indoor ski slope with real snow, and even an indoor artificial ocean complete with wave machine for people to surf. Mike had looked as if he'd died and gone to surfing heaven when I'd shown it to him. Since then, he'd gone surfing every free moment, showing off his moves to Jodie – who was trying to learn how to stay on a board for more than thirty seconds before wiping out.

The two of them had become quite the item over the last month. I'd even spotted Jodie sneaking out of Mike's room early in the morning.

But I was getting increasingly worried about Jack. He seemed prone to mood swings – either really happy or moping around with a face as long as a horse's. He had almost completely shut me out and always seemed to be with Alice. There was definitely a natural friendship between the two of them. Whether it was anything more than that, who knew. I kept telling myself it was none of my business, but my heart still twisted every time I saw them together, which was a lot as we were still staying in Alice's house. Maybe she liked having us around...or maybe it was specifically Jack. I was glad of the training to distract me from my stupid thoughts.

Now I stood outside a room with Niki, waiting for my next training challenge with my Mossad .22 LRS in its holster on my hip.

'OK, Lauren, are you ready to raise your game to the next level?' Niki asked. Tom had been busy investigating further sightings of Astras, so Niki had taken over some of our training.

'You mean being able to shoot a bullseye at fifty metres isn't good enough for you?'

'A static target on a range is one thing, but moving targets are a whole other level. Beyond this door are kinetic targets that will stretch your skills to their limits. Just like an enemy soldier, they won't wait around for you to target them.'

'Don't I know that.'

'Then you'll also know that it's important we're realistic – there are some civilians in there too. Hit any of them and that will be the end of the round.'

'Understood.'

'Good. You should know that Jack managed the course in three minutes with a score of five hundred and fifty. He's quite a skilled shot.' Niki smiled.

'And so am I, thanks to all the recent weapon training.'

'So let's see these skills of yours in action.' He opened the door and I found myself standing in a long rectangular room about a hundred metres long. The area was mostly featureless, with padded grey walls and ceiling. Spotlights illuminated a polished black floor criss-crossed with slots, some straight, some curved. An observation room with a thick glass window was built into the room behind us, beside a matrix display leader board. Jack was in third place with a score of 650, Niki second with 880. At the very top was someone called Ruby Jones with 1,560.

'So this Ruby is the woman to beat,' I said.

'That will be near impossible, but if you do there's a beer on me at the Rock Garden tonight.'

'Make it a margarita and I'm in.'

'A margarita it is.'

'One small detail. Where are all the targets?'

'Oh, trust me, you'll have more than enough to shoot at in a moment.' Niki headed into the observation room, flipped a switch and his voice came over a speaker. 'Are you ready?'

'Born that way apparently.'

He chuckled. 'Then good hunting, Lauren.'

I slid the .22 LRS pistol out of its holster.

Niki had tried to persuade me to try out something heavier with 'better stopping power'. But I felt comfortable with the weight of the LRS in my hand. It might not have brought down a charging rhino, but it felt like an extension of me. I figured that probably counted for a lot in a combat situation when I had to move fast. At least that's what I kept telling myself. My theory was about to be put to the test.

I flicked off the safety and extended my arms forward, gripping the LRS with both hands.

Keep it smooth, Lauren...

I stalked into the centre of the room, senses needle-sharp and ready for anything. One step, two steps and then something at eleven o'clock shot up through one of the slots. The silhouette of a guy wearing a balaclava and holding a Kalashnikov rifle. I pivoted a fraction and squeezed the trigger. The crack of a round being discharged was followed by a perfect hole in the target's head as it slid back into the ground.

I allowed myself a quick glance at the leader board – there was my name with a score of fifty next to it. Oh, this was going to be easy.

You're going down, Jack Harper...

I took another step forward and this time a target raced out from a slot in the wall and curved along its track towards me.

I shifted my weight to my left foot, swinging the LRS round, anticipating the target's movement. I squeezed the trigger and sent the bullet straight through the heart of my would-be assassin. The target continued along its track and disappeared into a slot in the opposite wall.

My total ticked up to 250. A fast-moving target had to be worth more points.

Maybe I could even overtake this legendary Ruby...

I headed farther into the room and more targets jumped up. I dispatched them quickly and my score crept up to 500.

I was getting into the rhythm of it, sure I'd beat at least Jack, when three targets shot up from the floor simultaneously at my ten, twelve and three o'clock positions. I dropped into a squat, firing, turning, firing and firing again, swinging my gun in an arc. I went for chest shots to make sure I didn't miss and a hole appeared in each of the targets as they disappeared back to the floor. I glanced back once more and saw my total was at 750.

Read it and weep, Jack Harper. Now to beat your score, Tom.

I caught a blur of movement just behind me at seven o'clock. I spun round and fired instinctively...

And froze as a klaxon sounded and the room's lights were turned up to full strength. I stared at the target – a woman pushing a pushchair. She had a bullet hole straight through her chest.

I turned round slowly and saw my score had dropped to 450. Fourth position. The observation-room door swung open and Niki came towards me. 'You can't say I didn't warn you.'

'But that wasn't fair – she popped up behind me and I shot before I realised who she was.'

'Exactly, Lauren. And that's the lesson. You have to be certain of your target before discharging your weapon.'

I stared at him, then nodded. 'Shit, you're absolutely right. Just as well this isn't the real thing. I wouldn't be able to live with myself if I'd done that for real.'

'Which is why you need this intensive training. But don't beat yourself up too much. You did really well. You certainly seem to be a natural with a weapon.'

'Probably something to do with all those hours playing combat games with old boyfriends back at uni.'

'Well, it obviously honed your marksmanship skills. They are exceptional.'

'But that alone isn't good enough, right?'

'Yeah. And unfortunately the greatest lessons of all are the ones learnt during actual combat.'

I pictured the cardboard targets replaced with real people. They wouldn't neatly disappear into slots in the floor after being shot. Real life would involve blood and guts – and an emotional aftermath.

Niki patted me on the shoulder. 'I can guess what you're thinking right now. It's a personal choice to carry a weapon into the field and there's always the option of a tranquilliser gun instead, as Mike and Tom have chosen.'

But I knew it was far less effective. I nodded at the leader board. 'I wouldn't mind another attempt to raise my score.'

Niki smiled. 'I'm sure you would, but you're needed elsewhere. There is the usual Friday-afternoon meeting in Alice's lab, and she has something important to brief you about.'

I slid my LRS back into its holster. 'Then I'd better get my arse down there and face Jack's ridicule at not beating his score.'

CHAPTER SEVEN

I took the small secondary lift down to Alice's lab and found Jack and Mike gathered round a bench with Jodie, Alice and Tom, all eating pizza slices from several large boxes and sipping beer. Alice had held informal Friday-afternoon show-and-tell meetings like this every week over the last month and she always brought food and beer.

I saw my Empyrean Key orb suspended on two cables strung between two metal pillars. Jodie was adjusting a camera on a tripod pointed towards it.

'You just missed a fantastic demonstration of your Empyrean Key, thanks to Jodie doing a test run before she presented her results to you,' Alice said.

Jodie shrugged. 'I can't take all the credit. Mike's been helping me out.'

He reached out and squeezed her arm. 'Hey, this is all you – I just helped with the brainstorming.'

'So have you had that breakthrough you told me you were edging towards?' I asked.

Alice nodded. 'In a way, or to be more accurate, the beginning of a breakthrough. '

'But it's still damned impressive,' Jack said, holding one of the pizza boxes out to me.

I helped myself to a beer and a slice of margarita pizza – with added black olives and anchovies, Jack's favourite. The pizza from Eden's kitchens were almost as good as Mario's – my food obsession when working at Jodrell Bank.

'Any chance of you running the demonstration again, Jodie?' I asked.

'Of course, Lauren. You're the star guest.' She bounced over to a console and spun a knob to the right. The lab speakers emitted a familiar low-pitched hum.

'As I'm sure you recognise, that's the trigger frequency for your synaesthesia ability with the orb,' Mike said.

I nodded. 'That sound is etched into my brain.'

'We thought it was as good a place to start as any with our acoustic analysis of the Empyrean Key,' Jodie said.

I gazed at the stone, but wasn't surprised to see no signs of lights dancing over it – there wasn't an Angelus micro mind nearby. It was something I could see and others couldn't, because I'd been born with a unique synaesthesia gift, which meant certain tones triggered a light show in my eyes. This was also the basis of the visual language of the Angelus, which I'd first discovered when Sentinel had tapped into it to communicate with me. And it had enabled me to use the Empyrean Key to make contact with Lucy – and learn of the Kimprak threat.

'I'm not seeing any activity round the orb, but then I didn't expect to,' I said.

'Try looking behind you,' Jack told me.

I turned round to a large monitor on the wall, which displayed the live feed from the video camera pointed at the stone orb. The camera view showed complex geometrical lines radiating around the Empyrean Key like the magnetic field of a planet.

'Very pretty, but what am I looking at here exactly?'

'It's the acoustic fingerprint of the Empyrean Key,' Alice said.

'Sorry,' Jack said. 'I know you already explained it, but I still don't really get what it means.'

'I'm with you on that,' Tom said.

'I'll walk you through it with a second demonstration,' Jodie replied. 'To start with, it shows how this specific tone triggers your synaesthesia ability, Lauren. The sound seems to act as some sort of acoustic carrier wave to bring what is otherwise a piece of inert stone to life and provides an interface for Lucy's computer systems. Just watch what happens when we slightly change the frequency.'

Jodie moved the knob a fraction farther and the pitch of the note started to rise and modulate.

The patterns of energy shifted on the screen as the pitch changed, transforming from petal shapes to spikes around the orb.

'So the acoustic reflection from the Empyrean Key changes according to the pitch that it's been hit with, is that right?' I asked.

'It's certainly looks that way to us,' Alice replied.

'And how is this significant?'

'We know this three-dimensional stone orb is somehow directly linked to E8, where Lucy exists,' Jodie replied. 'My hunch is that we're looking at some sort of visual mathematical language that the Empyrean Key generates according to the frequency it's hit with. Get it to radiate the right acoustic pattern and it unlocks the functions of the device that can bridge our reality to E8.'

Alice sat forward in her wheelchair. 'Basically we think it's acting like a transmitter.'

'But without a micro mind in close proximity, it obviously can't do anything else,' I said.

Mike nodded. 'That's true. But the other reason for pursuing these tests is you, Lauren. We believe your brain is acting like an organic interface to process the information being acoustically projected by the Empyrean Key. And that's something we'd love to build a greater understanding of.'

'With that in mind, I have a present for you, Lauren.' Jodie took a blue box from beneath the bench and handed it to me.

'What's this?' I asked.

'A reliable way for you to always be able to generate the key frequency to unlock the Empyrean Key.'

I pulled open the box. It contained a tuning fork that looked similar to one that I'd seen Aunt Lucy's piano tuner use. I took it out carefully and turned it over. It was beautifully engineered from a single piece of polished steel.

'Nice,' Jack said. 'No need to worry about running out of batteries.'

I smiled. 'Do you mind if I give it a whirl, Jodie?'

'Be my guest.'

I tapped the tuning fork gently on the edge of the lab bench. At once a low note that perfectly matched the one from the speakers hummed out. Just when I thought it would go on for ever, it eventually died away.

'It's certainly easier than trying to hum the right frequency.' I hugged Jodie. 'This is a perfect gift – thank you so much.'

She smiled at me. 'I'm glad you like it.'

Alice wiped her hands on a napkin. 'So now on to other business – before I get to some major news. What about our own neutrino-detector network? How is work progressing there?'

'The initial designs for the CubeSat photon detectors are almost finished and we're about to enter a rapid prototyping stage,' Mike said.

'With any luck we'll have the first batch ready for deployment within five months,' Jodie added.

'That's great news,' Alice said.

'Yet the clock is ticking,' Tom sighed. 'Every day we don't detect the next micro mind, the more nervous I get. Six years until the Kimprak arrive on our doorstep isn't exactly a lot of time. I wish we could get them up there quicker.'

'I know, but it's still good progress. We'll get there,' Alice reassured him. 'Jack, how about your ongoing research? Anything to report?'

'I've managed to trim down a list of Neolithic sites to about a thousand candidates.'

'That sounds manageable,' I said.

'If only it were that easy,' Jack replied. 'We're only looking at a thousand sites *if* the Angelus visited Earth only once during the same time frame as Skara Brae. If they visited our world on multiple occasions, we could be looking at a much wider time frame.'

'So you need to cast your net wider?' I asked.

'Yeah, which could easily increase the current list tenfold, if not more.'

'But at least it's a start,' Alice said.

'That it is.'

I looked at my friends with something approaching envy. I hadn't been able to help in the same way – apart from the odd times when Jodie had wired me up to see my brain activity when a sound sparked off my synaesthesia. Without a micro mind to interface with, I couldn't contribute much. So instead I'd thrown myself into the intensive training.

Alice's gaze tightened on me, and I wondered if she was a mind reader in addition to her other talents. 'Niki tells me you've been excelling in your training, Lauren.'

'He's a great teacher.'

'He said you've showed real prowess in all areas,' Tom added. 'Apparently, you're also quite the marksman now.'

'I actually surprised myself there. Must be all those old computer games. I couldn't beat Jack's high score, though,' I added. 'At least, not yet.' I grinned at him.

Alice switched her attention to Mike. 'And I hear you've been blowing things up?'

Mike gave her a crooked smile. 'Who knew it would be so much fun! If we need a demolition expert, it seems I'm your guy – as long as I don't have to hurt anyone.'

'And how's the hand-to-hand combat training been going?'

We let out a collective groan and gazed at Tom.

'I don't know what all the fuss is about,' Tom said. 'You've all acquitted yourselves very well, especially when you consider you're learning multiple martial arts from judo to jujitsu.'

'So, Tom, any more news about your team investigation?' Alice asked.

He nodded. 'Right now, we have a lot of intelligence about a major increase of sightings of TR-3Bs over Illinois. If that wasn't interesting enough, we've also been receiving reports about Tic Tac UFOs in the same region.'

'Tic Tacs?' Jack asked.

I already knew the answer. 'Tic Tacs were mentioned in the USS *Nimitz* encounter. They moved at incredible speed, running rings round the F15 pilots trying to track them. The footage of them defying all the usual rules of flight was even released by the Pentagon, before you write that off as fantasy from the UFO community.'

Tom nodded. 'The same craft have been buzzing all over Illinois. Whether it's connected to the other Astra activity, we're not sure, but we certainly want to find out. We're about to launch a major fact-finding mission to the area of highest activity to see what we can discover. That's part of the reason I've accelerated your training programmes.'

Mike's eyes widened. 'What, you want to send us on a UFO chase?'

'Actually no,' Alice said. 'Something else has happened more specifically linked to your own talents.'

My pulse quickened. Was this what we'd all been waiting for? 'Is another micro mind waking up?'

'Maybe – we're not sure, which is why we want your team to go in and investigate. One of Delphi's automated internet searches turned up a news story about a young woman in Peru with synaesthesia that sounds a lot like yours, Lauren.'

'OK...but it's not that unusual,' I replied. 'One in three hundred people have it.'

'She also reported seeing geometrical patterns floating over the famous archaeological site of Machu Picchu after hearing strange noises. And there have been reports of a weird light in the sky.'

'Bloody hell, this sounds promising,' I said.

Jack sat up straighter. 'Machu Picchu was on my list of possible micro mind sites. If it is, it obviously rules out the Neolithic period being the only time the Angelus visited our world.'

A thought struck me. 'If this is anything to do with a micro mind waking up, what about any new neutrino activity?'

'I've already taken the liberty of reaching out to Steve at Jodrell Bank,' Tom replied. 'His contacts at the IceCube detector confirmed there was a fresh burst of neutrino activity somewhere within the atmosphere just thirty-six hours ago.'

My shoulders rose to my neck. 'Why didn't you think to tell us before now?'

'I just wanted to be certain before raising anyone's expectations.'

'In that case, any reports of seismic activity?' Mike asked.

A wide smile filled Alice's face. 'Yes, a series of quakes hit Machu Picchu in the last twenty-four hours. However, it's not that unusual for that region to experience quakes, and I haven't had a chance to confirm they're monowaves, but when combined with the other data...'

'Holy crap,' Jack said. 'Machu Picchu is on the bucket list of every archaeologist I know – me included.'

'As the rest of the team are going to be caught up investigating the UFO sightings, I can't spare any of them for this mission, so I'm afraid the three of you will have to fly this solo. I don't see it as a problem, since you're gathering intelligence rather than getting involved. What do you say?'

'I'm in,' I replied as my gaze lingered on Jack.

He scratched his cheek. 'An expenses-paid trip to an archaeological location I've always wanted to see. Now let me think...' A wide grin filled his face. 'Hell, yes. It's a dream come true.'

'If there are active quakes in the area, I'm in too,' Mike said.

'In that case we'll leave on board an XA101 at one a.m. tonight,' Tom said. 'I'll accompany you on the journey.'

'Jesus,' Jack said. 'Why such a godforsaken hour?'

'Landing near Machu Picchu in the early hours is less likely to be noticed.'

'I'd strongly recommend you all try to get an early night,' Alice said.

But Mike shook his head. 'I have a date with a beer at the Rock Garden with Jodie. It's karaoke night and we fancy our chances of winning the duet trophy.'

'Damned right.' Jodie held up her hand and Mike high-fived her.

'Before you head off partying,' Jack said, 'I'll go and dig up what I can on Machu Picchu and put together a briefing for everyone. Let's say in a couple of hours?'

'Sounds good to me,' I replied. 'I'll go and put my kit together and take a nice luxurious bath. Who knows when the next one will be – and I need it after the sweat I worked up on the firing range.'

Jack raised his eyebrows at me. 'Oh, I thought that smell was the cheese on the pizza.'

'Watch it, mister,' I replied with a smile. Maybe he did have the hots for Alice, but he was still my mate, I decided.

'I'd better prepare the equipment you'll need for your mission,' Tom said. His gaze narrowed on Mike. 'Just please try not to overdo it tonight.'

'I'll do my best,' Mike said as he winked at Jodie.

CHAPTER EIGHT

WE'D BEEN FLYING under the cover of darkness for a good ten hours and all we'd seen on the cockpit screen was a view of snow billowing over Icelandic landscape – the screensaver that Tom had called up. I really would have to have words with him about his choice of in-flight movie before our next flight.

Mike, needless to say, *had* overdone it last night. There was a distinct lack of sympathy for him in the cabin, especially after he'd stunk the place out with the smell of vomit – which had thankfully stopped when he'd had nothing left to regurgitate. He and the others had sensibly taken the opportunity to grab some sleep, but I hadn't been able to shut my mind down. Obviously the overarching goal of saving the world was driving this mission, but the growing sense I might be getting closer to seeing Lucy again was also a very big deal for me. Yes, she was only an AI facsimile of my real aunt, but she helped to fill in the hole in the centre of my being left from the death of the woman who'd unconditionally loved me.

A gentle alarm came from the speakers in the ceiling of the cockpit.

'ETA ten minutes,' Delphi's voice announced.

Tom opened his eyes. 'Delphi, please relay the live feed to the cockpit walls.'

At once the Icelandic scene was replaced by a mountainous landscape under a night sky, once again giving the distinct impression that our seats were flying through the air by themselves. The effect was heightened by the XA101 itself being almost invisible, since its adaptive electronic camouflage on its external surfaces matched it to the surroundings.

And what a view it was. We were flying between the towering peaks of the Andes, snow visible on the tips of the highest peaks despite it being summer. Dark blues surrounded the mountaintops, and below was a carpet of trees, broken by the odd field around occasional isolated buildings. The lack of any street lights suggested a lack of people down below – hopefully meaning there weren't many eyes to pick out the disguised craft flying overhead. To the east a glowing band of gold hinted at the coming sunrise.

My chest expanded as my eyes drank in the view.

Jack stirred in his sleep and his eyes cracked open before springing wide. 'Holy crap, you could have warned me the external cameras were on. For a moment there I thought I was having a lucid dream of flying.'

I smiled at him. 'Best not to wake Mike then. He'll only freak out again and I for one could do without the fresh smell of sick added to the old in here.'

Jack sat up and shook his head. 'He should be all right – I dosed him up with extra meds to settle his stomach.'

'Maybe best not to take the chance,' Tom added.

'Good point.'

'I'm going to deposit you as close as I can to Aguas Calientes,' Tom went on. 'It's the town nearest to Machu Picchu, and where Cristina, our eyewitness, lives. I'll choose an area of jungle where hopefully no one should spot us landing. From there you can make your way into town and the rest of the mission will be down to you.'

'What do you mean, *down to us*? Surely you've put together a plan?' I said.

'No – you're going to decide how you track down Cristina and find out what she knows before reporting back. View it as an extension of your training exercise. I must head back, as the situation in Illinois is rapidly developing. And I wouldn't allow you to do this if I didn't have absolute faith in each of you.'

'I just hope that faith is justified,' I said.

'Oh, it is,' Tom replied.

'ETA five minutes,' Delphi's voice announced.

'Right, we'd better wake Mike up as you all need to get ready,' Tom said. He pulled a holdall from beneath his seat and took out three wigs and what appeared to be a make-up kit.

Jack peered at the dark ponytail wig and scowled. 'Are these disguises really necessary, Tom? Nobody will know us here.'

'This is just an insurance policy,' Tom replied.

'Against what?' I asked.

'In case the Overseers have picked up on the clues and decided to investigate too. Any field operatives working for them will have been given your profiles by now. Besides, you need to match your fake passports in case you're asked for ID.'

'You'll really rock the ponytail look, Jack,' I said, smirking.

'Next time, *I* get to choose my own look, otherwise I'm going to give someone hell for it.' He gave Tom a pointed glare.

After landing on the ledge of a mountain, we wheeled our Zero motorbikes down the cargo ramp from the XA101. Tom had assured us these would be ideal for the mission, with their long-travel suspension, rugged tyres and large metal panniers for all our kit. We'd had a few minutes to test them through the meadows around Alice's house the evening before we'd left, and the joyride had left me grinning from ear to ear.

From here, the town lights of Aguas Calientes were starting to disappear as the sunrise strengthened its hold across the golden-kissed landscape.

We put the bikes on to their kickstands, Mike and I doing our best not to laugh at the transformation of Jack the Viking to pony-tailed biker.

'You really should consider keeping that look after this mission,' Mike said.

'Look who's talking, Mr Hipster with a stuck-on beard,' Jack replied.

I shrugged. 'Actually, I think it suits him.'

'That's only because his eyes practically popped out of his head when you put that blonde wig on.'

I gave Jack my best Insta-pout. 'What, you think it suits me?'

'Maybe, but I prefer your usual dark-haired locks,' Jack replied.

Note to self, Lauren: no dying your hair. I mentally shook my head at myself as Tom carried a silver briefcase down the rear ramp of the XA101's cargo hold.

He opened it and handed us each a rugged mobile. They looked as if they could take some serious punishment. 'These are Sky Wires, which are basically satellite phones with a navigation app built in,' Tom explained. 'They also have a backup walkie-talkie function for the rare situations you don't have line of sight to a satellite.'

'So no posting selfies to Instagram up on Machu Picchu then?' Mike asked as he scratched his beard. It seemed to be causing something of a rash.

Tom just raised his eyebrows at Mike by way of a reply. 'You can use the Sky Wires to keep in contact with me and to arrange your eventual extraction when you've gathered all the intel you can.'

Jack gazed towards the distant town. 'It looks like quite a long ride down to Aguas Calientes. Will these motorcycles have enough charge to get us there and back?'

'Don't worry – these bikes have been modified by our techs with solid-state batteries rather than the usual lithium ones. Thanks to that, they have an enhanced range of nearly three hundred miles – and you can always plug them in if you need more juice. The crash helmets aren't exactly standard either; they're reinforced with Kevlar, enough to stop a bullet. They each have a full heads-up display system that is linked to your Sky Wires. Not only can you have a map and other key information projected on the display, but there's also a night-vision image-intensifier system, which can be activated from a menu. Please try not to lose them as each one is worth about a million dollars.'

'Bloody hell, we'll do our best,' I said.

'Also, talking of money, there's thirty thousand US dollars and twenty gold sovereigns in each of your panniers.'

'Not that I'm looking a gift horse in the mouth, but why do we need all that cash?' Mike asked.

'For bribes and stuff, I'm guessing,' Jack cut in. 'Am I right, Tom?'

'Absolutely. In my experience, greasing the palms in certain situations can make all the difference. The next thing I need to run through with you is your weapons. Each of you has been equipped with a sidearm, which you can keep hidden somewhere on your body. Mike, you'll find a dart pistol in your panniers.'

He nodded. 'You'll get no complaints from me about that.'

'And hopefully you won't object to the C4 explosives with remote triggers also in there, just in case.'

Jack made a low throat-growling noise. 'As long as you don't go blowing up any archaeological artefacts.'

Mike held up his hands. 'I wouldn't dare, mate.'

'So how about me?' Jack asked.

'You've got a good old Glock 19 – discreet and very reliable.'

'Yep, happy with that.'

'Just please tell me my LRS is in there,' I said.

'I wouldn't dare not to, Lauren. Besides, it's a nice compact weapon, favoured by Mossad agents for that reason.'

Jack held his thumb and forefinger a few millimetres apart. 'You're that close to that LRS, I'm surprised you haven't started writing it poetry.'

'Who says I haven't?'

Jack snorted.

'And I've also equipped you with your full lock-picking kit, Lauren.'

'Cool. I just hope I remember all my training.'

'It's like riding a bike. I've also given each of you a low-profile shoulder holster for your weapons, invisible under a shirt.'

We sped along the dirt track, weaving through the jungle on our Zero motorbikes. The vehicles were eerily quiet against the wildlife chatter around us. With no clutch, the bikes were incredibly easy to ride – just a twist of the throttle and go. And the torque the electric motors gave the bikes was a real head rush.

'How far until we get to Aguas Calientes?' I asked.

'We're about ten miles away according to the map on the HUD display,' Mike replied.

'How do you pull that up?'

'Ah yes, you were off in the jungle having a comfort break

when Tom told us how to use our helmets' functions,' Jack replied.

'Needs must. So what did I miss?'

'They use an active retina-scanning system,' Mike explained. 'Blink three times in rapid succession to pull up the main display and menu system.'

I did as instructed and at once a constellation of readouts appeared, overlaying the view in my helmet's visor. The battery-charge indicator was sitting at a reassuring ninety-eight per cent, no doubt thanks to the regenerative braking that actively charged our batteries. In the left corner of my visor was a scrolling map with three triangles, obviously representing our motorbikes' positions.

'Oh, that's seriously cool,' I said.

'Yeah, there's no shortage of cutting-edge tech now we're sponsored by Sky Dreamer Corp,' Jack said.

'Maybe we should get some T-shirts made up with their logo.'

Jack chuckled. 'Yeah, nice low profile and all.'

I noticed a readout below the HUD map.

Distance to destination: 5 miles.

'Not that far now, guys.'

'So what's the plan when we arrive in town, Lauren?' Mike said.

So there it was. Following on from Eden, I was the one in charge. Everything that happened would be on me. To say I already felt out of my depth would be an understatement, and we'd done nothing yet.

I marshalled my thoughts and replied, 'I think we do what any tourist arriving in a place without a pre-booked a room does. We head to a bar and ask if anyone can recommend somewhere to stay.'

'I'm liking our illustrious leader's thinking here,' Mike said.

'Me too,' Jack agreed.

'Calm down, you two. This is about work, not getting hammered for breakfast. We can grab the opportunity to pick the brains of the locals and find out if anyone knows where we can find this Cristina woman.'

The track started to sweep to the right and ahead joined a tarmac road busy with traffic. A quick glance at my HUD map confirmed this would take us directly into Aguas Calientes on one of the few roads.

'OK, remember we're tourists here, guys, not weapon-packing spies,' I said. 'So no flash moves on your Zeros to draw attention to us.'

'Oh, you're no fun,' Mike said.

'Absolutely not at a time like this. Keeping a low profile is our motto from here on out.'

'Yes, ma'am,' Jack said.

I glanced in my rear-view mirror to see him snapping me a salute.

Idiot. But I smiled inside the privacy of my crash helmet.

A few moments later we'd merged into the steady stream of tour buses and local traffic, keeping religiously to the speed limit like good law-abiding tourists. But how long until our new motto would be ripped to shreds? Something deep down told me it would – it was just a matter of time.

CHAPTER NINE

THE BAR WAS PACKED out with a group of tourists, their piles of rucksacks and holdalls crowding the floor. According to the bartender, their trip to Machu Picchu had been cancelled – the site was currently closed to the public and had been all week since the quakes had started hitting. But that hadn't stopped the tour groups coming to Aguas Calientes as tickets for Machu Picchu had to be bought months in advance. The tourists wandered around gloomily, while the bar owner seemed much happier – business was brisk as the tourists sought different ways to fill their time and blow some cash.

Despite it only being ten a.m., the beer was in full flow. In an attempt to ingratiate ourselves, we'd already bought everyone in the bar several rounds of drinks and things had grown distinctly lively. A group of Germans had even organised an impromptu singalong that Mike had happily thrown himself into. But it was way too early in the morning for that sort of behaviour in my book.

I sat at the bar along from a young local guy with his head

down in a paper. I sipped my pisco sour that one of the Germans had insisted I tried – it was either that or being forced to dance with him to an ancient pop track. Pleasantly and much to my surprise, the Peruvian cocktail wasn't a million miles away from a margarita. I'd been distinctly suspicious of the whisked eggs whites until I'd tasted it. Of course, Jack and Mike were being very stoic about having to drink beer for breakfast too. *Needs must*, Jack had said.

But as I drank, I was painfully aware we were anything but tourists out for a good time. I'd already tried picking the brains of the bartender about Cristina, but despite the considerable custom I'd been throwing his way the guy was being uncommunicative. Meanwhile, Jack and Mike were embedded with the tour group to see if any of them knew anything about her. I wasn't sure how they were getting on, but the laughter seemed to be getting louder by the minute from their corner of the bar.

I pushed my pisco sour away and gestured to the barman. 'Could I grab a coffee instead?'

'Sure.' He turned his back to me to face an impressive-looking coffee machine.

Time to try again. 'Look, I'm not a journalist or anything like that, if that's what you're worried about. I would just really love to meet Cristina. Maybe you know someone who could get a message to her?'

The bartender shook his head without even bothering to turn round. 'As I keep telling you, I have no idea who this Cristina is.' His coffee machine started gurgling and he headed along the bar to a woman waving several dollar bills at him.

The young guy in the seat next to me angled my way. 'Look, you have to understand you're not the first tourist who's tried to track Cristina down.'

I spun towards him. 'You sound as if you know who she is?'

'She's my cousin,' he said bluntly, and extended his hand. 'My name is Ricardo. I'm one of the tour guides here, just like Cristina.'

A tingle of anticipation ran through me. 'So do you know where I can find her?'

'I do, but that doesn't mean I'm going to tell you where she is.'

The bartender materialised with a steaming coffee cup in his hand. I paid for it and took a long sip of excellent coffee, letting it sharpen my brain as I searched for the best way to approach this. Any friend of Cristina would be naturally protective towards her. I could easily imagine how her life had been turned upside down recently. And the poor woman was unlikely to be able to make any sense of what she'd seen.

'Look, if you are worried about me being a journalist looking for a great story, or even a religious crank, you can relax on both counts.'

'Oh, they all say that, trust me,' Ricardo said.

This wasn't going well. My intuition was that the truth, or at least as much as I could reveal, would be the only thing that might work here. 'OK, here's the deal. Cristina isn't the only one who has seen strange geometrical symbols at old archaeological sites.'

Ricardo stared at me. 'You know someone who's seen something similar?'

'I have – me. I have something called synaesthesia, which is trigged by certain sounds.'

He sat up straighter. 'For real?'

'I'll swear it on whatever Bible you care to put in front of me.'

'So how can I really trust you? Those religious nuts you mentioned are real. There are people out there who honestly believe Cristina's visions have angered the ancient Inca gods, hence the tremors. And some of those who have sought her out are anything but fans.'

I started to understand Ricardo's hesitance. Hell, I would have probably done the same in his position – protecting someone I loved from the crazies. So what would make me realise that I didn't mean any harm?

I gestured to the barman, who headed over. 'Hey, have you got a piece of paper and a pen I could borrow for a second?'

'Sure.' He dug out a pad from behind the counter and tore out a page. He handed it to me, together with a pen.

'What are you doing?' Ricardo asked.

'Drawing some of the symbols she may have seen.'

I started to sketch a series of icons – the wave symbol, the dot icon – but it was when I began drawing the star sign for E8 that Ricardo grabbed my wrist.

'You've seen this too?'

'Yes, I have – why? Has Cristina seen something like this?'

Ricardo stared at me. 'Seen it...? She has drawings of this shape all over her wall.'

Hope rose like a bubble into my chest. 'So will you take this to her? Cristina didn't ask for this and the world has gone crazy on her. I really want to help.'

Ricardo peered at me, then glanced over his shoulder at Jack and Mike currently taking orders for another round with much back slapping from the Germans.

'OK, I know Cristina will want to see your drawings,' he said. 'So I will take you to her, but if she wants nothing to do with you, you must promise me that you'll leave her alone?'

'If that's what it takes, then I promise.' I thrust out my hand and Ricardo reluctantly took it, his handshake firm. Of course I had no such intention – we were talking about saving the world here, and what Cristina knew might be a big step towards that.

'I just hope my usual good instinct is right to trust you,' Ricardo said. 'Don't make me regret my decision.'

'I promise, you won't.' I hoped duplicity wasn't showing behind my eyes.

He peered at me and slowly nodded. 'OK, Cristina lives with her husband Gabriel, another guide, and their baby girl in a house at the edge of town. I can take you to her now if you'd like?'

'Absolutely. Just let me round up my friends and we'll get going.'

Ricardo nodded. 'Sure.'

Relief surged through me and I felt my neck muscles relax. At this rate we'd be heading back to Eden with vital intelligence before the day was out. I finished the rest of my black coffee and turned round to see Jack and Mike getting started on another beer each. I was so going to have to have words with them later about keeping a clear head whilst on a mission.

We'd headed away from the bar up alongside a broad river running through the heart of Aguas Calientes. Ricardo led us on to a steeply sloping side street and we began to make our way between tall buildings painted with a bright palette of colours – from blues to yellows to deep oranges. We clung to the cooling shade on one side of the pavement to shield us against the already intense heat of the day.

The streets were crammed with tourists that should have been up on Machu Picchu but instead were wandering around looking for ways to kill time. Consequently, there was something of a carnival feel to the town. Yes, people were disappointed not to get to one of the great wonders of the world, but they were more than making up for it by spending their money.

Tom had told us Aguas Calientes lay at an altitude of 2,000 metres and my lungs were soon complaining about the thin air.

Mike and Jack's faces looked flushed too. By contrast, Ricardo hadn't even broken a sweat.

I gestured towards him as he strode ahead of us. 'Bloody hell, that guy is putting me to shame. I can barely keep up.'

'You're not alone,' Mike said, wheezing slightly.

'I wouldn't beat yourselves up,' Jack replied. 'A lot of the locals have a physique that's adapted to living at this altitude. Many of them have broader, more barrel-like chests, able to squeeze every last molecule of oxygen out of the thinner air.'

'So they're built for this altitude in a way that we simply aren't?'

'Yep.'

'OK, that makes me feel a bit better.'

We rounded a corner to see a five-storey building with balconies painted in a bright yellow ochre.

'This is where a lot of the other guides live,' Ricardo said. 'Just wait here and I'll check if Cristina is around.' He headed for a table outside the entrance where men and women were playing cards. He high-fived several of them and bent his head in for a conversation with the group. A few moments later Ricardo waved us over.

'Cristina is up in her room preparing her famous chicken stew for everybody. With Machu Picchu shut, none of us have been paid for the last week and we all pretty much live hand to mouth. Cristina offered to cook for the other guides in this apartment block who shared their ingredients with her. It's a way of saving money when things get this tight.'

It sounded like a tough existence to me. My fingers gently brushed the money belt beneath my shirt containing a wad of ten thousand dollars.

We followed Ricardo through the doorway into a courtyard. A covered staircase wound its way up to the floors. Criss-crossing the open space, washing lines fluttered their clothes in a gentle breeze, like pendants stretched between the balconies. We climbed up the stairs to the third floor and passed through the doorway into a dingy corridor. The only source of light was a single open window at the far end with a metal fire escape visible past it.

'This place looks really rundown,' Mike whispered to Jack and me as Ricardo walked ahead.

'Let's give Ricardo a substantial cash donation that he can share with the others,' I replied. 'Not just a sign of our appreciation, but to make things easier for them at the moment.'

'You've got a good heart,' Jack said.

I raised a shoulder. 'I try.'

Ricardo came to a stop in front of a peeling blue door and knocked. We could hear a baby crying in the room beyond.

'Sounds like my favourite little person needs a hug,' Ricardo said through the door.

The wailing continued, but there were no footsteps.

Ricardo rapped his knuckles on the door harder. 'Cristina, hey! It's Ricardo.'

Still no response. He knocked again.

'On the loo maybe?' I asked.

'She would still be able to hear – their apartment is tiny. She would have shouted something back.'

'Maybe she popped out,' Jack suggested.

'She'd never leave baby Nicole by herself,' Ricardo replied.

I gestured along the corridor to the fire escape beyond the open window. 'A quick ciggy break?'

Pedro shook his head. 'Cristina doesn't smoke.'

As he knocked again, a guy with dark eyes and a broad face appeared in the corridor behind us carrying a bag of groceries. 'Hola, Ricardo.'

'Hola, Gabriel. Tu esposa no responde y Nicole está sollozando con su corazón allí.'

'Ella no es?' Then Gabriel looked at Jack, Mike and me, and scowled. 'Hey, you know the deal, Ricardo. Cristina doesn't want to talk to anyone at the moment, especially strangers,' he said switching to English no doubt for our benefit.

'I know, we all know, but she'll want to talk to this lady.'

I stepped forward. 'I can imagine the sort of crazies that have been turning up at your door, but I promise you we're different. You see, I have a pretty good idea what Cristina has been going through as I have the same thing – an audio-visual form of synaesthesia.'

'You have?'

'Yes, and I've seen geometrical symbols hanging in the air at another archaeological site. That's why we're desperate to talk to her.'

Gabriel's eyes widened. 'Then please come in. She needs to talk to someone who understands what she's going through. She thinks she's been going crazy.'

'God, I can imagine.'

Gabriel shifted his bag of groceries to his left arm and fished out his key. 'Hey, Nicole, hush your tears, Papa is coming.'

He unlocked the door, pushed it open with his foot and let out a small gasp. He dropped the bag of groceries and darted inside. 'Cristina, where are you?' he shouted.

We followed Ricardo. A baby girl, tears streaming down her face, sat in the middle of the floor. She was surrounded by the scattered contents of the small room.

Ricardo scooped the girl into his arms to soothe her. 'Hush, Nicole.'

Gabriel stared around, his hands interlocked on top of his head, then rushed into the adjacent room.

I began to take in the chaos. Books had been thrown off a toppled bookcase, drawers emptied out on to the floor. A pot had been tipped over and a cooling puddle of stew slopped out over the worktop. A framed photo of Gabriel, Nicole and a pretty dark-haired woman with smiling eyes lay shattered on the ground. A sketch book was open on a sofa, some pages torn from it.

Ricardo bounced Nicole on his arm as he tried to quieten her.

Gabriel stormed back into the room, his eyes wide. 'Cristina isn't here.'

He spun round to stare at us. 'I find strangers outside my door and now this.'

Ricardo shook his head. 'It's nothing to do with them, I promise, Gabriel. They were with me the whole time – I brought them here. They can't have been involved.'

Gabriel slumped on the sofa and picked up the torn notebook, examining the missing pages. 'Whoever it was took her drawings.'

'You mean the symbols?' I asked.

'Yes – the ones she saw hanging in the air at Machu Picchu, just like a sign from god,' Ricardo replied.

My pulse amped. 'And this was triggered by a sound?'

He nodded. 'She was up there guiding a group last week when a tremor hit the mountain. It was followed by a strange animal-like cry from beneath the earth. Then these symbols appeared in front of her eyes. She filled that sketchbook with what she saw.'

'Her synaesthesia kicking in, it has to be,' I said.

Jack and Mike both nodded as Nicole held out her arms for her father.

Gabriel took Nicole from Ricardo, smoothing out her dark hair as he kissed her head. 'Shush, my baby girl. Mama's going to be OK, you'll see...'

But I could hear the fear behind every syllable of his words to his daughter. I twisted my fingers through the strands of my blonde wig. So what were we talking about here – had one of the fanatics who'd labelled Cristina as a devil abducted her and taken her drawings as evidence of sins against god? It sounded like a bad Dan Brown novel. And if so, what would they do with her?

A chill ran through me as I exchanged a loaded look with the others that told me they were thinking exactly the same thing.

CHAPTER TEN

WE LEANT against the wall of the corridor in Gabriel and Cristina's cramped apartment. It was crowded with a procession of people offering to help look for her. But no one had found any clues about who had taken her, or where. The police had been called and I'd agreed with Jack and Mike that we'd make a fast disappearance as soon as they arrived. Despite the seriousness of Cristina's abduction, we had an even bigger priority – discovering the whereabouts of the waking micro mind. We needed to keep away from the authorities' radars as best we could.

Ricardo walked past us to the balcony and lit a cigarette.

'I'm just going to see how our friend is doing,' I said to Jack and Mike. 'Cristina's his cousin after all.'

Mike nodded. 'Everyone is all over Gabriel and Nicole. Ricardo's been a bit forgotten in all this mess.'

I clambered out and leant on the railing beside him. The bright sunshine was a stark contrast to the gloomy corridor inside. 'How are you?'

He breathed out a wreath of smoke round his head. 'I keep

hoping this is a nightmare and that I'll wake up from it in a moment.'

'I know exactly what that feels like...' I paused, trying to find the right words.

'If anything's happened to her...' Ricardo crumpled into himself as he squeezed his eyes shut.

I patted his arm. 'Let's not go there yet.' He took some deep breaths and I looked out from the balcony into the rear narrow alley where people had already checked for signs of Cristina. A small van was trundling along it towards the back of an adjacent building. 'I can't believe that no one saw anything.'

'Me neither. There are lots of eyes in Aguas Calientes. For this to happen in broad daylight is impossible.'

The van reached the yard at the back of the building and parked up. An old guy climbed out and headed round to the vehicle's doors, opening them and revealing a stack of boxes inside. The man carried a box to a metal door in the building, and I saw a security camera was mounted above it... I stared at the camera and grabbed Ricardo's arm.

'That camera has a view of this rear alley.'

He blinked at me. 'Mary, mother of god, you're right.'

'Do you know who it belongs to?'

'A small shop round the corner. We should tell Gabriel.'

I shook my head. 'I think he has enough to deal with – and let's not build up false hope in case it hasn't captured anything.'

Ricardo nodded. 'You're right. So let's go and check that footage. Then if we learn anything, we can let Gabriel and the police know.'

I stuck my head back through the window into the corridor. 'Guys, we may have just found a lead about Cristina.'

Jack stopped pacing and stared at me. 'Which is?'

'I'll tell you on the way.'

The four of us headed down the fire escape, jumping it three steps at a time.

A short while later we were all crammed into the small grocery shop, standing among piles of vegetables, canned goods and an assortment of noodle packets. A Peruvian grandmother-like figure was peering over her specs at Ricardo as he negotiated with her to see her camera security footage. She would only agree to a surprisingly large amount of cash – supplied by us. There were no flies on this lady.

The old woman rotated a monitor on the counter towards us and gabbled something in Peruvian Spanish back to Ricardo, then disappeared into a storeroom at the back.

Ricardo pushed a fast-forward button. 'Here we go, my friends.'

The morning's footage began to play at high speed.

Children played some sort of ball game that looked a bit like hopscotch, followed by a flock of pigeons settling along the rear wall of the apartment. The birds were frightened off by a skinny cat as it attempted an optimistic leap to catch them. Followed by a delivery van pulling up and unloading several boxes of multi-coloured drinks into the yard. The everyday comings and goings of an alley in Aguas Calientes.

But then at last we saw something that stood out.

A grey jeep drove slowly along the alley and stopped next to the fire ladder we'd just climbed down. Two local looking people got out of the vehicle – a thick-necked man and a shorter guy. Both wore casual shirts and blue jeans. At first glance they were guys just going about their business. But there was something about the shorter guy and the way he moved that radiated authority, especially as the taller man kept nodding frantically to everything he said and wringing his hands.

Ricardo leant in and his eyes widened. 'Hang on, that short guy is Miguel Villca, the police commandant for this region. Why was he here in Aguas Calientes?'

'Would he have turned up if somebody had reported something suspicious?' Mike asked.

Ricardo shook his head. 'Normally it'd just be a couple of regular officers. We wouldn't usually see someone of Villca's rank unless it was serious, like a tourist going missing from the Inca Trail.'

'So something is already off about this,' Jack said.

'Absolutely,' I agreed. 'Let's see how this plays out.'

Ricardo pressed the normal speed playback button.

A tightness grew in my chest as the two men headed up the fire escape together to the third floor. Jack and Mike exchanged a silent look as we watched them clambering through the open window into Cristina's apartment.

Mike pointed to the timestamp on the video. 'Nine-fifty a.m. – roughly twenty minutes before we got there. This has to be linked.'

Villca and the other man re-emerged from the window a few minutes later clutching a woman with a bag pulled over her head. Her arms had been cuffed behind her back and she was struggling as they escorted her down the fire escape.

'Oh my god,' Ricardo whispered.

The men bundled Cristina into the back of their jeep and drove off just as slowly as they'd arrived, obviously not wanting to draw attention to their vehicle.

Ricardo stared at the monitor, his hands clawing the counter.

'But why in hell's name would the police commandant want to abduct a young woman like Cristina?' Jack asked, voicing what we were all thinking.

My body felt like it had drained of blood. 'To silence her?'

Jack nodded. 'If some people really do believe she's a devil, that's not out of the question. Machu Picchu generates most of the income for this whole region. So any negative publicity that might threaten that revenue stream is going to be bad for business, especially on top of the recent earthquakes.'

I stared at Jack, not wanting him to be right, but knowing he was making a strong point.

'Then we have to do something about this,' Mike said. 'This footage is solid evidence that something has gone down here. I say we show it to the authorities.'

'The authorities being the police,' Jack said. 'See any problem there?'

'We can't just let that bastard get away with this,' Ricardo said.

'And we won't,' I said. 'But we need to go higher up the food chain and take this over Villca's head.'

'But how do we do that?' Mike asked. 'It'll take time that we don't have. We need to do something right now, because if Villca really does see Cristina as that sort of threat...' Mike let his words trail away.

'Then we have to find her and fast,' Jack said.

They were both absolutely right, but a thought struck me. 'Hang on – the fact they didn't just murder her in her apartment has to be a good sign.' I caught Ricardo winced but pressed on. 'After all, they could have blamed it on some fanatic who'd taken the law into their own hands.'

Mike clicked his fingers. 'You're right. They must need her for something. And helping themselves to her drawings has to be linked to that.'

'But why would they be interested in those?' Jack asked.

An awful answer hit me. 'Guys, what if the Overseers have already beaten us here and have paid Villca off?'

'You mean they know Cristina has a synaesthesia ability like yours?' Jack said.

'It's certainly a strong possibility. If they've put two and two together like we did, they may have realised she's someone who could lead them straight to the micro mind.'

'Then we need to contact Niki and request a security team from Tom's investigation to rescue her,' Mike said.

I held up my hands to halt them. 'Guys, slow down and think it through. By the time a team gets here it could be too late. Besides, this is just a theory, not a known fact. I say we get ourselves up to Machu Picchu – if we're right, I'd bet good money that's where they've taken her.'

'The observatory, to be exact,' Ricardo whispered, still staring at the monitor.

'The what?' I asked.

'It's where Cristina had her visions.'

'That makes sense – it's part of the Machu Picchu site,' Jack said. 'The sky was important to the Incas, especially for their rituals, and the moon and the sun were both worshipped as gods. On the summer solstice, sunlight would shine through a specific window in the Solar Observatory, a date that was a big deal in the Inca calendar.' Jack rubbed his chin. 'And now Machu Picchu has been closed off because of –' Jack made air quotes – 'the danger of rock falls from the earthquakes.' It was a message we'd seen on a sign when we'd entered the town.

'We need to get up there and find Cristina,' I said. 'Before it's too late.'

'I thought this was just a reconnaissance mission?' Jack said.

'If needs must, we have to step in.'

Jack shrugged. 'You're the boss.'

I caught the slight edge to his tone. What was that about?

'We should also tell Gabriel about this,' Ricardo said. 'It's an important lead.'

'Not if we don't want a lynch mob heading after Villca.'

'And why is that a bad thing? He's more than earned it,' Jack said.

Exasperation rose through me. It was so obvious. 'Because if that man is prepared to kidnap someone in broad daylight, I doubt he'd pause in shooting other innocent people to keep things covered up. We need to stop talking and get moving.'

Jack rubbed his eyes with his thumbs. 'Right.'

Ricardo hauled his gaze away from the monitor. 'You'll need someone to guide you up the old mountain path that bypasses the roadblocks the police have in place.'

'Are you sure?' I asked. 'We don't know what we're getting ourselves into here. It could be very dangerous.'

'You said yourself that Villca might be capable of anything and this is my cousin we're talking about...' Ricardo hung his head.

'Now there's a motivation I think we all understand,' Mike replied, patting Ricardo's shoulder.

CHAPTER ELEVEN

WE SLOWLY WOUND our way up the less visited side of the mountain towards Machu Picchu. Even with the collapsible walking poles from our panniers, the ascent was tough-going up the steep mountain path. On a more positive note, we were well hidden by the trees as we approached the site.

We walked in silence, each of us lost in our own thoughts, the cicadas our soundtrack.

The jungle around us thinned, giving us a glimpse of the east slope of the mountain and the switch-back road that led from Aguas Calientes to Machu Picchu. It was empty of vehicles thanks to the roadblock we'd skirted past at the bottom.

'Let's take a break for a moment,' Ricardo said.

'Fine by me,' Mike said, breathing hard. 'Hey, Ricardo, have you any more of those coca leaves? They do seem to be helping.'

'Sure, my friend.' Ricardo took a single green leaf from a plastic bag and handed it to Mike who began to chew it.

'I still can't get my head around the fact it's the same leaf cocaine is extracted from,' I said.

'In its leaf form it's a very mild dose,' Ricardo said. 'It has been used for centuries to help with altitude sickness and to calm people. Just don't try to take these leaves out of Peru – your own countries are likely to throw you in jail if you try.'

'I don't much fancy getting locked up for accidentally smuggling drugs,' Mike said. He unhooked his binoculars and scanned the main road to our left. 'As expected, there's no sign of any rock falls.'

'Well, there's a surprise,' Jack replied.

Ricardo gazed out at the empty road. 'It's strange seeing the mountain this quiet. At this time of day there should be dozens of buses bringing the tourists back down to Aguas Calientes. The longer this goes on, the harder it will get for us tour guides to survive.'

I took a sip of water from the mouthpiece of a hose over my shoulder. What I would have given to be using our Zeros to climb this mountain. But Ricardo had been adamant about leaving them behind. He'd told us that, however great our bikes were, this route involved almost vertical rock faces that we would have to climb. Reluctantly we'd left the Zeros outside the bar with a promise from the owner that he'd keep an eye on them for us... which had cost us more cash. We'd discreetly loaded up with our weapons as an insurance policy and I also had the Empyrean Key on the off-chance it would come into its own once we got up to the site. Plus Mike had one of his portable monowave quake probes that Jodie had constructed, a device with a short metal corkscrew spike and a digital readout on the top. I hoped he wouldn't have a chance to try it out – I didn't much fancy experiencing an earthquake first hand.

I took another drink of the cooling water. Even under the cover of the trees, the combination of the heat and thin mountain air of the Andes made me feel like I'd run several marathons. No wonder most sensible people took the bus.

'OK, let's get going,' Ricardo said, putting away his own water hose.

I was even more grateful for the walking poles as we ascended farther. Just as Ricardo had promised, in places we had to tackle sheer slopes that would have challenged a mountain goat. There were far too many buttock-clenching moments, but the ground began to finally level out, much to my relief.

Ricardo pointed along the trees. 'This small path will take us straight to the site.'

I put my hands on my hips and stood before him. 'Then this is where we should part company, Ricardo.'

'What are you talking about? I'm coming with you.'

Jack shook his head. 'No, Lauren's right. You need to go down to Aguas Calientes and be with Gabriel. He needs a friend right now.'

I placed my hands on Ricardo's shoulders. 'If Cristina is here we'll rescue her, I promise.'

Ricardo looked between us. 'Are you really sure?'

'Just have a beer waiting for us when we get back down,' Mike said.

Jack unhitched his rucksack and shrugged it off his shoulders. He took out a roll of ten thousand dollar bills we'd already agreed among us and held it out towards Ricardo.

Ricardo held up his hands. 'I didn't help you for money. There's no charge for any of this.'

I gazed into his eyes. 'Use the money to make a difference for you and the other guides until Machu Picchu reopens, OK?'

He held my gaze for a moment but then took the roll and put his hand over his heart. 'Thank you, my friends, on behalf of all of us.'

'Just do us one favour,' I said.

'Name it.'

'Whatever happens, you never met the three of us.'

He peered at us. 'Who are you again?' A beaming toothy smile filled his face. 'And don't worry, the other guides won't say anything either.'

Ricardo pursed his lips, leaning into us, his mouth opening to say something. But then his shoulders dropped. He nodded to Mike and Jack, then leant forward and kissed me on the cheek. 'Be lucky, my friends.' He held our gaze in his. Then he held up his hand in farewell as he turned away and headed back down the mountain.

I waited until he was out of sight before I returned my attention to the others. 'Right, time to get ready for whatever is ahead.' I opened my rucksack and took out my LRS from its slim shoulder holster and strapped it on, trying to look a lot more confident than I felt. I was already feeling the weight of leadership pressing down on me.

'Just to remind you, this is meant to be a reconnaissance mission,' Mike said as he took out his dart gun.

'Sod that if Cristina's life is on the line, but I promise we'll only engage if we absolutely have to. Our first priority is to rescue Cristina if she's up here. The second will be for me to get close enough to this Solar Observatory to try out the Empyrean Key and see if it activates anything.'

'You think we'll find the micro mind there?' Jack said as he slipped on a lumberjack shirt to hide his Glock's holster.

'Well, Cristina's encounter bears a lot of similarities with my own experience at Skara Brae, so there's every reason to be hopeful.'

As I dug through my pack for my sports top, my eyes fell on the Empyrean Key nestling in the bottom. I ran my fingers over it, anticipation growing in me. Hopefully not much longer until I saw Lucy again. See her, rescue Cristina, save the world. If only it were that simple. Experience had taught me it would be anything but.

I took out the tuning fork from its leather pouch and slipped it on to my belt in readiness.

We began to thread our way through the trees that cast welcome dappled shade over us. Ahead was a small rock face with plenty of handholds. Yet it was a surprisingly strenuous climb, no doubt altitude playing a big factor, and Jack was the first to reach the top of the ledge.

'Holy crap,' he said, staring ahead of him.

I crested the top at the same time as Mike, my eyes eating up the astonishing view stretching away before us.

Framed against the mountain peaks of the Andes, Machu Picchu lay above us across a series of stepped terraces that followed the contours of the mountain to the top. Buildings ringed a grassy plateau, llamas wandering everywhere across the site. The sheer beauty of it in the spectacular mountaintop setting stole my breath away. It certainly exceeded any of the photos I'd seen of this place. No wonder so many people sought it out as a bucket list experience.

'Now that is seriously cool,' Mike said.

'Oh, Machu Picchu is far beyond cool,' Jack replied. He waved a hand towards it. 'All the greatest thinkers among the Incas civilisation lived up here. In their culture it was brains not brawn that was held in the highest esteem.'

I wrapped my hands round the back of my neck. 'Building something like this so high up must've taken incredible amounts of effort.'

'You'd better believe it, although of course the top of a mountain is exactly where you want to be when a quake hits. The way these buildings are constructed is an astonishing feat of engineering. The gaps between the interlocking stonework of the walls are almost millimetre perfect and have survived centuries of quakes. Even today researchers are still mystified about how they achieved such high standards.'

Mike pointed a finger to the sky and whistled the opening tune of *The X-Files*. 'Maybe they had help?'

'I hope not,' Jack said. 'I like to think that Machu Picchu was all their own work – another great example of human ingenuity.'

'But can you imagine if the Angelus did visit here?' I said.

'Yeah – the Incas would have probably thought it was their sun god putting in a house call,' Jack replied with a smile. 'If that's true, once again everything I thought I knew about archaeological history will be turned on its head.'

'It gives me goosebumps just thinking about it, so let's go and find out for sure.'

We started forward again, climbing up another slope through the trees towards the first of the terraces.

I unhooked my binoculars and peered through them.

Among the structures on the slope above us, I could see the distant specks of several people clustered round one that had curved walls, unlike the rest. Blue and white tape stretched round it, cordoning it off from the rest of the site. Uniformed police officers, along with a number of workers in dusty grey coveralls, were carrying red boxes and stacking them up on the main plateau, much to the interest of several llamas.

'What are they up to?' I asked.

Mike peered through his binoculars. 'I don't want to worry you, Jack, but those are transport boxes for dynamite. They've got enough there to level Machu Picchu.'

'Why the hell would they do that?' Jack asked, now looking through his binoculars. 'Hang on, isn't that Villca and...shit. He's got Cristina with him.'

I swung my binoculars to where Jack was looking and saw Villca talking to an older woman as they walked together. She had silver hair and was wearing a khaki shirt, trousers and wide-brimmed hat. The police commandant was pointing to the explosive boxes and shaking his head. Meanwhile, Cristina was being pushed along after by the thin policeman we'd seen with Villca on the security-camera footage.

'So that confirms he brought her up here with him,' Mike said.

'I'm still hoping that doesn't necessarily mean he's working with the Overseers,' I said.

'Possibly, and that woman with the silver hair is none other than Professor Evelyn Fischer,' Jack said. 'She's notorious among archaeologists and makes Indiana Jones look like the model of restraint. She doesn't give a damn about destroying a site if she can plunder the artefacts and peddle them to the highest bidder on the black market. The fact she's here at all is very bad news for Machu Picchu. She's brought those charges for a reason. There are rumours going way back that a hoard of Inca gold is hidden somewhere here. And maybe that's why Cristina is here too, to show Fischer exactly where she saw her visions in case they were a sign of a hidden chamber.'

'A sign from the Inca gods, you mean?'

'Maybe for Villca. But for Fischer money is the only god she worships.'

'She'd go as far as blowing holes in one of the greatest wonders of the world just to follow a hunch?' Mike asked.

'I'm sure I don't need to remind you how the Spanish plundered sites like this back in the sixteenth century. The Incas started to hide their treasure because of it. And if a hidden chamber exists, maybe that's where any hidden Inca gold is too. Fischer is certainly the sort of woman who will follow through on even the vaguest clue, however weird.'

'But surely Villca won't stand by and let her destroy Machu Picchu. It's the lifeblood to the whole region,' Mike said.

'It could be as simple as money, and probably lots of it,' Jack replied. 'The Inca gold could be worth countless billions. It could turn a lot of heads to do something like this. Fischer has almost certainly offered Villca a share of the profits.'

'Some people make me truly sick,' I said.

We watched through our binoculars as the group headed for the curved building.

'As we expected, they're making straight for the Solar Observatory,' Jack said.

The thin policeman pulled the hood off Cristina's head. Fischer came up to her, cradled Cristina's face in her hand and asked her something. Cristina shook her head and Fischer slapped the younger woman hard on the face.

I stiffened as Cristina glowered at her, a trickle of blood running down over her chin from her split lip.

'That bloody bitch,' Mike said.

The thin policeman shoved Cristina hard in the back and she took several faltering steps forward towards the Solar Observatory. She gestured with her chin towards the curving wall.

'I think she just told them where she saw those symbols,' I said, lowering my binoculars.

'I'm starting to think the Overseers are behind this after all,' Mike said. 'They must know your synaesthesia has something to do with being able to interact with a micro mind.'

'Unfortunately, I think you're probably right,' I replied. 'When I was interrogated by Alvarez he already knew about it. Although I didn't tell them that had anything to do with how we crossed over to E8, they must have put two and two together, particularly as that was how I communicated with Sentinel back at Jodrell Bank. Thankfully, when we were captured they didn't realise how significant the stone orb I had on me was.'

'So you're saying they picked up on the same clues that we did, which led them here?' Mike asked.

'That's not too much of a stretch, especially as they must also be aware of the recent neutrino activity.'

'So this could be fishing trip for the Overseers,' Mike said. 'Follow up a few leads on the off-chance one might lead to a micro mind. Plus throw in the added incentive of a possible pot of gold at the end of the rainbow.'

'Guys, I really don't like the look of this,' Jack said, still peering through his binoculars. 'Evelyn has just had her people set those charges all around the Solar Observatory. We should get up there and try to stop this before it's too late.'

He started to climb up on to the terrace but I grabbed his arm. 'Jack, we can't and you know it. There are only three of us against all of Villca's and Fischer's people. We need to keep cool heads and choose our moment, rather than charge in.'

'But we could try drawing them off with a diversion or something. Anything to stop them blowing those charges.' Jack stared at me with pleading eyes.

Something in me twisted as I shook my head. I knew what this meant to Jack. 'Do that and they'll know someone else is up here. They'll come after us and we'll blow our chance to help Cristina. We'll probably lose the micro mind – if it's up here – to them too.'

Mike chewed his lip and nodded. 'I know it's difficult to sit by and let this happen, Jack, but you've got to listen to Lauren. She's absolutely right on this.'

Jack tipped his face towards the sky, fingers interlocked round the back of his neck. He finally groaned and looked at us both. 'OK. I'm so not happy about this, but this is your call, Lauren. You're the one in charge of this mission.'

'This is the right move, even though it might not feel like it right now.'

Jack gave me a *whatever* shrug.

There was nothing I could say that would make this any easier for him. And I prayed this *was* the right move. The out-of-my-depth feeling was only getting worse.

We continued to watch Fischer's workers hook up the explosives and then trail their wires up to the plateau. Villca waved his arms round at Fischer wildly even as they headed over to a low wall to take cover. Bribery or not, the man obviously wasn't happy about what she was planning to do. But Fischer carried on walking away to take up position behind sandbags with everyone else.

I glanced across at Jack. His knuckles were white on his binoculars. The poor guy had seen the Overseers wreck Skara Brae, a site that had been his whole life, and was about to relive it all over again.

A distant siren started up and a few llamas around the Solar Observatory scattered.

'Get down – they're about to blow it,' Mike said.

We ducked behind the wall. I focused on a bead of sweat running down the back of Jack's neck as he hung his head, and resisted the urge to reach out for him. Alice aside, when had things become so tricky between us?

A massive boom shook the ground and a shock wave rattled through the trees around us. Seconds later, small stones rained down like hale, shredding the foliage and showering us with stinging impacts as we hunkered against the wall.

The roar of the explosion rolled away, echoing between the peaks as a tidal wave of dust rolled over us. Choking, I pulled up my T-shirt to cover my mouth as the dust began to swirl away slowly, revealing the destruction. Where the Solar Observatory had stood only a moment before was now a gaping hole in the ground.

Jacked growled. 'Those fucking bastards, if I get my hands on them...'

'You'll forget your Hippocratic oath again, right?' Mike asked.

'Damn right I will,' Jack replied.

Wiping the dust off my binoculars with my T-shirt, I peered

through them and saw Fischer striding back towards the blast site. Villca was close behind her, shaking his head.

Around us the leaves began to tremble. For a moment I thought a smaller secondary explosion had gone off. But then the ground shook and the mountain trembled with the song of grinding rock.

'Earthquake!' Mike said over the roar. He grabbed the probe spike from his pack and screwed it into the ground as it started bucking beneath us. 'Get down!'

We threw ourselves flat as the trees whipped around and the ground jerked.

A large boulder tumbled past us and bounced down the slopes, joining an avalanche of scree. In that moment the rock almost felt like liquid as it pulsed beneath my body, a living monster awoken by Fischer's explosives. I clutched my hands over my head, my heart hammering in my chest as it answered the cry of the quake.

The minutes stretched forward as the mountain continued to tremble. Then slowly, so slowly, the world became still again. We began to hear distant sirens drifting up from Aguas Calientes far below us.

I spat out the bile that had flooded my mouth. 'Is everyone OK?'

'Yeah, I'm good,' Jack said.

Mike nodded as he pulled his spike out of the ground and peered at the display on top. 'That was four on the Richter scale. More importantly, it was definitely a slow-moving monowave.'

In the middle of all this craziness, a flicker of excitement surged through me. 'Yet another sign that one of Lucy's micro minds really is here.'

'Not necessarily. I can't be certain the quake originated in this mountain. To be sure, I would need to place a number of sensors around it and triangulate them when another quake hits.'

'We haven't got time for that.' I peered over the terraced wall, but there wasn't any sign of Evelyn, Villca, Cristina or the others.

Mike gestured down the mountain. 'Those damned idiots – looks as if they got the hell out of here because of the quake.' He shook his head. 'The safest place they could be is up here on the mountain. The real problem will start when all those big rocks begin landing in the valley below.'

I looked down and saw a convoy of trucks and police vehicles speeding along the mountain road towards the town.

'Then we should grab this opportunity to find out what we can and then look for an opportunity to rescue Cristina later,' I said.

'Damned right,' Jack replied.

Together we scrambled over the edge of the terrace and walked towards the shattered stones of the Solar Observatory and the plume of smoke drifting up from a gaping hole into the bright cobalt-blue sky.

CHAPTER TWELVE

ALTHOUGH THE AIR was now clear of dirt thrown up from the explosion and I'd drunk half of my aqua pack, I still had a dusty tang in my mouth. The jungle soundtrack had stopped dead and there was no sign of the llamas anywhere. Apart from us, Machu Picchu was deserted. It made it easier to imagine this site as a bustling community of the Incas living here five hundred years ago, their elite of the elite.

We were on the eastern side of Machu Picchu, stone paths criss-crossing the network of buildings. Despite the severity of the quake, with the notable exception of the Solar Observatory, I couldn't see any fresh debris that had fallen from the many sturdy-looking walls. At least Fischer's wanton act of archaeological vandalism had been limited in that way.

Mike trailed a hand over the smoothed wall beside us as we walked up some steps. 'The earthquake hasn't left so much as a scratch on these.'

Striding out ahead of us, Jack nodded. 'Like I said, Machu Picchu has survived every quake in history. That makes what Fischer just did an even bigger crime.' He reached the shattered remains of the Solar Observatory and clenched his hands into fists as he took in the damage.

We joined him at the rim of a sloping basin where the building had stood only a few minutes before. Now there was just scree sloping down to the dark hole in the middle. The rising column of smoke had begun to fade away.

Tears beaded Jack's eyes. 'I don't have the fucking words right now.'

I patted his back. 'I know.'

Together we picked our way carefully down the scree slope and peered into the inky hole of darkness in the centre.

'Did you know that was down there, Jack? It appears to be some sort of room?'

'There's no mention of it in any of the records I've seen.'

'We might not agree with her methods, but it looks as if Fischer really might be on to something,' Mike said.

'And if the micro mind is down there she may have just blown it up,' Jack groaned. 'I can't see that sitting well with her bosses.'

A sinking sensation passed through me to my toes. 'Let's find out.' I dug a torch out of my bag and shone its powerful LED beam down into the blackness. Partially buried by rubble, there appeared to be stone steps descending from the small hidden room and a corridor sloping away into the darkness.

'Do you want to give the Empyrean Key a go to see if you can communicate with the micro mind, Lauren?'

I nodded, taking the stone orb out of my rucksack and the metal tuning fork from its pouch. I gave it a sharp tap on the orb. A deep chiming note rang out but nothing appeared over the Empyrean Key.

'I'm not seeing anything,' I said. 'But I wouldn't panic just yet – I'm guessing that corridor leads somewhere.'

'Tombs possibly, or something like that. If so, there may be a significant amount of gold down there too.'

'Well, there's only one way to find out – let's go and explore,' Mike said.

I shook my head. 'Not all three of us. Villca and Evelyn could arrive back at any moment – once they decide this mountain is safe from further quakes. We need somebody to remain up here and warn us if they're returning. And as Jack is the archaeologist and I'm the one who can use the Empyrean Key, that means...'

'You guys get to have all the fun, in other words.'

'Those are the breaks,' Jack said.

'Yeah, tell me about it. Never mind – I'll set up more seismic monowave probes and take some readings whilst I'm keeping guard. There are likely to be some milder aftershocks and the more data we can gather the more there'll be for us to analyse afterwards.'

'I really wanted to hear that another quake might hit whilst we're underground,' I said.

'Relax, Lauren,' Jack said. 'You can see for yourself how Machu Picchu coped with a serious earthquake. We can be reasonably certain that any underground passage will too.'

'Then let's get going,' I said.

With our torches' light beams illuminating the way, Jack and I slid down a sloping slab of rock that had been split in two by the blast.

We landed on the rubble floor below and found ourselves at the entrance to a sloped tunnel with perfectly smooth stone walls. There was no sign of any weathering, unlike the structures on the surface.

Jack took a deep breath in. 'As I thought.'

'What?'

'Taste the air.'

I drew in a large lungful but got nothing. 'I'm not picking up on anything unusual.'

'Exactly. The air isn't stale. There isn't even any lichen growing on the walls. My guess is that this was hermetically sealed until Fischer blew a hole through the Solar Observatory. Once again testament to the stone-crafting abilities of the Incas.'

'If they didn't have help that is...' I pointed to the sky as Mike had earlier.

'If the Angelus built this place, I'm pretty sure they would have been able to melt straight through the rock with some sort of souped-up laser. But the wall is constructed from stone slabs, suggesting human work.'

'In other words, one made by our species and not alien visitors.'

'Exactly. Maybe there's hope of turning you from a UFO fangirl into an archaeologist yet.'

'Sorry, I'm too far gone for that.'

Jack laughed and my heart lifted at the sound, especially after the sharpness of his earlier tone with me.

Mike's silhouette against the bright blue sky appeared above us. 'How's it going down there?'

'There's no obvious sign of whatever triggered Cristina's visions, so we'll need to head deeper down this passageway,' I replied.

'Don't go too far. I doubt even Sky Dreamer Corp's state-of-the-art Sky Wire phones can work through solid rock.'

'So we'll need to maintain a line of sight to each other,' I said. I directed my torch beam along the corridor that sloped away into darkness. We could use the walkie-talkie function on the phones for this. 'Mike, place your phone near the entrance and we should be able to stay in contact.'

'And if you go round a bend?'

'Then we lose contact.'

'So try not to do that, hey, because you'll worry me sick. Here, catch.'

Mike lobbed his phone down to us and I caught it one-handed, the muscle memory of my years of playing ball games at school kicking in. I pulled up the walkie-talkie function and toggled it into speaker mode before placing it on the step.

'Just give us plenty of warning to pull out if there's even a hint of company on its way,' I called up to Mike.

'I will. Good hunting, guys.'

I nodded and turned to Jack. 'I know what a big deal this is for you, so you'd better take the lead.'

'It could be the archaeological discovery of the century, so thank you...'

His eyes had a faraway look as he stepped past me into the passageway. A man about to realise his dreams. He so deserved this after what had happened at Skara Brae.

We started down the steps into a corridor of darkness so long it was beyond the reach of even our torch beams.

Jack seemed lost in a world of his own as we headed down into the heart of the mountain. I could only begin to imagine how his excitement was building.

For me, it felt eerie knowing that we were probably the first people to walk down here since this secret passageway had been closed off centuries before. What would be waiting for us at the bottom? I just prayed with every fibre of my being that it would be another crystal facet of Lucy's artificial consciousness. Certainly whoever had built this had gone to a serious amount of trouble to stop it being discovered.

'Bloody hell,' I said after a while. 'This is even harder work than the climb up to Machu Picchu.'

'There's probably even less oxygen down here. I've not felt so much as the faintest breeze, which suggests a lack of airflow. If you get too lightheaded, tell me, and we'll have to head back to the surface.'

'But we may not get this chance again,' I replied.

'I realise that, but as much as I want to know where this leads to, I'm not prepared to put your life on the line.'

I knew Jack was being sensible, but with each step the idea that we might be closing in on another micro mind powered my determination to see this through. 'I'm good for now, so let's keep going.'

But as we continued forward I could almost feel the weight of the mountain pushing down on us from above.

'Guys, are you there?' Mike's voice rang out from my Sky Wire phone.

I unclipped it from my belt and pressed the talk button.

'All good, although I'm half expecting to see Bilbo Baggins and Gollum down here, we're that deep beneath the mountain.'

'*The Hobbit*, right?' Jack asked.

I nodded. 'That and *The Lord of the Rings* are two of the greatest stories ever told.'

'If you say so.'

'Oh, I do.'

Jack shrugged. 'Anyway, Mike, please don't tell us we need to head back up to the surface already?'

'Nope, no sign of the bad guys yet. You're good for a while longer. I was just checking in to see you were both doing OK.'

'Yeah, we're fine,' I replied.

'Good. Over and out.'

We started forward again and soon the stitch in my side became a burning knife of pain. As the air grew even leaner, spots of light started to dance in front of my eyes. I had to put a hand on the wall to steady myself and dragged in a breath, my lungs burning. I couldn't carry on much longer, but then Jack came to a stop ten metres ahead of me.

'What's that?' he said, not realising the state I was in. His torch beam was no longer disappearing into the darkness but playing over something solid ahead.

'Thank god.' I pushed myself off the wall as Jack strode down two steps at a time and I forced myself to hurry after him. By the time I caught up, Jack was standing before a slab of polished stone that completely blocked the passageway.

'This must be some sort of doorway, but damned if I can see any obvious mechanism to open it.'

'You think it might be a sealed tomb or something?' I asked.

'No way to be sure until we get through it.'

'If this were an Indiana Jones film, there'd be a special hidden trigger to open it, probably in a nest of creepy crawlies,' I said.

Jack shook his head at me. 'You really do watch too many movies.' He continued to probe the edges with his fingertips. 'Nope, this looks permanently sealed. As far as I can tell it was never intended to be opened again.'

'So what do we do now? Head back to the surface and grab some C4 to explode it open – if there's time?'

Jack's eyes narrowed on me. 'No – it would probably cave the whole corridor in. The proper archaeological approach here would be to excavate round this very carefully with a good old-fashioned chisel.'

'And you think Fischer will do that when she eventually turns up here?'

'Of course not. She'll blast through this and excavate through any resultant rockfalls to help herself to whatever is on the other side.'

I stared at him and felt like slapping myself. 'I've missed the most bloody obvious thing here! If there is a micro mind just the other side of that door, then...'

Jack's eyes lit up. 'Try it, Lauren.'

I grabbed the Empyrean Key out of my rucksack again and

struck it with my tuning fork. The crystal-clear tone rang out, seeming much louder in the confined space. I stared at the stone orb, willing it to activate.

'Come on, come on...'

A flicker of light danced over the Empyrean Key and then a single icon appeared – an arrow pointing upwards.

I punched the air. 'Yes!'

Jack stared at me. 'You've found a way to open it?'

'Only one way to find out for sure...'

I rotated the arrow into the selection window and flicked my wrist forward.

The icon turned green and a grinding sound came from the slab of stone as it began to slide up into the ceiling.

Jack whooped and drew me into a fierce hug. 'You genius!'

I laughed. 'Why, thank you, kind sir.' His hands hung on to me and I felt a tickle of electricity. But too soon his arms dropped away and he gave me a lopsided smile before turning away to peer into the inky gloom beyond and the hint of a large chamber.

My insides sank as the moment slipped away, and my Sky Wire burst into life.

'We've got serious trouble,' Mike said between pops of static.

I pressed the speak icon. 'What's happened?'

'I've been trying to get hold of you for the last five minutes. Villca and the rest of them are back. They're on their way to the Solar Observatory right now.'

'Shit, then get the hell out of there,' I said.

'But what about you?' Mike whispered.

'We've just discovered a chamber. Hopefully we can find another way out from it or hide inside. We'll wait for the coast to clear before making a break for the surface. Get back down to Aguas Calientes and if we haven't turned up by tonight, contact Niki and tell him to bring in the cavalry.'

'Right...' There was a pause and I heard voices in the background growing louder. 'Got to go. Good luck to us all.'

'Amen to that,' Jack said.

A faintest pinprick of light that was barely a star appeared at the top of the shaft behind us.

'I'm guessing that's not Mike,' Jack said.

'Fuck, we need to kill our torches!' My breathing seemed impossibly loud as we turned them off and plunged ourselves into darkness.

'You know you opened the door – do you think you can close it behind us in the same way?' Jack whispered.

'Let me try.'

Heart racing, I gripped the Empyrean Key and struck the tuning fork against it. A deep note hummed out and an icon blazed into existence over the orb – a downwards-facing arrow. I quickly selected it and rotated my wrist forward, my jaw tensing.

A low grinding sound came from the passageway and the door slid shut behind us.

'Oh, thank god,' Jack said from the darkness.

'At least that will buy us some time,' I said. 'Now let's see where we are.' I turned and flicked my torch back on. Jack and I gasped at what lay before us.

We were standing in a large vaulted chamber about five hundred metres wide. At the far end towered a giant stylised stone figure with hollowed-out eyes, holding a skull in its hand. But it was what lay before it that stole all the attention. Surrounded by a moat was a large plaza. A vast ziggurat stood in the middle, covered in what appeared to be solid gold stretching up towards the ceiling.

I turned to Jack, slack-jawed. 'What the hell is this place?'

Jack stared at me. 'Exactly that, Lauren. I think we've just stumbled into the Inca version of hell.'

CHAPTER THIRTEEN

IF THE SCENE before us was overwhelming for me, I could only begin to imagine what it was like for Jack. He stared at the view open-mouthed. A gurgle of water gently echoed throughout the room from the small streams emerging from holes ringing the chamber. They cascaded in a series of small waterfalls down into the rectangular moat below.

The faintest breeze brushed my face. I sucked in a lungful of the fresh air and the light-headedness began to evaporate.

Jack put his hands on top of his head. 'This is beyond anything I could have ever imagined.' His words amplified as they bounced around the chamber.

'Bloody hell, talk about an acoustic effect,' I whispered, my words coming back at us in just a murmur this time.

'Interesting,' Jack replied, also in a hushed tone. His torch beam played over the ceiling, revealing scallop shapes carved into it. 'I bet you that those have something to do with the echo effect.'

'You think this chamber was deliberately designed to amplify sounds?'

'It could have been, especially if the Angelus had anything to do with it.'

'I thought you said aliens hadn't built this place.'

'Up there maybe, but down here I'm not so sure. Anyway, whatever else this might be, I'm pretty certain this chamber represents the Inca version of the underworld – Ukhu Pacha. The symbolism down here is a whole area of research in itself. Even the moat round that temple is significant.'

'How so?'

'Like many cultures, the Incas believed that hell was where bad people ended up. But in their religion Ukhu Pacha also represented rebirth, symbolised by water, hence the significance of a moat. They called our physical world Kay Pacha and, going by the location of Machu Picchu directly overhead, this probably represented that. Then there was Hanan Pacha, the upper realm of the Inca sun god and moon goddess in the sky – so where else would they build one of their most sacred cities but as close to heaven as possible.'

'And what's the deal with that huge statue?'

'That's Supay, leader of the demons. But he isn't like the Christian version of the devil. Ukhu Pacha can also be thought of as their earth mother and even our own inner world, so it's not all bad. Man, I'd need several lifetimes to study what's down here.'

I gestured back to the corridor we'd emerged from. 'Unfortunately, we don't have long before Fischer and her team try to blast their way in here. Our priority must be to locate the micro mind. Everything else is secondary to that, even one of the most significant archaeological discoveries since Tutankhamun's tomb. After all, the fate of our world is hanging in the balance.'

Jack sighed. 'Don't I know it.'

Together we headed down the steps and over a bridge crossing the moat to the large open plaza in front of the gold ziggurat.

Jack took out his Sky Wire and began taking photos. He caught me giving him a sideways glance.

'Something for me to study afterwards,' he said. 'I'll probably never get a chance to see this place again.'

'I can already see your TED talk to a packed room of people about your archaeological discovery of the century. But to admit to the world that we'd been here at all would open up a can of worms about who we are and what we were doing here.' I didn't voice my other worry that grew by the second – I couldn't help feeling that we'd just created a trap for ourselves. There was no other obvious exit out of this chamber. I also couldn't see anywhere obvious for us to hide. That meant we would have to leave the way we came. And how would that work out if Fischer, Villca and their people were on the other side of the door?

I kept my concerns to myself as we crossed the plaza to the golden ziggurat glinting under our torchlight.

Jack gestured to the Empyrean Key still in my left hand. 'Is it worth trying your magic eight ball again?'

'Definitely.'

I took hold of the tuning fork and gave it a sharp tap on the stone. The orb lit up with two icons hovering over it. Next to the door control, a stylised sun icon was now blinking.

'Oh, this is new,' I said. I rolled the sun icon into the selection window and flicked my wrist forward. Golden light shimmered into existence from a dozen crystal spheres mounted in the ceiling, making the gold-covered temple almost incandescent. It also revealed a series of frescoes carved into the walls of the chamber. In the panel directly over the doorway, a stylised version of Machu Picchu with its stepped terraced construction clinging to the top of the mountain had been carved into the rock. But it was what was in the next panel that made my pulse amp.

I grabbed Jack's wrist and pointed at the inverted tetrahedron shape hanging over Machu Picchu. 'Look!'

Jack gawped at it. 'Holy crap. If we needed confirmation that the Angelus once visited this site, that pretty much seals the deal.'

My gaze swept hungrily to the next pictogram. In it, the micro mind was now floating at a forty-five-degree angle to Machu Picchu, a light beam blazing out from its tip towards the ancient city. And where the beam struck the ground, figures were on their knees with their heads down and arms extended.

'That looks like an act of worship to me,' Jack said.

'Me too. The gods from the sky making that house call we talked about.'

In the next pictogram, a cross-section of the mountain showed a group of people following the light beam's path as they dug a tunnel down it into the mountain.

'That has to be the shaft we came through,' I said.

Jack nodded. 'Which suggests that the Angelus were instrumental in directing the Incas to this chamber. It had probably formed naturally. In other words, the Angelus gave them the highway straight to Ukhu Pacha.'

Together we gazed at the next panel. It showed thousands of workers building inside the underground temple, constructing the giant statue of Supay. The final panel depicted the chamber as it was now, but with one major difference – there was a starburst blazing from the summit of the temple.

My back tingled as I gestured towards it. 'Do you think...?'

'That X marks the spot for the location of the micro mind? I certainly pray so. But you should give your magic eight ball another tap to see if it turns up anything else.'

I struck the tuning fork again. This time another icon appeared and this one was familiar – a circle with an arrow left and right of it.

A slow smile filled my face.

'What is it?' Jack asked.

'You remember that galactic map back at Skara Brae? I think I might have just found something similar here.'

'So try it already.'

'Oh, I'm all over it.'

I selected the reverse arrow and activated it. At once, hundreds of beams of light burst from the orbs in the ceiling, illuminating the chamber like a disco. But rather than stars, ghostly figures appeared where the beams danced over the plaza, then vanished. The scene stopped and a crowd of ghosts – at least a thousand – froze in place as they headed over a bridge and on to the plaza. There were men and women, bare-armed and -legged, all wearing embroidered cloths and large ornate necklaces.

'I wish you could see what I'm seeing, Jack.'

Jack turned towards me with a stunned expression. 'Don't you worry about that, Lauren Stelleck. This isn't your synaesthesia. Those orbs in the ceiling must be some sort of holographic projectors, because I can see this as well as you can. These people have to be the original Aztecs who built this place.'

'But as supremely cool as that is, why are we being shown this, Jack?'

'It has to be for a reason.'

'So let's find out for sure...' I gazed at the circle now pulsing in between the two arrows and rolled my wrist forward.

Like a movie fast-forwarding, all the figures burst into sped-up motion and moved towards the ziggurat temple where they gathered at its base. A figure in long robes stood in front of a doorway near the top of a stepped structure, arms spread wide as he gazed down at the people below him. Then the holographic movie slowed to normal playback speed.

'Is that guy some sort of priest?' I asked.

Jack nodded. 'The Willaq Umu, the high priest – and usually the brother of the emperor. That suggests that this was some sort of important ceremony.'

The figures in the plaza knelt down like some sort of choreo-graphed flash mob, all eyes on the priest, who slowly raised some-thing shiny into the air. For an awful moment I thought it was a knife and we were about to witness a human sacrifice.

Jack grabbed his binoculars and peered through them at the shimmering figure above us.

He grinned and pointed to the Empyrean Key in my hand. 'I think he's holding one of those. And that's a huge deal because, as far as I'm aware, one of those stone orbs has never been found outside Europe.'

Anticipation was now running circuits in my stomach as we moved forward towards the edge of the holographic crowd. We began to pick our way among the people now raising and lowering their hands. Many had the same physique as the modern-day Peruvians we'd met in the town.

Finding his path blocked by a closely packed group, Jack was forced to walk straight through a woman who was bowing. She shimmered slightly as he passed through her. I managed to make my way round her. There was no way I was walking through her – far too weird for me.

We reached the edge of the golden temple, almost blinding now under the lights. My heart began to accelerate as we ascended the oversized steps. Were we really about to find another fragment of Lucy's consciousness?

The priest thrust the round stone orb aloft. The holograms of the gathered crowd threw themselves flat to the ground.

'Whatever this ceremony is, it looks as if it's about to reach its climax,' Jack said.

As we finally reached the same level as the priest, he turned and went through the open doorway behind him.

Every fibre of my being tingled with excitement as we followed the ghostly apparition inside and found ourselves in a little room with a smaller version of the holographic projector set into the ceiling. The priest stood in front of a raised stone plinth that held a model Inca city about three metres wide. It was intricately carved, from the statues to the buildings with frescoes on them. All it needed was miniature llamas and it would be set. But although similar in style to Machu Picchu, its layout was different.

'Talk about a letdown,' I said. 'I really thought we were about to discover the micro mind. Do you think it's buried beneath this ziggurat?'

Jack shook his head and tapped his finger on his lips. 'There's something familiar about this model – and look at the priest now.'

The holographic man held his Empyrean Key carefully over the model city. I could now see it was almost identical to the one in my own hand. Eyes closed, he appeared to be chanting.

Jack let out a sigh. 'I knew I recognised this place. This is a model of Choquequirao. It was a contemporary of Machu Picchu and about sixty miles from here.'

'So why place a model of that city in this chamber?' I asked.

'Whatever the reason, it has to be significant,' Jack replied.

As if in answer, the priest's eyes snapped open and he lowered his Empyrean Key towards a building in the top-right-hand corner of the model city.

I noticed a semi-circular depression in the building's roof, in which a real-life Empyrean Key was already nestling. The priest placed his holographic version over its counterpart, his image flared with light and he and his phantom orb disappeared, leaving just the physical version behind.

Jack turned towards me. 'Did you just stop the playback?'

I shook my head. 'It has to be the end of the recording. And this must be significant.' I reached out and took hold of the other stone sphere.

'Stop!' Jack shouted.

But I'd already started to lift the other Empyrean Key. At

once, a rumbling came from outside. I bit my lip and dropped the stone orb back into the depression.

The rumbling grew louder.

'Shit!' I said.

We both dashed outside. The holograms of the crowd had vanished, presumably at the same moment the priest had. The small streams that had been flowing out of the walls had turned into major torrents, making the moat rise fast. The thunder of the water bounced around the walls, making my ears ring.

'Jack, I've got a bad feeling that this situation is about to get a lot worse.'

'Me too. That stone orb must have been booby-trapped in case someone helped themselves to it.'

'What the hell have I done?' I was meant to be the leader and already I'd screwed things up for us.

'Never mind beating yourself up right now,' Jack said. 'We have more pressing matters!'

The rapidly rising water had already covered the bridge and was now surging over it towards the temple. I scanned the room, but still couldn't see any obvious exit.

Jack was staring round too. 'We need to get to the highest point.'

I gestured to the top of the temple. 'That's going to be as good a place as any.'

We climbed the final steps to the summit of the ziggurat. Even though it took us moments, by the time we'd reached the top the water was already lapping about the base of the temple, starting to swallow it step by step.

'We're going to die down here, aren't we?' I said.

'As they say, hope is that thing with wings,' Jack replied.

'I'd settle for a bloody life jacket right now.'

Despite the tension in his face, Jack chuckled. 'You're quite a woman, Lauren Stelleck.'

'So you keep telling me.'

The water rose ever quicker, surging up until it lapped round our feet. Icy numbness spread through me as it covered our thighs, waists and chests until we were floating up from the ziggurat, treading water.

Jack grabbed on to me. 'Isn't there an override for any of this on your Empyrean Key?'

I had to shout over the deafening roar of water. 'Damn it, I didn't think to check!'

Kicking hard, I lifted the stone clear of the water and raised it above my head. Jack wrapped his arms round me for support as he kicked hard to lift me. I kept my hands clear of the frothing water and raised the tuning fork. *Please, god, make this work.*

I struck the tuning fork against the orb.

My stomach balled into a hard lump when no icons appeared over the orb. There wasn't even the open-door command, which would at least have released some of the water.

'It's not working, Jack!'

'But it doesn't make sense to lure someone with the right key into a death trap.'

The water surged again, lifting us farther towards the ceiling decorated with carved star constellations.

Why wasn't the bloody Empyrean Key working?

My gaze snapped back to the tuning fork. Of course, I couldn't bloody hear it over the deafening roar of water. We were going to die because I couldn't hear the vibration of a tuning fork... Wait, vibration! That was all sounds waves were, so...

I struck the tuning fork again, but this time I pressed its handle against the top of my jawbone just beneath my ear. A deep note filled my eardrum, humming through me, and the icons blinked back into existence round the orb, plus a new mouth-shaped icon that blinked rapidly.

I spun the Empyrean Key and selected the icon, managing to

grab a last lungful of air just as the water surged up over our heads. The mouth icon turned green and I flicked my wrist forward underwater.

We were buffeted by currents from every side, the world a confusion of swirling bubbles and muted howling. The only constants in the chaos were Jack's arms still clasped round me and the stone orb held tight in my hand.

Then I heard a new sound – a rumbling noise somewhere ahead of us. A vortex of bubbles reached out and grabbed hold of us, pulling us towards the far side of the chamber. I caught a glimpse of the top of the temple skimming past, the head of the Supay statue rushing towards us. Through the swirling haze I could make out his mouth had pivoted open to reveal a black hole behind. The current strengthened, pummelling our bodies as the dark cavern of nothingness rushed towards us. The maelstrom sucked us into the mouth and we sped away along a dark underwater tunnel.

My chest burned as my lungs used the last of the oxygen. Unknown things crashed into me, but still Jack and I hung on to each other, two souls fighting for life.

A pinpoint of light quickly grew brighter and wider. In an explosion of water, we were swept out into daylight. Still clinging to each other, we dropped at least fifty metres into a pool of foaming water, hitting the surface hard. The impact knocked the air out of me as we slid beneath the water. But our momentum was killed rapidly. We kicked upwards together desperately and burst through the surface in a shock of air and sky.

I gulped in fresh oxygen as I began to make out where we were. Behind us the waterfall that had carried us into the pool was tumbling from a cave mouth in the side of the mountain.

Together we swam for the shore and crawled up on to the embankment into the shadow of the surrounding jungle. Every part of my body felt as if it had been pummelled. We both slumped on to our backs, staring upwards, me still miraculously clutching the Empyrean Key and the tuning fork to my chest.

Then, of all things, Jack started to laugh, tears filling his eyes. He whooped and pulled me into a tight hug.

A second later, he pulled away, grinning. 'We're fucking alive, Lauren!'

I was half laughing, half crying, as we grabbed each other in another hug. I felt the beat of his heart against my chest and I felt a surge of love for this man. Instinctively, I turned my face towards his, my lips almost brushing his neck. But then he pulled away and it felt as if a part of me was missing.

A bubble of sadness rose through my body as I gave him a forced smile. His eyes skated away from mine and I sighed. Whatever it was we had between us, we were so not on the same page.

CHAPTER FOURTEEN

WE'D BARELY SPOKEN as we headed deeper into the jungle, not wanting to alert any eyes on the mountain to our escape. Confusion about what had just happened with Jack clouded my mind. I'd felt the guy soften into me, our edges merging, and the next he was pulling away like I was an ancient warty grandmother who'd just tried to kiss him. Thankfully, I had other things to focus on, and tried to ignore the crippling embarrassment.

Despite both being soaked through, we were drying quickly in the heat of the day, thanks to our high-tech wicking clothing. Fortunately, the rest of our belongings had remained intact and dry inside our rucksacks, our Sky Wires as sturdy as ever. I'd already tried contacting Mike on both the walkie-talkie and the phone, but so far he wasn't picking up. I was trying not to automatically jump to the worst conclusion: that he'd been captured.

Amazingly, our disguises were still in place too, although Jack's ponytail now resembled the tail of a drowned cat and I really needed a brush to drag through my blonde locks.

My gaze wandered back to the side of the mountain, just

visible through the thick trees. The waterfall that had spat us out of the cave mouth was now just a small tumbling stream.

'I guess that means the chamber has emptied itself of water,' I said, nodding at it.

Jack glanced at me for the first time since the almost-kiss, his eyes meeting mine. 'Which means Fischer and Villca won't have too much trouble getting in there. And by the time anybody else outside their inner circle realises what's going on, it will be too late to stop her spiriting all that gold away.'

'You think?' I gestured towards Jack's Sky Wire phone clipped on his belt. 'Didn't you take lots of photos? Wouldn't it be a shame if somehow they got out into the public domain...'

Jack slowly smiled. 'Wouldn't it just? Then all that gold could be claimed by the Peruvian state rather than lining the pockets of Fischer and Villca.'

'Exactly. We can hand the photos over to Ricardo when we get back to town. I'm sure he can make good use of them.'

'But what about Cristina? We have to help her somehow,' Jack said.

'Ricardo has access to that security-camera footage directly linking Villca to Cristina's abduction. Combine that with the photos of his involvement in setting the charges that blew up the Solar Observatory and I suspect he'll end up rotting in a Peruvian jail for the rest of his life.'

'That bastard deserves everything that's coming for him,' Jack replied. 'So what do we do about locating the micro mind? I'm worried it might still be hidden in that chamber somewhere. I doubt we'll be able to gain access again, as at least in the short term it will be swarming with Villca's and Fischer's people. As much as I hate to admit it, we may have reached the point of handing this mission over to Tom and his security team.'

I shook my head. 'I'm as certain as I can be now that it's not at Machu Picchu. My money is on Choquequirao. Why else would they have built that model of the city inside and gone to the trouble of booby-trapping it?'

'That does make sense—'

Jack's words were cut off by animal cries erupting all around us as hundreds of birds took flight. A moment later a tremor shuddered though the ground. It was a lot less powerful than the last one, but still strong enough to whip the trees about. Then a deep tone vibrated from the mountain and my whole body buzzed in sympathy, as if I were a tuning fork.

'Another monowave quake?' Jack asked, staring at me.

But I ignored him because light was bursting over the Empyrean Key in my hand. However, rather than the usual menu items appearing, it showed just a circle round the stone orb in a horizontal plane. An arrow in its circumference pointed to the left of us and I followed it, seeing a distant mountain range. As the ground continued to shake, I reorientated my body towards the mountains. The arrow remained pointing straight towards them, like a compass needle locked on to magnetic north.

Jack peered at the Empyrean Key and then me. 'Is that sound from the mountain triggering your synaesthesia?'

I nodded. 'I'm seeing this arrow pointing towards that mountain range in the distance.'

The quake started to subside and the deep humming from the mountain faded. The arrow began to flicker round the orb.

Jack unclipped his Sky Wire and pulled up the map function. A green dot indicated our position on the northern slopes of Machu Picchu. He zoomed the map out to show a large section of the surrounding area and typed 'Choquequirao' into the search bar. A red marker appeared to the west of us. He zoomed in on that until we could see a satellite view of another Inca temple on a mountaintop.

'Is that the direction your marker is pointing to?' Jack asked.

I nodded as my heart expanded with fresh hope. The sound

from the mountain faded away to silence and the icons vanished. 'Hopefully we'll find that micro mind in the building the other Empyrean Key was placed in.'

'OK, but what if it wasn't a micro mind at Machu Picchu that triggered your ability?'

'It has to be something to do with the shape of that chamber. Remember that echo effect inside it? If the Angelus were involved in its construction, I expect the acoustic effect was far from an accident. It must have been designed to trigger a visual response in someone with synaesthesia.'

'But what created it?'

'Without something to generate the sound, like a tuning fork, how about a slow-moving monowave originating at a different location?' I replied. 'We know that sound was amplified within that chamber. So what if, like my tuning fork being struck, when the right vibration hits the chamber it creates a resonance, which is channelled through the rock?'

Jack's eyes widened. 'And then anyone near the mountain with your form of synaesthesia would start to see visions, just like Cristina did when a monowave quake hit.'

'Bloody hell. This is going to blow Mike's mind when we tell him. Talking of which, we should try checking in with him again.'

Jack nodded, put his Sky Wire on to speaker mode and dialled Mike. A moment later we heard it ring... Ten seconds became thirty... Jack was about to give up when there was a click.

My heart leapt. 'Oh, thank god, we were wondering what had happened to you.'

But there was only silence at the other end of the line. I frowned at Jack.

'Hey, buddy, can you hear us?' Jack asked.

'Who are you?' asked a male voice with a Peruvian accent.

Jack hit the call end button. 'Crap, that can't be good.' He pulled up the map and toggled to an option at the side of it. A location marker for Mike appeared, showing that he, or at least his phone, was now in the police station in Aguas Calientes.

My gut twisted. 'Shit!'

Jack's hand trembled and his expression zoned out. It made me think of a training exercise we'd completed back at Eden. We'd had to cross a fast-moving river in a deep gorge with a rope we'd managed to string over it. I'd thought it was Mike who would freeze because of his fear of heights, but of all people it was Mr Hero himself who'd had a bad case of the shakes halfway across. So bad that I'd ended up stringing a second line across and headed out to him to talk him across to the other side. Nothing about it was mentioned afterwards by any of us – it was just one of those things. But back then I couldn't help but wonder whether the stress of what we'd been through was starting to get to Jack.

'Jack, are you OK?' I asked.

His eyes focused on me and he blinked. 'Sorry...what were we talking about?'

I stared at him, feeling rattled that he could tune out something so important. 'Mike. Best case, he's lost his phone and it's been picked up and handed in.'

'Worst case, he got himself captured at Machu Picchu,' Jack replied, seemingly back to his usual self.

'But if he's fallen into Villca's hands...' Fear bubbled in me.

'Let's just pray he's sitting at the rendezvous point in the bar wondering where his phone is.'

'I bloody well hope so, but my instinct is that this is bad, Jack.'

'You're not the only one.' He stepped out again and my eyes lingered on his back for a moment. Where had he been in his head just now?

We checked in with Niki as we headed down the mountain towards town and filled him in on what was happening. He gave us strict instructions not to engage, even if we discovered Mike was in trouble. If that happened, we were to contact him again and he would call back a security team from the UFO investigation and send them in to secure Mike's release. I wasn't thrilled at his plan – it would no doubt delay any rescue attempt – but I also understood the sense in it.

I told him I'd email him photos of Villca's abduction of Cristina, plus Fischer destroying the Solar Temple. Niki promised to get the word out via social media – using secure, untraceable routes that Tom had already set up. One way or another Villca and Fischer would face the music.

Once I'd emailed Niki the photos and hung up, Jack and I accelerated into an almost full-blown run, yomping through the jungle back to the city. With every passing minute, my anxiety levels ratcheted up. What if Mike had been captured and tortured to reveal what he knew? What if we were too late…? My looping thoughts only quietened down once we'd arrived at the edge of the town and started to make our way towards the bar. Everywhere seemed to be swarming with police vehicles, their blue lights flashing as they rushed around.

My thoughts also kept returning to Jack's strange reaction to the news about Mike. I discounted what had happened at the waterfall – I'd obviously misread the signs. But Jack zoning out like that was so similar to what had happened over the ravine. I'd put that down to stress, a panic attack even. But what if it was something more? Even if he didn't want to talk about it, I needed to know, if only for my peace of mind.

I gathered my resolve. 'Jack, I need to ask you something.'

Jack glanced round at me. 'What is it?'

'I'm worried about you.'

He stopped dead, his gaze falling to the jungle floor. 'Why's that exactly?'

'You seemed to have some sort of moment when you heard about Mike. Something similar happened during the training exercise back at Eden. Is there anything I should know about as your team leader? Something that might affect your performance on this mission?'

His gaze slowly lifted from the ground back to me. 'You know at Skara Brae how I went charging into everything without a care in the world?'

'I put it down to you being a naturally heroic Viking.'

'No, I'm afraid that, like any person with half a brain in their head, I was scared to death. But I was able to blot that out – and there was a reason for that.' He looked at his hands. 'Have you ever noticed me with the shakes?'

I nodded, and a swirl of worry passed through my stomach. 'Please don't tell me you have some serious medical condition?'

'Not in the way you mean.'

'So what then?'

'It's one of the withdrawal symptoms of coming off Prozac too quickly.'

The huge knot of anxiety in my stomach loosened. 'So you were on antidepressants – big deal, Jack. It's not an issue. After all, half the world takes something to numb the pain from time to time – from booze to drugs and everything in between.' A new thought surfaced and I found myself staring at him. 'Hang on, is this something to do with the death of your wife?'

'No, I was on Prozac long before Sue died.'

'Right... So you're telling me that you freezing up over the ravine was down to you taking Prozac?'

'Actually the opposite. I knew I had to clean up my act so I could stay sharp enough to help you take on the Overseers, so I stopped taking my meds when I arrived at Eden. It was a chance for a fresh start and I didn't want to screw things up again. I'd done OK until that ravine crossing. One of the possible symptoms of Prozac withdrawal is dizziness and a real doozy hit me on the bridge. The world was literally spinning round me, so I had to keep my eyes shut. You know the rest. It also happens at moments of shock, like thinking Mike has run into serious trouble.'

The missing pieces of the Jack Harper puzzle were starting to make sense at last. 'You poor guy. You should have said something before now, Jack.' I would have reached out to hug him, but I wasn't sure my heart could take a fresh rejection so soon.

'I find it difficult to talk about this to people, Lauren. There's only one other person who knows about it.'

'Mike?' I asked.

'No, I've never told him.'

'Who then?'

'Alice.'

I couldn't help staring at him. Jack had chosen to share his most intimate secrets with a woman he'd only just met. Why hadn't he told me before? Wasn't I a good enough listener – or maybe he just didn't see me as a close enough friend?

Jack hung his head. 'I told her I've been suffering from post-traumatic stress disorder.'

Another piece of the puzzle. 'Something to do with your time in the military?'

He nodded, still not looking at me.

'But I thought you were a trauma surgeon and not on the front line?'

He let out a hollow laugh. 'The thing about a military front line is that they move suddenly. Our field hospital was in a military compound supposedly far away from any insurgent activity. But the guy who snuck into the back of a supply truck wearing an explosive vest beneath his jacket obviously didn't get the memo.' Jack started to shake as he stared at the floor. 'The explosion

ripped apart our medical tent where I was operating on a marine
who'd just had his leg blown off. And the explosive vest had been
packed with ball bearings...'

'Oh god!'

Jack's eyes filled with tears. 'Friends and colleagues were
ripped apart in front of me. I was only saved thanks to the metal
gurney that shielded me from the blast. If the shrapnel that
slammed into it had been two inches higher it would have sliced
me in half...'

I took Jack's hands in mine and massaged them with my
thumbs, forgetting the barriers he'd previously thrown up
between us.

'I got to live that day when so many of my friends died,' Jack
continued. 'Later I wished I'd been killed with them, because I
couldn't cope with living. I had a complete breakdown – I
couldn't sleep, couldn't eat, couldn't function. The military
understood and gave me a full honourable discharge.'

'Jack, I'm so sorry. And then there was Sue's death on top of
that.'

'Oh, that was just the icing on the cake,' Jack said. 'That's
when I switched to archaeology, like my dad, to try to leave the
ghosts of my past far behind.' Tears were now rolling freely down
Jack's face.

'Then I turn up and crash into your world, bringing the Overseers with me, destroying the peaceful life you'd carved out for
yourself. You probably wish you'd never met me.'

Jack shook his head. 'None of this is on you, Lauren. You're
as much a victim in all of this as I am. Besides, I owe you a lot.'

I peered at him. 'In what way?'

'You were a one-woman tornado crashing through my life, but
you also woke me up. It was an accident leaving my Prozac
behind the first time I accompanied you to Skara Brae, but I also
knew I couldn't keep on just numbing the pain. You, Lauren,

were the catalyst to kick my reliance on a drug that had slowly stripped my soul away.'

I gazed at the man before me, so much more complex than the carefree Viking I had first taken him for. What did it matter if he'd spoken to Alice about this before me? At least he'd opened up to someone and now he was choosing to confide in me too. Whatever else Jack was, he was a damned good friend.

I nodded, giving him a broken smile. 'Thank you for telling me this, Jack. I'm here for you in any way you need me.'

Before I knew what I was doing I reached out and wrapped my arms round him, wanting to take his pain away. I felt him relax in my arms, hugging me back, and everything that had happened at the waterfall was forgotten. God, when had this guy started to mean so much to me?

CHAPTER FIFTEEN

By the time we reached the town, worry about Mike had taken centre stage in my mind again and nausea was swirling through my gut.

'I keep hoping it's just the quake that's stirred up this hornet's nest of police and we're going to find Mike having a beer in the bar,' Jack said.

'I would love that to be true, but I have a feeling it won't work out that way,' I replied.

'What happened to your endless supply of optimism?'

'It had a reality check.'

He nodded. 'Same old.'

We rounded the corner to see a group of police officers. They were showing every person they ran into a piece of paper. A group of young men who'd been cornered by a female officer walked away, shaking their heads. One of them screwed up the sheet of paper they'd been given and threw it into a bin. As they passed their eyes lingered on us for a moment too long. Nothing was said, but my instinct was screaming at me that we were in trouble.

Jack gave me a sideways glance. 'Maybe they just recognised us from earlier?'

'No, it's more than that. I can feel it.'

I stooped down as we drew near to the bin and scooped out the crumpled piece of paper. The air caught in my throat. On it were drawings of a man and a woman, with a vague resemblance to a disguised Jack complete with ponytail and me with my blonde locks.

'Crap, how do they know what we look like?' Jack said.

'Maybe Ricardo or one of the others blabbed. Or...'

'Or maybe Mike gave our description to the police.'

'You're doing nothing to stop my paranoia here,' I said. 'Let's get to the bar and find out for sure. We can ditch our disguises there too, since they've served their purpose.'

'I am so not going to miss this rat-tail hairpiece. Next time I'm choosing my own disguise.'

'Dark glasses alone really won't cut it.'

'Yeah, yeah.'

We headed along the street, trying to mingle with the other tourists, doing our best to avoid eye contact with anyone else. At last we reached the bar where, much to my relief, our three Zero motorbikes were still standing outside.

'That could be a good sign,' Jack said. 'At least they haven't seized those yet.'

'Maybe Mike just hasn't cracked about them in an interrogation so far.'

'I'm really starting to miss Miss Optimistic.'

'Me too,' I replied.

We went inside to a bar full of angry people, not so much in conversations but shouted exchanges. I scanned the room but there wasn't any sign of Mike or Ricardo. On the plus side, whatever was causing the arguments, nobody was paying any attention to us.

I gestured for the barman who came over. 'Have you seen our friend Mike? He was in here with us earlier.'

The guy gave me a wary look. 'No, haven't seen him.'

'What about Ricardo, the guide who hangs out here?' Jack asked.

The guy's expression became fierce. 'Why are you looking for him?'

'Because he might know where our friend is,' I replied.

'You're going to have a hard time asking Ricardo. He got himself arrested. He was seen being dragged into the police station. Add that to the disappearance of Cristina and the whole town is in uproar.'

Jack nodded. 'The truth is—'

I put my hand on his arm to stop him and shook my head. This wasn't the time for that conversation. Instead, I took out a hundred-dollar bill and slipped it over the counter. The barman narrowed his eyes at me.

'We were never here, right?' I said.

'You do know the police are looking for two westerners who were seen with Ricardo? Something about trying to smuggle out some rare Inca artefacts.' A thin smile curled his lips.

I scowled at the guy and slipped another hundred-dollar bill towards him. 'Just so you know, that's a lie someone has cooked up.'

The guy peered at us. 'I know Ricardo well enough to be sure he had nothing to do with it. You, I'm not so sure about.'

I sighed and added another bill to join the other two.

His smile widened. 'Ah yes, now I remember, nothing to do with you either.' He took the money and stuck the notes into his back pocket.

I turned away from the bar just as the door burst open and Gabriel came rushing in. His gaze swept the room and he came pushing through the crowd towards us. 'You guys have to get out of here now. The police are on the way. Someone recognised you in the street and told them that you were in here. My sister-in-law works in the station at the desk and took the call when it came in. She let me know as I'd mentioned you to her.'

'Thanks for the heads-up, but why are you helping us?' I asked.

'Ricardo got a message to me before he was arrested. He told me who really abducted Cristina and now I've seen the security-camera footage for myself. Anna also told me they have your friend Mike in a cell next to Ricardo's.'

'Shit!' I said. 'But thanks for telling us, Gabriel. Now it's our turn to return the favour. Cristina's fine, but Villca still has her hostage. We saw them up at the Solar Observatory.'

Gabriel stared at me. 'Why has he kidnapped Cristina?'

'To get her to locate exactly where she had her visions.'

'But why would he be interested in those?'

'Because your wife's visions contained a clue to the location of a secret underground temple beneath Machu Picchu,' I said.

Gabriel looked between us. 'You're winding me up?'

'As crazy as it sounds, it's all true,' Jack replied. 'Villca is involved with someone called Evelyn Fischer, who's basically a grave robber. Thanks to what Cristina told them, they just blew up the Solar Observatory. Beneath it there's a passage that leads down to a hidden chamber. Inside is an Inca temple covered in solid gold.'

'You mean the rumours are really true?' Gabriel asked.

'They are, but you need to get the word out about what Villca and Fischer are doing. Otherwise you can be sure that Machu Picchu will remain close until they have stripped the temple of its treasure.'

I looked into Gabriel's eyes. 'And more importantly you need to get up there and try to rescue Cristina.'

Gabriel squeezed the bridge of his nose and slowly nodded.

'Leave it to me. The people of this town will deal with our corrupt commandant and his new foreign friend.'

The door swung open again and two police officers headed into the bar. Gabriel blocked their line of sight to us with his back.

'We need to get out of here now,' he hissed. 'There's an exit through the doorway behind the bar.' Gabriel said something in Peruvian to the barman, who nodded and stepped aside. We ducked behind the bar, herded by Gabriel, then crept past him and out through the door, finding ourselves in a back alley.

I quickly pulled off my wig as Jack did the same.

Gabriel's eyes widen. 'Sure you're not the artefact smugglers they say you are?'

'Anything but that,' Jack replied.

He slowly nodded, his gaze brightening. 'But what are you going to do now?'

'We need to scout out the situation at the police station,' I said. I turned towards Jack. 'Then we can supply solid intel to Niki for a follow-up strategy.'

'And if things move too quickly for our backup to get here in time?' he asked.

I turned the thought over in my head. This was another leadership call and I tried to make myself sound as confident as I could. 'Then this stops being a reconnaissance mission...'

Jack gave a sharp nod. 'Hell yes. After all, it would be a shame not to make use of all that training we've had.'

Whatever my apprehension, I knew this was the right call. There was no way either of us would wait for someone else to rush in to save the day if an opportunity presented itself to do it ourselves.

Gabriel looked between us. 'It sounds like you think Ricardo and Mike's lives are in danger?'

'I'm certain of it,' I replied.

'And Cristina?'

'Her ability is useful to them, so I think she'll be fine for now.'

'But when she isn't?' Gabriel asked.

I could dress this up for him, but he deserved to hear the truth. 'I would be worried if I were you. That's why you need to get up to Machu Picchu as soon as possible. We would go ourselves, but we need to get to the police station.'

'You do what you need to do to save Ricardo and your friend. Leave the rest to me and the people of this town.'

'Good, but I need your help for one other thing, Gabriel,' I said.

'Name it.'

'Can you ride a motorbike? We need to get Mike's bike as near as possible to the police station. If things go as I think they will, we'll need to make a fast exit.'

'Do Peruvian bears shit in the woods?'

'I guess?' Jack said.

'Of course they do and of course I'll help you,' Gabriel replied. 'My grandmother once said I was born on two wheels.'

'Then let's get over to the police station,' I said.

CHAPTER SIXTEEN

A SHORT WHILE LATER, the three of us were weaving through the back streets of Aguas Calientes on the Zero motorbikes, the helmets adding a useful layer of disguise for Jack and me. Thankfully, with all the tourists filling the town, the police didn't even register three bikers as we slid by the crowds.

By the time we reached the police station, for some reason I was feeling totally calm. Maybe being exposed to one too many dangerous situations had rewired my brain for ever. Jack seemed to be doing OK too, with no sign of his Prozac-withdrawal shakes. It was almost as though both of us had started to thrive under stress. If we could bottle it, we'd make a fortune, I thought.

We followed Gabriel as he turned off the street into an alley. He came to a stop, dismounted and put his motorbike on to its kickstand. We did the same and slipped our pistols into our hidden shoulder holsters without Gabriel noticing, before following him towards the end of the alley.

Gabriel turned to us. 'The police station is just round the corner and across the street.'

'OK, one final favour,' I said.

He nodded.

I pulled up the video call button on the Sky Wire and rang Jack's phone. A moment later his phone chirped.

Jack gave me a questioning look as he accepted the call.

'Just hang on and I'll explain.' I swapped the camera view from the front facing one to the rear camera and handed my Sky Wire over to Gabriel.

'What do you want me to do with this?' he asked.

'I want to keep the risk of us being recognised to a minimum. So if it's OK with you, you're going to be our eyes and ears for a moment. Can you get close to the police station without drawing any attention to yourself and show us what we're up against?'

'No problem.' He rounded the corner of the building, gazing at the Sky Wire's screen as if he was a normal guy just casually checking his social media.

Jack's phone showed a perfect video surveillance of what Gabriel could see as he crossed the street.

The concrete-walled police station ahead was surrounded by vehicles and at least a dozen police officers were gathered outside. Gabriel wandered past them and none of the officers gave him a second glance, as I'd expected.

Jack peered at his phone's screen. 'That place might as well be a fortress. There's no way we're getting in there past all those cops.'

I nodded. 'Gabriel, is there any way into the back of the station, avoiding the front door?'

In answer, the view bounced as Gabriel headed down an alley along one side of the station. The camera view was turned to a wall and then pivoted upwards. We could now see – through barbed wire on top of the wall – a rear yard. Two windows on the ground floor were barred and a heavy-duty lock held a rusting door in place. Suddenly the phone view dropped back down and all we could see was ground.

'What's happening?' Jack asked.

There was no reply. Jack's hand went for his Glock.

'Wait a moment,' I whispered.

The camera view swung back up.

'Sorry, guys, a police officer just walked past the alley and nearly caught me,' Gabriel said.

'OK, that's more than enough,' I said. 'Get yourself back here.'

'On my way.'

Once again the view bounced as Gabriel retraced his steps. He'd just reached the other side of the street when the roar of several cars approaching echoed between the buildings. The video view swung round to show an old man who'd been crossing the street jumping out of the way of three black SUVs with tinted windows. The vehicles screamed to a stop just outside the police station and a group of men and women leapt out. They were openly carrying Uzi sub-machine guns, which I recognised instantly thanks to my training with Tom. The police officers eyed the group suspiciously, but did nothing to stop them, while I only had eyes for a guy who'd emerged from the middle SUV.

'Holy crap, that's Alvarez,' Jack said, staring at the screen.

'Damn it, that confirms the Overseers are pulling the strings behind this operation,' I replied.

Gabriel appeared at the entrance of the alley. 'Hey, did you see all those cars pull up and people with guns pile out of them?' He handed the Sky Wire phone back to me.

'Unfortunately we did,' I replied. 'Look, Gabriel, your job now is to spread the word around town and get as many people as possible up to Machu Picchu. But please watch yourselves, as they'll be armed.'

Gabriel nodded. 'We'll have phones,' he said. 'We'll live-stream the entire thing to make anyone up there less likely to try anything. Just do your best to get Ricardo and your friend Mike out of there.'

'We will, I promise,' I replied. I felt a surge of admiration for the guy, not showing even a flicker of fear about going up against Villca and his people without any weapons. In my book that took real guts.

Gabriel hugged me and then Jack. 'Good hunting, my friends.' With a final wave he disappeared along the alley, out on to the street opposite.

'So what's the plan, Lauren?' Jack asked.

'We confirm that Mike and Ricardo are still in the police station and then spring them.'

'In other words, it's too late for Tom and the cavalry to get here.'

'What do you think?'

A smile curled the corners of his mouth. 'We both know the answer to that. But we need to go in prepared.'

'I agree. We'll try to gain access to the police station through the back door. I just hope my skill at picking locks is as good as Tom thinks it is.'

We headed back to our motorbikes and I took out my lock-picking kit. In addition to my LRS, I helped myself to Mike's spare dart gun, while Jack loaded his rucksack with smoke, flash-bang and tear-gas grenades – as well as several extra magazines for his Glock.

He gestured towards the tranquilliser gun in my hand. 'You're going to use that instead of your LRS?'

'You know I'm not keen on killing someone even at the worst of times. It's likely that many of the people in that station won't be corrupt, but just following orders like Gabriel's sister-in-law. So I want to be careful.'

'True. We can also use some of those fancy martial-art moves Tom taught us, especially those pressure points that'll knock somebody out for a while. But what about those Overseers mercs or Alvarez himself? What happens if we run into them?'

'Oh, that's why I'm still packing my LRS. My moral objections to killing will quickly disappear if that bastard is standing in front of me.'

'So we're going in there without a disguise?'

I handed him a baseball cap and some dark glasses. 'This will have to do for now. Hopefully, no one aside from Alvarez will recognise us. And if we see him, it all becomes a bit academic anyway, as it will surely turn into a shooting match.'

Jack nodded and checked his bullet magazine in his Glock.

I threw on my baseball cap, pulled the peak low over my face and slid my sunglasses on. 'Let's do this thing.'

Taking a large breath, I hooked my arm through Jack's and together we walked out of the alley into the street. Just everyday tourists doing touristy things.

As we rounded the corner, I saw every police officer out the front now warily watching the armed Overseers guards standing among them. Though Alvarez's mercs didn't seem to care what impression they were making as they scanned every vehicle that passed intently. One of the Overseers' gazes soon locked on to us.

'Keep it casual,' I said from the corner of my mouth as we began to cross the street.

'I wasn't planning on anything else,' Jack replied.

'Hey, you,' the Overseers soldier with blond cropped hair called out.

I forced myself to stay relaxed and not automatically reach for my LRS. The merc began walking over to us.

'The barrel of his Uzi is still pointing down,' Jack whispered, 'which suggests he hasn't recognised us.'

'Here's bloody hoping,' I said.

My heart was pounding by the time he reached us.

'Hey, amigos, have you got a light on you?' He waved a

cigarette at us and then gestured his chin towards the police officers. 'None of those clowns have one between them.'

The tension across my chest released a fraction. 'Sorry, you're
out of luck. We both gave up a week ago. And my boyfriend here
is all cranky because of it.'

Jack sighed and spread his hands. 'You know how it is,
buddy.'

'Dude, I feel your pain,' the soldier said. 'I tried to give up
several times, but hey.' He shrugged. 'Thanks anyway.' He
nodded and headed back to the other mercs.

'As cool as a bloody British cucumber,' Jack said from the
corner of his mouth.

'I'm not sure I was that cool. I swear a little bit of wee just
dribbled out.'

Jack suppressed a smile as we reached the sanctuary of the
alleyway running down the side of the police station. Soon we
were standing beneath the wall to the rear yard.

Jack narrowed his gaze at the barbed wire on top of the wall.
'That's going to be a real bitch to get over.'

But I'd already spotted a large wheeled rubbish bin at the
back of the bar and pointed to it. 'That's why we're going to use
that.'

'See, you're so the brains in this operation,' Jack said.

'If you say so.'

He winked at me as we went over to the bin. We wheeled it
back, me wincing at every clatter of the wheels on the uneven
ground. But thankfully no curious faces appeared to investigate
and at last we had the bin pushed up against the wall.

I glanced back along the alley to the street to check it was still
clear, hopped on to the bin and peered over the wall. It was a
good three-metre drop on the other side. The overgrown yard
contained a number of rusting chair frames and a pile of scaf-

folding poles stacked up at the back of the building. It looked as if no one had used it in a very long time.

I mentally thanked Tom for all our assault-course training, then barely hesitated before leaping over the wall. I dropped down the other side, going straight into a roll to absorb the impact. I sprang back to my feet, eyes already on the rear of the police station. I spotted some upper-storey windows looking out over the yard, but the blinds had been closed, presumably to keep out the bright afternoon sunlight.

'How's it looking?' Jack whispered from the other side of the wall.

'All clear so far,' I replied.

Within a few seconds Jack was over the wall and crouching by my side.

I took out my lock-picking kit and unrolled it. 'Hopefully this won't be the shortest rescue attempt in history when I can't get past that lock.'

'I have every faith in you.'

We crept towards the metal riveted door, its black painted surface bubbling with rust spots. It had a substantial lock that looked as if it had come straight from a medieval dungeon. I put my ear to the door but couldn't hear anything on the other side. I tried the handle but as I expected it was locked.

From the pouch I selected the larger of my lock-picking tools.

'You've got this, Lauren, just take your time,' Jack said.

Unfortunately, time is one thing in short supply at the moment, I thought.

I inserted the tension wrench – a metal bar that I would need to rotate the lock's barrel. Next, I pushed the second bar with a bent end, called the short hook, into it. I probed the keyhole and felt the first pin give way as I applied a light pressure to it. Then I pivoted the hook and felt the pin click into place. The tension across my shoulders relaxed slightly. Now I had a real chance of pulling this off.

As I worked on the remaining pins, Jack kept guard, casting an eye to the windows in case anyone chose this moment to open their blinds. I listened out for his voice, but the only sound was the faint murmur of trucks and cars passing on the other side of the building. The minutes ticked past before the next pin locked into place, but that was quickly followed by the third. Time for the last pin...but it wasn't shifting.

'It must be rusty,' I whispered.

'Anything I can do to help?' Jack asked.

'Can you grab that small aerosol of oil from the pouch and squirt it into the lock for me?'

Jack did as I asked and oil was soon dribbling out of the keyhole. I smeared the lubricant over the tip of my hook tool and pushed against the last stuck pin once more. With a sudden click it released and locked into place. I chewed my lip as I carefully rotated the wrench. With a graunching sound, the barrel turned.

'That was damned impressive, Lauren.'

'Maybe, but now comes the really hard part – the actual rescue.'

I withdrew the dart pistol as Jack unholstered his Glock and screwed the silencer on. I started to open the door a crack but its hinges squealed. I grabbed hold of the oil aerosol and sprayed them. 'Ready?'

'Now would be a good time for some Prozac, but I'll survive.'

With one hand on the handle, I raised the dart gun with the other. I slowly pulled the door open, which now gave out only a slight protesting groan. The strong stench of sweat and urine hit my nostrils as we stepped into a short dimly lit corridor. The yellowing walls were pitted and there were some very dubious stains on the floor. A number of large cockroaches scuttled away at our appearance. Yes, this definitely had the *je ne sais quoi* of a cell block.

Another door stood at the junction in front of us. My guess was that this probably led into the main area of the police station. Two corridors went left and right of the junction, presumably leading to the two cells with barred windows we'd seen from outside. Voices came from beyond the door, too indistinct to make out, but one was definitely shouting. I hoped that whatever was going on out there would prevent anyone in the police station hearing what was happening in the cells.

We crept to the junction and glanced left and right to the solid-metal cell doors on either side.

I gestured to the right-hand cell.

Jack nodded and we walked towards it. I lifted the hatch set into the door and we both peered inside. My heart jumped to my throat – Ricardo was sprawled on the floor in a pool of blood.

'Lauren, quick, get me in there,' Jack said. I grabbed my lock-picking tools and worked as quickly as I could while my mouth dried out. Thankfully this lock was far easier than the last and within a minute I had it open.

Jack rushed into the cell and rolled Ricardo on to his side. I had to stifle a gasp as I took in his blood-soaked face. Ripped flesh exposed the white bone of his jaw.

Jack checked for a pulse, and sagged on to his haunches, shaking his head. 'What did those bastards do?'

Tears threatened my eyes, any hint of the soldier-like calmness of before gone. 'He's only in here because he tried to help us.' The ache inside me hardened into a ball and I swapped the dart pistol for my LRS.

Jack glanced at me. 'What happened to not taking innocent lives?'

'You're telling me that no one in this station knew what was going on back here? Of course they fucking did, but no one stepped in to help Ricardo. As far as I'm concerned, they're all complicit.'

'That's quite a sweeping statement, Lauren. What about Anna, Gabriel's sister-in-law?'

I knew Jack was right, but my fury was in control now. 'I don't fucking care any more.'

'Trust me, you don't mean that.'

'Oh, but I do. I promised Gabriel that we'd save Ricardo, and now this.' I flapped my LRS towards the corpse.

'Right...' Jack said, his eyes slipping away from mine.

I couldn't help but feel he was judging me, even though he had a weapon clutched in his own hand. He was a doctor too. Talk about being a hypocrite. What gave him the right? A tinge of anger burned through my blood and I had to turn my back on him to avoid saying something I might regret. This little conversation would have to wait for another time and right now I needed a cool head.

'Let's check on Mike,' Jack said to my back.

My anger was swept away by sudden cold dread and I clenched my jaw as I pulled the door closed behind us. We rushed to the other cell and I braced myself as Jack opened up the hatch in the door. I sagged in relief. There was Mike, very much alive and sitting on a bunk. His head hung down between his shoulders as he stared at the ground, his wig gone.

I gripped the edge of the hatch. 'Mike, are you OK?'

He lifted his face to us and nodded. His cheeks were streaked with tears. 'You're here! I've been worried sick about you. But...Ricardo?'

Jack shook his head. 'I'm so sorry, buddy.'

Fresh tears tumbled down Mike's face. 'That bastard Villca tortured him. I don't think I'll forget Ricardo's screams as long as I live. But he didn't say a word, not one.'

'Fucking hell. He didn't deserve any of this,' Jack said. 'But why did Villca leave you alone?'

He shrugged. 'Maybe they need me alive. After they realised I was in disguise, they took some photos of me. Then a guard told me someone else would come to question me, but, whoever it is, they haven't turned up yet.'

'Shit, I think they were talking about Alvarez,' I said.

'He's coming here?'

'Already is,' Jack replied. 'We need to get you out of here fast.'

I had just inserted the lock-pick wrench into the door when the shouted conversation in the police station grew distinctly louder. Then we heard footsteps approaching.

Jack stared at me. 'Fight or hide?'

'Hide. There are too many trigger-happy mercs with Alvarez. And, as angry as I am, we need to pick our moment if we want to stand a chance.' I pulled the wrench out of the lock. 'Mike, you'll have to play along, but we're going to be right next door.'

Mike gave us a pale look and nodded.

Jack and I rushed back to the other cell and dived inside, pulling the door quickly closed behind us. As we pressed ourselves flat against the wall in case anyone glanced in, I looked anywhere but down at Ricardo's dead body sprawled on the ground. The metallic smell of blood crawled up my nose.

We heard Mike's cell door being opened.

'I can assure you, Commandant, that our methods will be more effective in getting this prisoner to cooperate,' a man said.

Fresh anger surged through me as I recognised Alvarez's voice.

'I still say you should let me deal with him,' another man said. Villca?

'You've done more than enough already, Villca,' Alvarez replied. 'You've learnt absolutely nothing and that guide is now dead – what were you fucking thinking? But we keep our promises – a share of the treasure is yours, especially since you delivered Cristina into our hands. I'm certain she'll prove a useful asset to us.'

I exchanged a tight look with Jack. What did he mean? But at least it sounded like she wasn't in immediate danger.

'That may be great for you, but your damned archaeologist has brought me some serious trouble by using explosives.'

'That *damned archaeologist* will make you very rich. Now, is there any news about Mr Palmer's accomplices?'

'No reports back yet.'

'Pity. They are almost certainly Jack Harper and that bitch Lauren Stelleck, who I have a personal debt to settle with.'

I tightened my grip on my LRS. Alvarez wasn't the only one. I still vividly remembered what his mercs had done to the guys on the oil rig.

'Guards, make sure no one disturbs us whilst I interrogate the prisoner,' Alvarez said.

'Yes, sir,' they replied in unison.

Jack raised his head a fraction to peer through the hatch in the door, then ducked back down and leant towards me. 'Two armed mercs are standing guard outside the cell,' he whispered.

'Then we just charge out of here and take them down.'

Jack shook his head. 'Think it through, Lauren. You're the one who said we needed to take a stealthy approach to this mission. If we go in loud now, there are a lot more armed people around here. And even if we do manage to take out those guards, Alvarez will use Mike as a hostage to gain leverage over us. I'm afraid our best option is to wait this out and grab the chance to free Mike when we can.'

I gestured towards the body on the ground. 'And what if it sounds as if Mike is heading towards the same ending as poor Ricardo here?'

'Then to hell with it and we go in guns blazing. But this is your call – you're the one with the most level head when the shit hits the fan.'

'Not sure I believe that right now.'

'Well, I do, even as angry as I know you are.' He reached up and gently touched my face.

I allowed myself a moment and cradled his hand in mine. I breathed in and slowly nodded. 'Yes, we hold fire...for now.' I squeezed my eyes shut and lowered my gun.

CHAPTER SEVENTEEN

MY EYES KEPT SKATING over Ricardo's body as we listened to the conversation coming from the adjacent cell. The problem was that, even with my ear pressed to the door, I couldn't quite make out what was being said as Alvarez and Villca questioned Mike. I was also painfully aware of the hulking presence of the Overseers guards just outside in the corridor.

'So what now?' Jack whispered.

'This is where the other bit of my lock-picking kit comes in,' I said.

'What do you mean?'

'This.' I took out a bendy black rod with a fisheye lens on the one end and slotted the data plug end into the slot on my Sky Wire phone.

'And that is?'

'It's a flexible camera, normally used to investigate tricky locks. But in this instance it will give us a look at what's going on outside and is less likely to be spotted than you trying to peek through the hatch.'

'Neat.'

I slipped it under door, slow and steady, praying that neither of the two Overseers soldiers noticed the snake-like device. With my breath held, I toggled the camera on via the Sky Wire's screen and a clear fisheye view of the corridor appeared. Jack frowned at the two mercs with Uzis in their hands. These guys obviously took guard duty seriously.

The door to the main police station opened. At once both soldiers turned to face the police officer who walked in. He was carrying two buckets heavy enough to stretch his arms out, a towel hung over his shoulder.

The officer raised his chin at the Overseers soldiers, who nodded and pushed the cell door open for him. The officer disappeared into the cell, out of our view. But we could hear Alvarez's voice through the open door.

'So how is it that you've turned up here, Mr Palmer?' Alvarez asked.

'Like I've said a hundred times already, I'm not going to tell you a thing,' Mike replied.

'That's what you think...'

We heard a chuckle. 'You'll be singing like a canary after we begin to waterboard you,' Villca said.

'That's where they make someone feel like they're drowning by pouring water over their faces, right?' I whispered to Jack.

'Yeah. I've had to deal with soldiers who'd been captured and had that done to them. They all told me it's bad – real bad. Anyone will crack given long enough if they feel like they're choking to death. We've got to do something.'

'And we will, but we still have to choose our moment.' I caught the smirk that one Overseers soldier gave the other. This was all a game to them. The utter bastards.

'Leave me alone, you fuckwits!' Mike shouted before his voice became muffled.

I might not have been able to see what was happening, but in my imagination it was a vivid movie based on every torture scene that I'd ever seen on TV. Mike was being held down flat on the floor, a wet towel draped over his face. Villca had taken one of the buckets of water and was pouring it over Mike's head. Almost on cue, a gurgling scream reached us.

'Jesus...' Jack whispered.

'What can he actually tell them?' I replied. 'As far as Villca knows, you and I are still lost somewhere beneath Machu Picchu.'

'It won't take Fischer and her team long to work out we're not there.'

'So we're already out of time?'

'Probably.'

On the Sky Wire's screen, the door to the main police station opened again. A female Overseers soldier nodded to the two guards and rushed through Mike's cell door.

'There's been a development, General Alvarez,' we heard her say.

'What sort of development?'

'Fischer has just reported that they've successfully gained access to the hidden underground chamber.'

'I'd better head up there immediately,' Alvarez said.

'What about the prisoner?' Villca asked.

'I'll leave him in your hands for now. However, if your techniques don't work, mine most certainly will. And I suggest you keep a tight guard around him in case his accomplices launch a foolish attempt to rescue him.'

'I can assure you that my police station is a fortress,' Villca replied.

'That's what he thinks,' Jack whispered.

On the screen we saw Alvarez and the female soldier emerge from the cell.

Villca appeared right behind them. 'And what about our little arrangement, General?'

Alvarez narrowed his eyes at the man, making the scar radiating from one of them deepen. 'You'll be paid in full, as we agreed. Fifteen per cent of any gold that Fischer recovers.'

The corners of Villca's mouth curled upwards as he spread his hands wide. 'I thought after I've been so helpful that you might increase that figure to twenty per cent...'

Alvarez's gaze tightened on the man. 'Don't get greedy, Commandant, or I can assure you that you'll regret it.'

For the first time I saw a look of fear crossing Villca's face.

He quickly raised his hands in an apologetic gesture. 'No problem – fifteen per cent will be just fine, my friend.'

'I'm glad we understand each other,' Alvarez replied.

Before the commandant could respond, the general turned on his heel. He and his three mercs headed out of the door and into the main police station.

Villca scowled at Alvarez's back, then rolled up his shirt sleeves and walked back into Mike's cell. The corridor was now empty of people and it was just him and the other officer inside the cell.

I turned to Jack and nodded.

I quickly drew my fibre-optic camera back into the room and stowed it in my rucksack along with the Sky Wire.

The sound of someone choking echoed along the corridor.

'Let's go,' I whispered.

We slowly stood, weapons in hands. I took hold of the cell door's handle and opened it a crack.

Tom had taught us the basics of squad combat movement for clearing a building and I used them now, entering the corridor first and taking up a lead position to the left-hand side of Mike's cell door. Jack came behind me.

'Just tell us where your friends are and we can stop this,' we heard Villca say, followed by the sound of someone snatching in a large gulp of air.

'I'm not telling you a fucking thing,' Mike replied.

'Then let's see if we can loosen your tongue.' The sound of splashing water and more choking came from the cell.

My jaw stiffened and I aimed my LRS towards the door, nodding to Jack. He yanked the door open.

Villca and the police officer spun round as we barged into the cell. Mike was sprawled on the ground, his face covered with a towel, water bubbling up through the wet fabric as he struggled to breathe.

White-hot fury burned through my veins. Villca and the officer reached for the guns on their belts, but I gestured with my pistol towards them. Both men raised their hands.

Jack squatted by Mike's side and yanked the towel off his face. 'We've got you, buddy.' He helped Mike gently into a sitting position and slipped a knife through the plastic ties binding his wrists behind his back.

'You came for me,' Mike said, his voice wavering.

I gave him a smile as I fought back the threat of sudden tears. 'There was never a question that we wouldn't.'

In the split second my attention had been on Mike, I caught the police officer's hand dropping to the gun on his belt.

My weeks of training at Eden kicked in instantly. Adrenaline powered through my bloodstream as I brought up my LRS to shoot. I squeezed three shots straight into the guy's chest before his hand had reached his gun, remembering the target shooting with Tom. But this was no cardboard target. The officer stared at me, a shocked expression filling his face as he clutched his chest, blood dripping between his fingers. Then he slumped to the floor, the life flowing out of him.

I couldn't help but wince as Jack checked the pulse in his neck and shook his head.

The old Lauren would have been appalled, but this new version just felt a cold, hard focus and pushed the rising nausea back down. This was a mission and it was my duty to get us all out of here alive.

Villca just stared at me, his face ashen. 'Please don't hurt me. I have a family.'

'Everyone's got a family,' Jack said. 'It's just a shame you didn't remember that with Ricardo.' He reached forward and grabbed Villca's gun from its holster, holding it out towards Mike who just blinked at it.

'Humour me here,' Jack said.

With a faint nod, Mike took the weapon and cradled it in his lap.

I glared at the commandant and a feeling of pure hatred rose up through my icy calmness. This guy so deserved a bullet in the brain. I took a deep breath. No, I needed to keep my emotions in check and not let this situation get out of control. Besides, we could use him.

'OK, Jack, can you cuff the commandant?'

Jack peered at me. 'No summary execution?'

Villca grimaced.

'I haven't become that person, not yet at least.'

'Good to hear. So what are we going to do with this bastard?'

'We're going to use him as a hostage.'

'Oh, now I'm liking your thinking,' Jack said as he helped himself to the cuffs hanging from the dead officer's belt. He pulled Villca's hands to his back and snapped the cuffs shut round them.

I moved behind the commandant and stuck my LRS into the small of his back. 'If you don't do exactly what I tell you, you're a dead man walking. Do you understand me?'

Villca gave me a frantic nod.

'OK, this is how it's going to work,' I said. 'We're going to head out into the yard like we're the best of friends. If you do anything to make anyone suspicious about what's happening, you'll get a bullet through the back of the head.'

'OK, OK!' he replied, his shoulders shaking.

Whatever else Villca was, I was becoming increasingly certain that hero wasn't among them.

'Mike, can you walk?' Jack asked.

Mike took a steadying breath. 'Yeah, I think so.'

'Good man.'

I handed my baseball cap to Mike. 'Put that on and pray that nobody recognises you on the way out.'

'You got it,' Mike replied, pulling the cap's peak low over his face.

With our weapons hidden, I propelled Villca ahead of me and we stepped out into the corridor.

My plan instantly fell apart as the door to the station opened and a young policeman appeared. For a split second he stared at us. Then he reached for his pistol.

Jack was already raising his Glock.

'Stand down!' Villca shouted.

The young officer just stared at him, his gun shaking in his hand.

'You heard what I said, officer!' Villca said.

The guy nodded and lowered his weapon.

Time seemed to stand still for a moment. I felt the uncertainty creeping back in, but I had to make a call.

I raised my chin towards the young policeman. 'OK, you, back to where you came from. We're about to come through after you and if anybody so much as blinks, your precious commandant is history. Now go and warn everyone.'

The officer blinked rapidly and stepped backwards through the door, shutting it behind him.

Villca stared at the closed door. 'Your plan is shit, you know. If you shoot me, it will be over for you.'

'Oh, I have other plans for you,' I replied. I raised my LRS and struck him hard across the back of the head. Villca slumped to the floor and stilled.

'I thought we wanted him as a hostage?' Mike asked, gazing down at Villca.

'That's what we want the officers out there to think,' I said. 'They'll be expecting us to try to walk through that door. And we all know it takes just one person with an itchy trigger finger to send everything rapidly south. So here's the real plan, guys. Jack, get ready to throw flash-bang grenades – and anything else you fancy – through that door. Meanwhile, we'll exit the way we came, as originally planned.'

'Really liking your style,' Jack replied with a smile as he took tear-gas, flash-bang and smoke grenades out of his pack.

Supporting Mike, I headed to the rear door. As I opened it, I gave Jack a thumbs up. He pulled the pin on three grenades and jerked the door to the station open. He lobbed the grenades through and slammed the door shut again.

Guns sounded, bullets peppering but not piercing the door. A split second later, we heard three muffled bangs, followed by shouts and cries. Smoke began billowing through the gap beneath the door.

Still hanging on to Mike, I stumbled out into the yard towards the rusting chairs. I glanced back to see Jack lobbing another smoke grenade into the cell block. Then he raced out and slammed the outer door behind him.

'Jack, can you stack those chairs and help Mike over the wall?'

'Sure, but what about you?'

'I'm going to slow down our pursuers.'

'Go knock yourself out.' Jack began to pull the chairs from out of the weeds, stacking them to form a ladder over the wall.

I raced towards the scaffolding poles, grabbed a couple and jammed them at an angle against the rear door. Hopefully this would buy us precious seconds.

I ran back just as Mike scaled the chairs up on to the wall. Jack had draped an old rubber doormat over the barbed wire and Mike crawled over it and dropped down the other side. A moment later Jack and I followed him.

So far, so good.

'OK, guys, we need to act as casually as possible and get back to our motorbikes.'

Jack and I stowed our pistols as Mike offered the police officer's weapon to Jack.

'Best keep it,' Jack said.

'Please, mate,' Mike replied.

Jack sighed, took it off Mike and stowed the pistol in his rucksack.

We stepped out of the shadowed alley into the sunlit street. Onlookers crowded round the entrance to the police station, watching smoke billowing out from it. A number of police officers were sitting on the pavement coughing and wiping tears from their eyes. Fortunately, no one noticed the three westerners heading across the street and disappearing into the alley opposite.

'Mike, are you good to ride your bike?' I asked as we headed for the parked up Zeros.

'Just about, although I could so do with a stiff drink first,' he replied.

'Later maybe,' I said as Jack and I shoved our kit into our panniers.

I pulled my crash helmet on and pulled up the navigation system. A quick search later, the destination was locked in:

Choquequirao. I selected the menu option to share it with the others.

'Where the hell is Choquequirao?' Mike said over the intercom.

'We think it's where the next micro mind has been hidden,' Jack replied.

'You mean you didn't recover it from beneath Machu Picchu after all?' Mike said.

'No,' I admitted. 'There's a lot to bring you up to speed on.'

We were soon weaving our way through the traffic, following the GPS markers on our helmets' HUDs. All the roads out of town were crammed with vehicles heading the other way. Through a gap in the buildings I saw why. A huge line of traffic was snaking up the road to Machu Picchu. There were also what looked like thousands of people heading up the walkway on foot to the ancient site.

'Looks as if Gabriel has made good on his promise to get the town up there,' Jack said over the intercom.

'It'll certainly make life difficult for Alvarez, not to mention Villca, when the locals discover what they've been up to.'

'My heart bleeds for them,' Jack said.

'The main thing is they get to Cristina and that she's OK,' I said.

'Amen to that,' Jack replied.

The few minutes it took us to reach the edge of the town felt like hours and I had to fight the urge to open up the throttle and race out of town like a scalded cat. At last we reached the main road and sped away along the tarmac between the towering mountains. It was only then that a weight lifted off my shoulders.

CHAPTER EIGHTEEN

WE'D JUST PASSED through a small town called Cachora and were now on a road gently weaving its way along the bottom of a rocky valley. There were only occasional mountain goats to witness our near silent passage on the electric Zero motorbikes as we drove past. After five hours, it was still a good forty-five minutes to the site of Choquequirao. Above, the deep blue sky was tinged with gold, hinting at the coming sunset. There wasn't much in the way of daylight left before nightfall.

On our journey I'd rung in and updated Niki on what was happening. He wasn't at all happy when we'd told him Alvarez had turned up and we'd had to rescue Mike. He was going to recall one of the security teams and would be sending them to support us as soon as possible. It had done nothing for my leadership confidence; Niki clearly didn't think we could handle this by ourselves.

On the plus side he'd told me that various social media sites were now alight with what had been discovered at Machu Picchu and that an unnamed high-level police officer had been implicated in corruption – fuelled by the photos of Villca abducting Cristina.

High in the sky, a large lone bird circled in the dying thermals of the day. Jack quickly informed me this was an Andean condor. I glanced in my rear-view mirror at Jack and Mike in our motorbike convoy.

'Anyone else notice the distinct lack of other vehicles on the road?' I said over the intercom.

'It's really not that strange,' Jack responded. 'There are plans to create better access to Choquequirao for tourists, but it's currently still a remote site. Although I'm surprised we haven't seen anything in the way of a pursuit by now. Whenever Villca came round, he would have been as annoyed as hell. I would have expected him to throw every resource at tracking us down.'

'Not forgetting what he'll do when they eventually work out the micro mind isn't at Machu Picchu after all,' I said.

'Hopefully, Gabriel and the townspeople are making life as difficult as hell for them,' Jack said.

'But Alvarez is like a cat who always lands on his feet. Experience tells me it's just a matter of time before they find us.'

I realised then that Mike hadn't said a word. In fact, thinking about it, he'd hardly said anything since we'd fled the town, even when we'd finished bringing him up to speed on what had happened while he'd been captured.

'Mike, are you OK back there?' I asked.

There was no response. I glanced in my rear-view mirror again, but it was impossible to see his expression through his visor.

'Are you OK, buddy?' Jack asked.

This time a reply came, his voice sounding strained. 'Sorry, I zoned out there. What were you saying?'

'Lauren was talking about the company we're expecting before long,' Jack said.

'You can count on it...' Mike replied, his voice trailing away.

He sounded distracted, and of course he was. We'd all had a taste of torture courtesy of Alvarez. But being waterboarded would probably haunt Mike for the rest of his life. Maybe Jack, after caring for traumatised soldiers who'd suffered similar experiences, would have ideas on how we could help him.

I returned my attention to the GPS display on my helmet's HUD. According to the map, we'd another mile left until we hit somewhere called Capuliyoc. There, we'd leave the tarmacked road behind us and would be on the trail itself. Jack had already briefed us that this was only used by mules and tourists heading up to Choquequirao on foot. We'd have to take it easy, as apparently the trail was treacherous in places. Hopefully, our Zero bikes would be up to the challenge; without them it would be a six-hour trek.

The mountain peaks either side of us cast long shadows across the valley, dropping it into a deepening gloom. It wouldn't be long now until night descended. I felt shattered after the day's events. We'd all certainly earned a good night's sleep. But that wasn't on the cards for a while yet.

Ahead of us the road came to an end in a car park, from where a lone minibus was just departing. A glance through the windows revealed a number of sleeping tourists with suntanned faces. As the vehicle drew level with us, it slowed to a stop. The minibus driver, a young guy in his thirties, wound his window down.

'If you're thinking of trekking up to Choquequirao, don't bother,' he said. 'A series of tremors hit earlier today and everyone has been evacuated off the mountain until things calm down.'

Electricity tingled through my veins. This had to be a good sign. 'Thanks for the heads-up. Was anyone hurt?'

The guy shook his head. 'No, but the tremors got stronger

and there have been some strange sounds coming from the mountain too.'

Mike sat upright on his motorbike and cracked his visor open. 'What sort of sounds?'

The driver made the sign of the cross on his chest. 'A wailing noise...' He glanced in his rear-view mirror at the sleeping tourists and dropped his voice to a whisper. 'Some of the locals are convinced it's demons that have been woken up in the mountains.' He rolled his eyes at us. 'Anyway, I have some tired walkers in desperate need of a bar. *Adios*, my friends.'

He started up the minibus and drove away – along the road we'd just come up.

I peered at Mike. 'What are you thinking?'

'It certainly sounds promising. And if another quake hits whilst we're here, I'll stop and take a reading to see if it's the source of the monowaves.'

'At least Choquequirao itself should now be empty of people,' Jack said.

'Hopefully, but we should turn off our headlights and use the night-vision systems built into the helmets just in case.'

'Bloody hell, do you two have a death wish or something?' Mike asked.

'You know us,' I replied.

'Yeah, I do,' he said with a hint of a chuckle in his voice.

My heart lifted at the sound. Maybe Mike was starting to surface from wherever he'd been.

The three of us killed our headlights and dropped into the growing darkness.

I hunted through the menu system on my HUD and activated the night-vision mode. At once the gloom around us became shaded with greens, revealing details in the shadowed areas. Even the faint stars that had started to appear now shone as vivid points of light.

'Great kit – probably military grade,' Jack said.

'Would you expect anything else from Sky Dreamer Corp?' I asked.

He chuckled. 'Hell, no.'

'So are we ready to head out, guys?' I asked.

'Yes, but let me lead the way,' Mike said. 'I did a fair bit of scramble biking back in my teens, so, unless you object, I'm probably the most experienced to lead us on what could be a tricky ride.'

'Fine by me,' I said.

'Me too,' Jack added.

Mike nodded and manoeuvred his bike on to the narrow trail ahead of us.

As we set off behind him, if anything the night-vision system did a better job than our headlights of turning night into day, albeit a very green one. I could easily see the dirt track was littered with small stones and potholes as we started to descend towards the bottom of a valley.

'We just need to keep our speed down if we don't want to lose a filling,' Mike said over the intercom.

'I had no other intention,' I replied, already shaken to my core.

Cicadas chirped in the trees around us, only briefly stopping as we passed them. Despite my closed visor, the heady aroma of the jungle, a combination of rich compost and heavily scented mountain flowers, managed to seep into my nostrils.

I noticed that our GPS marker on the map was still located back where we'd run into the departing minibus. 'It looks like we've lost GPS coverage.'

'Maybe the mountains are blocking the signals from the satellites,' Jack said.

'Not the best moment to lose our map position, though.'

'We should be fine – this trail leads straight to Choquequirao.'

'You reckon? I can get lost in a car park.'

Mike and Jack laughed over the intercom.

The trail became increasingly uneven. I ended up standing up in the saddle, trying to help my body absorb the lumps and bumps in the trail, whilst also trying to restore some circulation to my legs. Slowly I started to get into the rhythm of the bumpy track by focusing on the trail ahead and weaving my way between the potholes rather than dropping straight into them.

Suddenly a small mountain slide reduced the path to just a tyre's width. I jumped off the Zero and tiptoed along the section, following Mike's lead, and we all made it through unscathed. Back on the bikes, our speed didn't get much above ten miles per hour, still faster than walking but not the speed I would have liked. It was a good two hours before we finally drew level with what appeared to be a deserted campsite. Above us, stars blazed in the sky. Maybe one day I'd return here for some serious camping with a small portable telescope. But that would probably have to wait for another life...if we managed to save the planet.

After about another twenty minutes, we reached a bridge crossing a river. We drew to a stop next to another deserted camp-site on the shore.

On the opposite side of the river, the trail led up the mountain ahead of us. 'Please tell me it's not much farther? My bum is numb enough already.'

'We're on the last leg now,' Jack replied over the intercom. 'Once we're over this bridge, we'll begin a steep ascent up to Choque-quirao. But even on the Zeros, it will take us a couple of hours.'

'Bloody hell. I'm going to need a long soak in a hot bath to iron out all the knots in my muscles after all this.'

'You're not the only one,' Jack replied.

Mike turned to look at us, his face one huge smile behind his visor. 'You mean you're not enjoying this ride of a lifetime?'

'At least someone's having good time,' I said.

Mike's smile widened even further. 'Damned right I am.'

Whatever lay ahead of us, the mood of our group was getting lighter. Maybe it had something to do with the mountain air, but also because we were finally closing in our target, I hoped.

Following Mike, we crossed the bridge one after the other and began to crawl up into the jungle again.

This was by far the hardest riding yet. I had to use every gram of concentration to stay on the narrow path to avoid tumbling down the slopes. My clothes were covered with fine dirt kicked up from the trail. I desperately wanted to stop to take on water, but I was far too aware that time was ticking on.

At last the jungle petered out, and we were on the exposed steep mountainside, the number of switchbacks and false summits only adding to my tension. The altimeter in my HUD had ticked up past 2,500 metres and I was definitely starting to feel light-headed.

But despite the numbness in every limb, anticipation grew inside me about what we might discover up at Choquequirao. Though there was also a nagging worry lurking in the back of my mind. What if we'd got this wrong and there was actually another secret chamber back at Machu Picchu? Maybe that was the real reason Alvarez and the others hadn't turned up here yet. Maybe the micro mind was already in the hands of Alvarez? Maybe...

There you go again, Lauren. Just stop it already.

Yes, maybe this was a wild goose chase, but maybe we were really on to something at last. I couldn't keep speculating about what might be ahead. No, I needed to stay focused and deal with the here and now, rather than try to second-guess *maybe* situations. I would have talked about it with the others, but being the team leader weighed down on me. This probably wasn't the best time to voice my anxiety.

As I rounded the next switchback bend, I saw a brief flash high in the sky. Yet when I screwed up my eyes, even with the assistance of the night-vision system, I couldn't see anything. Probably just a meteorite burning up. Then a tremble ran through the bike, growing rapidly stronger.

'Quake! Off your bikes now!' Mike called through my helmet's speakers.

We all braked hard and dropped the Zeros to their sides as the mountain began to shake beneath us.

Mike threw open a pannier and took out one of his quake sensors. While small stones skittered down the mountain slope around us, he quickly twisted it into the ground.

I lay flat, grateful for the crash helmet's protection, as stones began to strike us and our bikes like large hailstones hitting a tin roof.

The ground groaned beneath my body. Farther down the mountain, boulders shaken loose tumbled down end over end, gathering speed. Some had already reached the river we'd crossed earlier, sending up plumes of water as they cannonballed into it.

'It's subsiding!' Mike shouted as he stared at the probe's readout.

With almost a sigh, everything slowed to a stop and the mountain became quiet again.

Mike blinked as he peered at the display, leapt to his feet and let out a long whoop.

'We're near the source of the monowave?' I asked.

'The most powerful monowave yet – five on the Richter scale. We have to be close to the source.'

A surge of relief passed through me, but I couldn't relax completely until I laid eyes on the micro mind. 'Then let's get a shake on, people.'

We remounted our bikes that, apart from a few stone chips, looked fine, and started up the mountain again.

The slope soon became almost vertical, the trail barely a thin ribbon for us to follow. One slip and we'd be history, tumbling back down the mountain to join the boulders in the river.

My mouth became bone dry as I leant over the handlebars to try to maintain the motorbike's centre of gravity. If I had felt tired before, my legs were jelly now, the back of my throat sandpaper. The thin air was certainly doing nothing to help. Any chatter on the intercom had fallen away. We were all feeling it.

At last, after what had felt like an impossibly long time, we climbed up through another section of jungle and the slope finally became more gentle as the vegetation thinned. Dead ahead of us was a tin shed and large sign signalling our arrival at Choquequirao.

'Thank god for the sake of my numb arse,' Mike said.

'You're telling me,' I replied.

Jack flipped up his visor. It was his turn to have a huge grin on his face. 'I know it's been tough getting here, but goddamn this is one hell of a day to be an archaeologist.'

'You'll certainly have a lot of material to put into your TED talk now,' I said.

He snorted. 'Aren't I just. So what next, Lauren?'

There it was again – I was the one who was meant to know what to do. I quickly gathered my thoughts. 'We need to get these bikes out of sight and keep as low a profile as possible around here. Just call me paranoid.'

'As I've always said, a great characteristic in a leader,' Jack replied.

I smiled at his vote of confidence.

Following Mike, we rode along a track towards the start of some steps cut into the cliff. We dived into the trees next to it and, after a few minutes, parked up.

'So let's get going,' Jack said.

'Not yet,' I said. 'We need to take on some much needed water and food. You'll be no good to anyone if you collapse before we find the micro mind.'

Jack pulled a face but nodded.

I noticed Mike now had his back to us, his hands hanging down like a rag doll as he stared out across the valley. His lighter mood during the ride up here seemed to have evaporated.

I exchanged looks with Jack, who grimaced and nodded. One unspoken conversation later, I was heading over to our friend.

I stood before Mike, but he gazed through me. Was part of him back in the cell reliving what had happened to Ricardo?

'Are you OK?' I asked.

His eyes focused on me and he blinked. 'Sorry, Lauren... You know, my brain keeps looping back...'

'Of course.' I reached out and squeezed his shoulder. 'If you need to sit this one out – stay with the motorbikes until we get back – neither of us would judge you for that.'

He glowered at me. 'No, I'm done with waiting. Look where that got me at Machu Picchu.'

'Mike, relax. I get it, I really do.'

His shoulders dropped. 'I know you do. Sorry, I didn't mean to snap.'

'It's already forgotten. But let's get this thing done, hey?'

Mike nodded and slowly drew himself up as if recharging himself from some hidden source. He headed back to his bike and opened up his side pannier boxes.

'OK, we'd better be prepared for anything, so load up with whatever you might need,' I said. 'We should probably keep our helmets on – their night-vision systems might come in handy.'

'Good call,' Jack said.

After we'd finished refuelling with energy bars and water, we filled our rucksacks. Mike took his dart gun, whilst Jack and I loaded up with our respective pistols and several extra magazines. Jack gave Mike several flash-bang and smoke grenades and I was pleased to see that he was happy enough to accept them.

With the tuning fork pouch clipped on to my belt and the Empyrean Key safely stowed in my rucksack, I took out my Sky Wire phone. 'Time to alert Niki that we're here and to get an update on our evac. I don't fancy staying on this mountain any longer than we have to.'

Jack looked up as he finished loading an assortment of grenades into his rucksack. 'Yeah, me neither.'

I listened to my phone but there was no connection tone. When I glanced again at the screen I saw the lack of reception bars for the satellite phone. 'Shit, it's not just the GPS signal we've lost. There's no phone either.'

Mike gestured to the mountains around us. 'These can't be helping. We must be in a dead zone. We may need to go to the car park where we know the GPS was still working. We'll probably also get a phone signal there.'

'Oh, that's flipping great – it was hairy enough getting up here. I don't want to think about trying to get down those breakneck slopes,' I complained.

'If it comes to it, I can go alone,' Mike said. 'To be honest, you two would just hold me up.'

'What happened to sticking together?' Jack asked.

Mike shrugged. 'Needs must, but as always, this is Lauren's call.'

'Guys, maybe we're getting ahead of ourselves,' I said. 'Let's see how we get on before we decide to send anybody off to call home. We know they're on their way anyway.'

'Fair enough,' Mike replied.

Five minutes later, with our Zeros hidden in the bushes, we were at the steps that lead up to the site.

Now we were clear of the trees, I checked my Sky Wire

phone just in case, but it still had no reception bars. 'This place is as bad for phone reception as the metal-beamed night club I used to hang out at in Macclesfield.'

Jack peered at his Sky Wire and frowned. 'That means that we haven't got map coverage either. We're going to have to rely on our memory of the model of this site from the hidden temple.'

'That shouldn't be a problem, should it? It was a lone building near the top right-hand corner. That should be easy enough to track down, right?'

'It would be if seventy per cent of Choquequirao wasn't overgrown with jungle that hasn't been cleared yet. This place is not Machu Picchu.'

'Hang on, forget the Sky Wires – if a micro mind is nearby, it's time for the old tech,' Mike said.

I felt like slapping myself. 'Of course.' I fished the Empyrean Key out of my rucksack and flipped up my visor so the helmet's night-vision system wouldn't interfere. I gently struck my tuning fork against the stone.

As the low tone hummed out, the effect on my vision was immediate – a green arrow shimmered into life over the orb. It pointed north-west of our position, up the jungle-covered slope of the mountain.

'Is it working?' Jack asked.

'Like a charm,' I replied. 'So here's the plan. Jack and I will head up to the site and, Mike, if you could...' My words trailed away as I spotted a bright flash of light in the sky again, but this time it lingered. The point of light seemed to get bigger as it raced towards us. 'Hey, what's that thing up there?'

Jack's eyes tightened on it as it grew ever larger. 'A missile with our fucking names on it.'

Mike paled. 'You mean the Overseers have found us?'

'No time for conversation – shift your arses!' Jack said.

The three of us sprinted for the jungle as the missile raced towards us. My mouth tanged with bitterness as I kept running... panting...running... *Keep going, keep going...*

Five, four, three, two, one...

A blinding flash of light turned the jungle bright white for a moment. A split second later a shock wave smashed into our backs, throwing us to the ground. I clutched my hands over my head as debris rained down. My heart thundered as the explosion's roar echoed away across the valley.

We picked ourselves up slowly, scraping the grime from our helmets' visors.

'Shit, that was too close,' Jack said.

'But where the hell did that missile come from?' Mike asked.

'That sneaky bastard Alvarez probably had something like a Reaper drone keeping an eye on the police station. Most likely it trailed us the moment we escaped Machu Picchu. And if it is a Reaper, it will have more missiles on it.'

'Going by that little demonstration, I don't think they're interested in taking us prisoners this time round,' Mike said.

'So we've led the Overseers straight to the pot of gold at the end of the bloody rainbow?' I asked.

'I guess so,' Jack replied. 'We can expect company any moment now.'

'Right, that's it,' Mike said. 'I'm going down the mountain to try to contact Niki to let him know he's flying into a hostile situation. The XA101 is unarmed.'

'You're not going anywhere with that damned drone circling up there,' I told him. 'There are too many open slopes on the way down for you to be spotted.'

'But we're going to be stuck up here without any backup.'

'Then we'll just have to press on and take our chances to locate the micro mind,' I said. 'With everything at stake, the priority is getting the micro mind repaired and launched. Even our lives are secondary to that. Remember, we're saving the world here.'

They gave me a grim look and then both nodded.

'If the Overseers know we're here, I bet that explains the lack of phone reception,' Jack said. 'I expect they're jamming all the frequencies around the site like they did back on Orkney.' He glowered up at the sky through the canopy of leaves and raised his middle finger towards it.

'I couldn't have put it better myself,' I said. I hitched my rucksack up higher on my shoulders and struck my tuning fork against the Empyrean Key. 'Let's move out, guys.'

CHAPTER NINETEEN

As we crept through the jungle, my body aching with every step from the aftermath of the missile strike, I kept the Empyrean Key clutched in my hand. But whenever I checked it with a tuning fork strike, the arrow hovering in front of the orb still showed a steady bearing to the northwest.

We made sure we kept the cover of jungle canopy over our heads the whole way. As we worked our way up over the overgrown stone terraces, the knowledge there was a Reaper circling above us weighed down on me. I kept glancing skywards through gaps in the leaves, looking for any sign of the killing machine. Not that I would be able to see it – Jack had told us that drones like the Reaper flew too high for the human eye to spot. The first we would know that we'd been seen would be a missile streaking towards us. No wonder these machines were so feared – if they could dispatch death with hardly any warning. But something puzzled me about the flash of light I'd seen, which I'd thought was a meteor. Could that have been the Reaper? That didn't stack up if Jack was right. What if it had been Lucy? Though that didn't make sense either – surely she would have made contact if she was keeping an eye on us?

'How long until we reach the building we're aiming for?' Mike asked.

'It can't be much farther,' Jack replied over the intercom. 'We must be almost at the edge of the site by now and...' His words trailed away as he pushed through a large bush to reveal a moss-covered mound straight ahead of us. Jack turned towards me. 'Please tell me this is it, Lauren?'

I glanced at the Empyrean Key and struck the tuning fork again. Sure enough, the arrow pointed straight at the mound. To make doubly sure, I tried sidestepping left and right as the note faded and the arrow kept pivoting back.

I smiled and nodded.

'Oh, thank god for that,' Mike said.

Jack's expression became pure focus as he moved forward and ran his fingers over the moss covering the rock, probing it with his fingertips. 'Yes, there's definitely some sort of structure beneath this.'

'So what now?' Mike asked.

'Working on the assumption there's a doorway under all this overgrowth, we need to clear the surface,' Jack replied.

'Then let's get this thing done,' I said.

Together we began to scrape away the moss. Moment by moment, a series of grooved markings in the stonework was revealed. Within a few minutes we had uncovered a winged figure carved in a Mayan style.

'I didn't know Incas had angels in their culture,' I said.

'They don't,' Jack replied.

'So what is it then?'

'As we're pretty certain the Angelus visited this site, maybe this is what they looked like.'

Mike and I exchanged wide-eyed stares.

'So this is where stories of angels originated from?' I asked.

'That's quite a mental leap, but it does makes sense,' Jack said. 'We've seen winged beings crop up in many cultures throughout the ages all around the world, so why not Inca too?'

'So rather than mythical beings dreamt up by a high priest, these were actually depictions of visitors from beyond our world?' I asked.

'I guess so.'

Mike whistled. 'That's seriously mind-blowing, guys. I'll be looking at all those old paintings of angels in a new light.'

'Well, it's made me even keener to discover what other secrets this building will reveal,' Jack said. He took out a black-bladed knife from a scabbard on his belt and began to scrape away the mud in the recesses of the carving. He worked for several minutes, his forehead ridging, before leaning back on his haunches and smiling. 'I thought so.'

'Thought what?' I asked.

'Oh, you'll see in a moment.' He worked the blade along the edge of the angel carving, revealing a rectangular outline in the wall. 'There we go, my friends – one door at your disposal.'

I peered at it. 'That's great and everything, but how the hell do we open it? I can't see a lock or any handle.'

'Are you sure?' Jack said. He pointed to a small round recess set between the hands of the angel.

I stared at the Empyrean Key I was holding. 'You think?'

'Well, the other one worked in the hidden temple, so why not?'

A tingle ran through me as I gently pushed the stone orb into the recess. My heart shuddered as a faint hum came from behind the carved angel. With a tremble, the door began to drop open, revealing a darkened room beyond.

'Blimey,' Mike said.

I placed my hand back on the Empyrean Key, but Jack

grabbed my wrist. 'Hang on, it could be booby-trapped like the other one.'

'But that orb was already there – and this one is ours. I think we're good. But to be on the safe side, maybe you two should back up a bit.'

Jack and Mike exchanged looks and stayed exactly where they were.

I sighed, but couldn't help notice how they both tensed a fraction as I tightened my grip on the stone orb. I yanked it out as if tearing off a plaster.

Exactly nothing happened.

'Talk about an anti-climax,' Mike said.

Jack chuckled. 'Makes a pleasant change when you hang out with Lauren.'

'Hey, I can't help it if life has a habit of getting interesting when I'm around.'

Jack gave me an eye-roll.

We peered through the doorway. Despite the night vision, the room inside was pitch-dark.

'I can't see a thing,' Mike said.

'Our helmets' vision systems, like the military ones, can only amplify what little light is around, even if it's only starlight,' Jack said. 'So when there's absolutely no light source, you can't see a damned thing – unless you have a secondary infrared system.'

Mike fished out a torch from his pack. 'So we need to go low-tech in other words.'

'Good idea,' I said. 'But best not to turn them on out here, in case that unfriendly eye in the sky spots it.'

'God, yes.'

Jack and I dug out our torches and, feeling our way with our hands and feet, we stepped into the room.

'Toggle your night vision off before you turn your flashlights on, otherwise they'll blind the helmets' systems and you won't see a thing,' Jack said.

I found the menu option and did the blink thing to kill the night vision. At once everything plunged into shadowy darkness.

'Everyone ready?' I asked, my pulse amping at the thought of what we were about to discover.

'All good,' Jack replied.

'Me too,' Mike said.

'OK, let's see what's inside.'

We flicked on our torches and three cones of light lanced out into the darkness. Any sense of excitement was quickly swept away by crushing disappointment. The room was utterly feature-less with just a dirt floor.

'Goddamn it,' Jack said.

'Not another bloody false trail,' I said.

'Or maybe someone else got here first?' Mike said.

'But there's no evidence of tampering around the entrance,' Jack replied. 'For anyone without an Empyrean Key, I would expect to see at least some chisel marks showing an attempt to force the door open.'

There had to be something here.

I held out the Empyrean Key and struck the tuning fork against it. The deep note hummed at the edge of my hearing and the arrow reappeared, but with one significant change. Rather than pointing out ahead, the arrow pointed down at the floor.

I grinned at the other two and gestured to the ground.

'Now that's more like it,' Jack said.

'OK, we all know the drill. Let's clear the dirt away to see what we're standing on.'

We began to work together again to scrape away the soil.

As a child, Lucy had bought me a dinosaur bone excavation set from the Natural History Museum in London. This was a lot like that – moving soil to reveal the treasure buried beneath.

Glimpse by tantalising glimpse, a spiral motif started to reveal itself.

I squatted on my haunches and ran my fingers over the raised surface. 'You know where we've seen a symbol like this before, don't you, guys?'

Mike gave me a sharp nod. 'The crystal rune markings on Orkney formed a spiral pattern. And we all know what was at the centre of that.'

'Skara Brae, where Lucy's original micro mind was buried.'

'So we just need to locate the centre of this pattern,' Jack said.

We worked quickly to scrape away soil at roughly the centre of the room.

A round recess appeared dead centre, sending my pulse skyrocketing. The cavity was exactly the same size as the one in the door outside.

I glanced at the other two. 'Only one way to find out.'

'What, no health and safety check?' Mike asked.

'Stuff that,' I replied.

I lowered the Empyrean Key into the hole and at once a pulse of blue light shot through the carving. With a glow that warmed the air, any remaining dirt was vaporised in a trail of rising smoke that left the spiral completely clear of debris. The light faded away, followed by a vibration from the floor.

We stepped back as a grinding sound, like a clock powered by stone gears, grew louder. Then the floor slabs started to lower in a radiating pattern, like the petals of a flower. It was only when they'd fully descended that I realised what we were looking at: a stone spiral staircase.

Mike punched the air. 'Pardon my French, but oh fucking yes!'

I gestured towards Jack. 'As our resident archaeologist, I think this is your moment again, so lead the way.'

Jack winked at me. 'Sure thing, Lauren.' He shone his torch

downwards and began to descend the steps. A moment later he called out, 'You'd better get yourselves down here!'

We headed after him into a round room about twenty metres wide. Pure unfettered elation surged through me as I saw Jack's torch spotlighting a micro mind mounted on stone pillars in the middle of the room. But where was the internal light that should have been glowing within the crystal?

Jack knelt to peer at it. 'Is it dead?'

'If so, I doubt we'd have been experiencing the monowave quakes,' Mike replied.

'And let's not forget the Empyrean Key is active around here,' I said. 'But there's an easy way to check. Just turn off your torches for a few seconds.'

A moment later we were plunged into darkness...but it wasn't complete. As my eyes adjusted to the gloom, I saw a faint bluish glow radiating around the micro mind.

I switched my torch back on. 'It looks as if we've hit the jackpot.'

Jack high-fived me. 'Way to go, Lauren.'

So this was it. We'd really found the micro mind. Any moment now I might get to see Lucy again, something I'd dreamt of ever since our last meeting.

'I need to get this thing rebooted,' I said. 'Then we'll haul our arses out of here before Alvarez turns up.'

Jack nodded as I took out the tuning fork and struck it against the stone orb. The arrow had vanished and two icons now appeared. One had wavy lines that I knew from experience would pitch us into what we'd nicknamed the twilight zone. Next to that was an orb with concentric circles radiating out – the reboot icon.

The buzz of anticipation grew inside me like a trapped bee as I rotated the icon into the selection window. I flicked my wrist forward and the icon turned red as four inward-facing arrows appeared round it. A faint humming filled the room as flickers of light, visible even in our torch beams, began to grow stronger within the crystal.

'Houston, we are starting the countdown to launch,' Jack said with a smile.

'And now the waiting begins,' I added.

'At least it should be quicker than back at Skara Brae when you put a bullet through the micro mind.'

I winced. 'Please don't remind me. Anyway, we can take it in turns to watch over the micro mind whilst catching up on some well-earned sleep.'

But Mike was frowning. 'I don't think so – listen.'

At first all I heard was the chatter of insects in the jungle drifting down the stairwell. But then I caught the faint clatter of rotors beating the air.

'Oh god, no.'

We killed our torches, powered up our night-vision systems and headed back up the stairs.

Silhouetted against the starry sky, three squat helicopters were coming in to land on the plateau next to the blast crater that the missile had created. Through my night vision I could see gunners in each of the helicopters' open side doors, training their weapons down towards the site.

'Black Hawks,' Jack said.

'Damn it, the micro mind is nowhere near finished rebooting yet,' I said.

'So we need to buy it some time,' Mike said.

With a rumble the three Black Hawks landed. As soon as they touched down, soldiers came during pouring out, taking up defensive firing positions around the helicopters. There were at least thirty, heavily armed, all wearing body armour and night-imaging headsets clamped on to their helmets. Then, to top it all, Alvarez himself got out from the last helicopter.

'What the hell are we going to do now?' Mike asked.

I chewed my lip and my eyes fell upon the stone still clutched in my hand. 'Hang on, I've got an idea.' I struck the tuning fork against the wall and there it was, the icon with wavy lines.

'You remember that time we dropped into the twilight zone, Jack?'

'What about it?'

'Well, I think that's gonna give us the edge we need right now.'

He peered at me and his eyes widened. 'Hell, yes!'

'What?' Mike asked.

'Oh, you'll see.' I rotated to the icon and selected it. In an instant the physical world of the jungle, Choquequirao and even the helicopter and soldiers all blurred around us. Our own bodies shimmered and shifted like mirages, the only constant our eyes staring at each other through the visors of our now out-of-focus helmets.

'What the actual fuck?' Mike said.

'This is what we nicknamed the twilight zone,' I told him.

'The waveform version of our world you recovered me from when I pulled that vanishing trick at Skara Brae?' Mike asked, his face defocusing around his eyes.

'The very same,' I replied.

'Good god. I mean, we knew that when particles aren't observed they're in a waveform state, but to see this for myself is...' He flapped his blurring hands, trying to find a word big enough and failing.

'As great as it is seeing you enjoy this road trip to the other side of reality, why are we here, Lauren?' Jack asked.

'Because, as we discovered back at Skara Brae, we're effectively invisible within it to anyone in our particle reality.'

'Oh, that's just genius,' Mike said.

'And we can sneak up on Alvarez and his soldiers to take them out before they know what's happening,' Jack said.

I shook my head. 'You're forgetting we can't do much to interact with the physical world whilst we're in the twilight zone.'

Mike nodded. 'That makes sense. Everything in this wave-form universe hasn't been collapsed into its particle form. Try your gun, Jack, and you'll see exactly what Lauren means.'

Jack peered at his Glock, which ghosted in and out in his hand. He raised his arm and closed his finger on the trigger. There was dull click, but nothing else.

'Crap,' Jack said. 'So we can watch but not touch in other words?'

'As much as I hate to advocate violence, don't be so sure,' Mike said. 'After all, we can shut down the orb for a moment, drop back into our world, do what we need to and then shift back to this crazy alternative universe.'

'A bit like a Klingon ship in *Star Trek* where they have to decloak to fire?' I said.

'That's a pretty good analogy,' Mike replied.

'OK, here's the plan. Let's make every moment count to buy the micro mind enough time to repair itself and power up. At the very least, we should try to even up the odds a bit.'

'Sound good to me,' Jack said.

'Just please try not to kill anyone you don't strictly have to,' Mike said as he took the dart gun from his shimmering holster.

'I can't promise, but I'll try,' Jack replied.

Our night vision was effectively redundant as everything glimmered with an aura of blurring bright energy. I raised my visor so I could breathe more easily as we walked towards the soldiers now in a defensive line round the plateau.

Alvarez waved his hand and his soldiers started to advance into the jungle, apart from one, who headed back to a Black Hawk. A moment later he escorted Cristina out from it.

'Shit, Gabriel obviously wasn't able to get to her in time,' I said.

'But why bring her here?' Mike asked.

'Maybe he's hoping she'll have one of her visions again,' Jack said.

I saw Alvarez place the stone orb into her hand. 'Oh shit, he's just given her the other Empyrean Key. They're going to use her like a bloodhound to sniff out the micro mind.'

Jack stared at me. 'So you think they've worked out the sound trigger to activate it?'

'Going by the fact Cristina's here, I think that's a pretty safe bet,' I replied.

'But we can't just stand by and let that happen.'

A hollow feeling filled my stomach. 'I know...'

'What's that meant to mean?' Mike asked, looking between us.

'Whatever we have to do to stop them,' Jack replied.

Mike squared up to him. 'You mean killing Cristina to slow them down, don't you?'

'I didn't say that.'

'You didn't bloody have to!'

I stood between them. 'Guys, let's just make sure it doesn't come to that.'

Mike glowered at Jack.

Jack sighed and shrugged.

I returned my attention to the scene on the plateau. Cristina was staring at the orb in her hand as the line of soldiers continued pushing out into the jungle.

'Time to lay on a reception committee for them,' I said.

We picked our way through the jungle until we were less than a hundred metres away from the two soldiers heading roughly in the direction of the building.

'OK, get ready, everyone,' I said.

I closed my visor, holding the tuning fork in my right hand, the Empyrean Key in the left. I waited until the soldiers had passed us, then I chose the dot icon that would shift us back into our particle-filled world. At once the real world swept back into focus and I activated my night vision.

Jack took out the guy on right, finding a gap in his body armour at the neck with a clean shot from his Glock. Mike's dart slammed into the other's soldier's throat as he spun round to fire at us.

I'd already selected the wave icon and flicked my wrist forward. As we shifted back, the merc's finger tightened on the trigger, but he was starting to lose consciousness. His carbine flashed with its fire, but the world was already ghosting around us. His bullets rippled, travelling on their way as though we weren't actually there...which in a sense was technically true. We'd become waveform energy patterns once again.

'Crap, this is better than invisibility,' Jack said. 'We're immune to fire as soon as we're back in the twilight zone.'

The soldier stared at where we'd been a moment before, then dropped to the ground as the dart did its work. But I could already see other soldiers closing in on their fallen comrade.

'OK, they know we're here now,' Jack said.

I shrugged. 'So let's dance.'

Initially, the firefight very much went our way. We kept moving, blinking back into existence, taking out a soldier where we could. But gradually a line of Overseers mercs closed in on us like a snare.

I caught some movement behind us farther up the slope. I'd been concentrating so hard on the fighting, I hadn't noticed the small breakaway group that had slipped round the side. Alvarez and another soldier were following Cristina, who was staring at her Empyrean Key and heading straight towards the building containing the rebooting micro mind.

'Guys, we've got to get back to the micro mind before Alvarez does,' I said.

Mike and Jack spun round and we began to race towards him, dodging several soldiers standing in our way.

We were on track until the twilight zone vanished just as we passed three soldiers, and the real world rushed back in.

The mercs opened fire. Their bullets raked the jungle as we dived for cover.

I stuffed the stone orb back into my bag. 'Retreat!'

We returned fire as best we could as we fell back into the jungle.

Jack turned to me. 'Did you shift us back, Lauren?'

'Nothing to do with me.' I glanced down at my Empyrean Key. All the icons had vanished.

'Damn it!' Mike said. 'Cristina must have stumbled upon a way to shut down the micro mind, which dropped us back the moment she did.'

As we ran deeper into the jungle, I stared across at him, not wanting him to be right, but knowing he had to be. The micro mind had been shut down and we were out-gunned. It seemed that Alvarez had won – for now.

CHAPTER TWENTY

I LOADED another magazine into my LRS as we retreated farther into the depths of the jungle, pursued by Alvarez's remaining mercs. 'We need to put some distance between us and them.'

'You mean we're simply going to give up on the micro mind after your big speech about doing whatever it took?' Mike asked.

'No, but we need to rethink our strategy. Our most immediate problem is that Alvarez's next move will almost certainly be to transport the micro mind out of here as quickly as possible on those Black Hawks.'

I heard the crack of a twig behind us. I spun round just as a shape loomed out of the bushes. Part of my brain registered the burly man's carbine as he swung it round towards me. I squeezed the trigger of my LRS and a single shot rang out with a suppressed hiss. A hole appeared in the guy's forehead, his eyes lifeless as if someone had flicked his off switch, as he sprawled at Mike's feet.

Mike pulled his helmet off and leant against a tree as vomit spilt from his mouth.

But I just felt numb, as if I were watching a war movie in

which someone had been shot – not the person responsible for taking a life. It seemed that crossing that line was becoming increasingly easier for me. I was becoming the soldier that the fate of the world needed me to be.

Jack raised his chin towards me, as if he knew exactly what I was thinking. He took the man's carbine from him and slung it over his own shoulder.

A rustle of leaves came from the jungle to the left, a few hundred metres above us on the slope. It was followed by a similar noise spreading out in a line through the thicket of greenery ahead, which was growing gradually louder.

I cracked open my visor so Mike could hear me. 'We need to even up the odds of survival,' I whispered.

'I'm not sure that I can,' Mike said.

'We all need to keep playing our part if we're to pull this off,' Jack told him.

Mike grimaced, scraped his hand across his mouth and pulled his helmet back on.

I had a momentary pang of guilt. Losing my grip on my own sense of humanity was one thing, but forcing Mike to do the same – even if he was only tranquillising them – felt like a step too far.

I beckoned him towards me and we crouched behind a boulder. Jack took cover behind one of the larger tree trunks. I listened to the murmur of the jungle around us, the sigh of the wind in the trees over the soundtrack of night insects. I strained my ears, searching for any hint of soldiers closing in on us. If we survived this mission, I'd be suggesting to Tom he might want to enhance the helmets with some sort of electronic listening device that could enable us to amplify barely there sounds.

Then I heard the faintest scrape of a boot on a rock. I glanced across at Jack and Mike, pointing in the direction of the noise to the right of us. They both nodded.

I held up three fingers and lowered each digit one by one. I needed to wait until this soldier was as close as possible. I lowered my final finger...

We all popped up from our hiding places, weapons facing forward, to see three soldiers creeping between the trees towards our hiding position.

Jack sprayed bullets from the carbine at two of the soldiers, who dived for cover.

Neurons fired at the speed of light as I aimed and fired at the third merc. The guy staggered backwards as my rounds smashed into his body armour, but he managed to squeeze off several shots. I ducked, but Mike, his hand trembling, aimed his pistol and fired. The dart buried itself in the guy's face below his goggles and he pitched forward.

Mike stood there staring at him, as if he wanted to be shot. The other two soldiers took aim at Mike, and I grabbed him and yanked him down behind the boulder. Their bullets hissed over his head.

'Time to light them up,' Jack said over the intercom. 'Turn off your night vision and cover me.'

I killed my image-intensifier with a blink. In the darkness, my training took over and I knew the exact location of the selector on my LRS. I pushed it to its semi-automatic mode, breathed in through my nose, stood up and sprayed bullets.

The strobe of my LRS firing lit up the boulder that our opponents were using as cover. Jack appeared from behind his tree and lobbed a grenade. It arced over the boulder and I ducked down as a bright burst of light cast shadows across the jungle, turning everything briefly to monochrome.

As the blinding after-image faded away, I powered my night vision back up. Jack was already standing over the two mercs who were writhing on the ground. He fired his carbine at them at almost point-blank range. Their bodies shuddered with the impacts of his bullets and a moment later they both stilled.

Mike appeared by my side and stared down at the dead men. 'Shit, Jack, did you really have to do that?'

'This is a combat situation, Mike. Kill or be killed. We have to make sure these people don't come after us.'

Anger flashed through Mike's eyes and his hand tightened on his dart pistol. Maybe he was considering putting a dart in Jack.

Jack shoved past him and aimed his carbine at the guy Mike had shot with the tranquilliser dart.

But Mike slapped the barrel down. 'You can't do this, Jack.'

'Just watch me,' Jack replied, his tone ice-cold.

I stepped between the two men. They were an almost perfect personification of the internal conflict within me – the civilian looking for a peaceful solution and the solider who had seen enough to be hardened.

Mike's eyes locked on mine. 'Please, Lauren, tell him.'

I felt the heat cooling in my blood. 'How long will your tranquilliser work, Mike?'

'He should remain knocked out for at least an hour.'

I ran the odds in my head. An hour in a fast-moving combat situation was a long time. Anything could happen. And if by any miracle we were still alive after that, then this guy...

Jack peered at me. 'I know how crap it is, but we haven't any choice. Not in this situation.'

My mind locked up. I didn't know what to do.

I slowly nodded and headed over to the guy. His eyes were closed and he almost looked peaceful. I took my LRS and placed the tip of the barrel to the temple of his head.

'Lauren, please don't do this,' Mike said. 'You'll never be able to forgive yourself.'

I forced myself to look at the guy's face, who was maybe in his mid-thirties. He had an old scar on his cheek and a fresh bullet hole in the side of his head. Somebody's son. Maybe somebody's father.

I closed my eyes as the part of my mind that was frantically agreeing with Mike tormented me. My finger trembling, I was about to pull the trigger when I felt a hand on my wrist.

I opened my eyes to see Jack looking at me. 'I'll do it.'

'But, Jack—'

He shook his head, and in one fluid movement, he placed his Glock against the side of the man's temple and fired. The guy let out a gentle sigh and died.

A deep grief tinged my numbness as I hung my head. There had to be a better way than this.

'You utter bastard. That guy was defenceless,' Mike said.

'Kill the attitude, buddy. Not everyone here can afford to be a conscientious objector like you, just along for the free ride.'

'Oh, you can fuck right off,' Mike said.

I had to deal with this before it got out of hand. I forced myself to stand between them. 'Stop it, both of you. We can tear a strip out of each other later, but not now. Got it?'

Both men looked anywhere but at me or each other.

'OK, now we've got that out of the way, you can be certain someone else will have spotted that flash bang going off in the jungle. No doubt we'll have more company any moment. We need to grab all the ammo we can.'

Jack immediately focused and I worked quickly with him, helping myself to one of the soldier's carbines as well as taking their ammo. But Mike stood watching us with his arms crossed. There was no point in trying to get him to take a weapon, especially after what he'd just seen Jack do.

Feet thundered through the jungle towards us, any pretence at stealth long gone. As Jack would say, we'd gone 'well and truly loud'.

I stowed my LRS and slipped a fresh magazine into the carbine. 'Time to get moving.'

'And then what?' Jack asked.

'We need to disable those Black Hawks to prevent Alvarez airlifting the micro mind out of here.'

'You know that's a real dangerous plan?' Jack said.

'It's always the way,' I replied as I took up the lead and began circling back through the jungle towards the plateau where the Black Hawks had landed.

'How are we going to take out those Black Hawks when they are almost certainly heavily guarded?' Jack asked. 'And let's not forget their damned Reaper drone up there ready to join in the party at a moment's notice.'

'We'll need to sneak in on our Zeros. Hopefully they won't hear us approaching until it's too late. Then we'll light those Black Hawks up with some of Mike's C4 charges and get the hell out of there.'

'And what if anyone in the helicopters spots us?' Mike asked.

'Then it will be the Charge of the Light Brigade all over again, so let's just pray they don't.'

'With all due respect, Lauren, I think I have a better idea,' Mike said. 'What if just one of us heads for the Black Hawks while the other two kept under cover. And as I'm not along for the *free ride*, I'll do it.'

'Buddy, I didn't mean what I said just now,' Jack told him.

'Yes, you did. Anyway, I have to do this for three reasons. Firstly, I'm the most experienced on a motorbike. Secondly, I won't be any good to you if you're going to ask me to shoot anyone. Helicopter with no one on board, yes, soldiers, no – even ones shooting at me. Finally, I am the expert with explosives.'

I looked across with fresh respect for Mike. 'Are you sure? Without wanting to point out the obvious, you seemed pretty shaken up just now.'

'I'm fine as long as I'm the one being shot at. It's killing others I have a serious problem with. I need to do this, Lauren, for all sorts of reasons.'

'You are definitely not just along for the free ride,' Jack said. 'You, my friend, have balls of steel.'

Mike snorted over the intercom. 'Let's hope so.'

In any other situation I would have given both of them a hug. But this so wasn't that moment.

'Then let's get ourselves back to our motorbikes and pray that our luck holds out long enough for Mike to implement his plan,' I said, then I led the way back into the dense jungle.

CHAPTER TWENTY-ONE

It had taken a good thirty minutes for us to work our way back towards the motorbikes, often crawling on our bellies to avoid the rest of Alvarez's mercs. Fortunately, we'd made it without any encounter, but my nerves were strung out like piano wires by the time we reached our Zeros.

Mike quickly opened one of his panniers and took out three of the C4 charges. He inserted the metal probes of the timer units very carefully into each pack, the tip of his tongue showing between his teeth as he worked.

'Are you really sure about this, Mike?' Jack asked.

Mike nodded. 'Look, demolitions is my thing now. If I can get close enough to set these charges, we can be back in the jungle before they blow up.'

I was starting to have serious second thoughts about sending Mike into such a dangerous situation alone. 'But what if you get spotted and a stray round hits the C4?'

'Then it will be thank you and goodnight.' Mike caught my horrified expression and waved a hand at me. 'Not really. Even if a bullet punched a hole straight through a pack, it wouldn't explode.'

'But if the timer unit is struck it'd be another matter, right?' Jack asked.

'Hey, I was trying not to worry Lauren too much,' Mike replied.

'Thanks for the thought, but I'm a big girl and part of my job as team leader is to worry. Jack and I will do our best to cause a big enough distraction to keep all eyes on us whilst you do the dirty on their Black Hawks.'

'Good stuff.' Mike nodded. 'I just wish I was religious at moments like this. I would definitely be praying to someone upstairs.'

'Hey, you've been a lucky son of a bitch so far, so I wouldn't sweat it too much,' Jack said with the hint of a smile.

The lines in Mike's brow smoothed out. 'Yeah, right.'

'We'd better get a move on before Alvarez recovers the micro mind and loads it on to one of the Black Hawks,' I said. 'Let's head to the edge of the clearing with the bikes. We can be certain of one thing – at some point the shit will hit the fan. So when it does, we hightail it out of here back down this mountain and to a place with reception so we can call Niki for help.'

'What happened to recovering the micro mind?' Jack asked.

'If the Overseers helicopters are taken out, it will buy us some time, hopefully enough for Niki to get here with the security team. Then together we can snatch the micro mind from the Overseers and airlift it to somewhere safe until it's had time to finish its self-repair.'

'Sounds like a good plan to me,' Mike said.

'So let's make this happen, guys.'

Jack cracked me a salute. 'Yes, ma'am.'

I smiled at him. 'Idiot.'

We began to wheel our motorbikes through the jungle towards the plateau.

As we neared the edge, Jack flicked a switch on his carbine's night-vision scope. 'Helpfully there are thermal-imaging scopes on the Overseers' weapons. We can use these to check whether anyone is guarding those Black Hawks.'

'Let's hope not. It'll make things a lot trickier,' I said.

Jack grimaced. 'Don't I know it.'

A moment later my heart sank. The first thing I saw as I peered through the carbine's night-vision scope was five soldiers gathered around the Black Hawks. Worse still, one was sitting on the edge of the open side door, within easy reach of the mounted mini-guns. The rest were standing a short way off and had carbines in their hands. Armed and dangerous.

'Oh hell,' Jack said. 'There's not a chance you'll be able to sneak up, Mike.'

He shrugged. 'We should have expected this, especially after Lauren blew the shit out of the last Overseers helicopters we encountered on Orkney. But I have an alternative plan.'

'What's that?' I asked.

'I'll sneak in on my belly, plant the C4, then crawl back out. Meanwhile you guys cause that distraction. Once I'm clear, I can use a remote trigger to safely detonate the C4 once we draw the soldiers away so they don't get caught in the blast.'

So there it was again, Mike doing what he could to protect lives, even of those on the wrong side of this fight. I envied him trying to hang on to his humanity in this extreme situation.

'That sounds incredibly risky to me,' I said.

'I've got this.'

'Are you sure?'

'I wouldn't suggest it if I didn't mean it.'

Jack shook his head. 'Yep, definitely balls of steel, buddy.'

'Even so, if you get yourself shot, I'm going to be seriously pissed off with you,' I added.

Mike laughed. 'Understood, *ma'am*.'

I rolled my eyes at him. 'OK, Jack, we'd better start the diversion. If everything goes according to plan, we'll rendezvous back here. But please be careful or I'll give you hell.'

'Oh, you can count on it.'

With a final nod to Mike, I cast a silent prayer to the sky that it wouldn't be the last time we saw him alive. Then Jack and I set off, wheeling our bikes round the edge of the plateau, using the jungle as cover.

There was still no sign of Alvarez or Cristina. Presumably they were still with the micro mind.

We crept through the jungle in silence until we were at last on the opposite side of the plateau.

'This should be far enough to draw the attention of those guards away from Mike,' I said.

'So what were you thinking exactly?' Jack asked.

'About half a dozen flash bangs and the same again of smoke grenades. Plus a few random shots to make them think they're being attacked from this direction.'

'I'm liking your style.'

I smiled at him. 'So you keep telling me.' For someone who was meant to be a mate, it was hard to ignore the spark that kept bursting into life between us, even in an extreme situation like this.

We parked up our Zeros and laid out the flash bangs along a thirty-metre stretch parallel to the edge of the plateau.

I picked up a flash-bang grenade. 'Let's get this show on the road, Jack.'

He scooped up another. 'Oh, this is going to get real interesting and fast.'

We pulled the pins on both grenades and lobbed them on to the edge of the plateau. I counted to three in my head as we both looked away and a blinding flash lit up the night sky. Then we turned back and sprayed bullets towards the helicopters, our muzzles popping with fire, shell casings emptying on to the jungle floor.

We were already running to the next grenades as the returning fire peppered the foliage behind us where we'd been just a moment before.

Once again we repeated the operation, but this time with smoke grenades. They quickly billowed across our side of the plateau and enveloped the Black Hawks behind a wall of smoke.

A crackle of fire shredded the trees with a hailstorm of bullets.

'Fuck, they're using one of those damned mini-guns on us,' Jack said over the intercom.

'At least we've got their attention now.'

'Yeah, maybe a little bit too much.'

We sprinted away, repeating our guerilla action over and over, until we'd reached the last grenades in our line. By now tracer rounds were lancing out in every direction across the plateau. We lobbed our last flash bang and smoke grenades into the melee.

'Good day at the office,' Jack said as we raced away, circling back to our Zeros.

'Now it's down to Mike,' I replied as mini-gun fire continued to shred the jungle on the far side of the Black Hawks.

When we reached our motorbikes, I opened my visor and raised the scope of the carbine to my eye. I saw brief glimpses of the guards fanned out and moving forward through the smoke.

'Mike, how are you getting on?' I whispered into my helmet's mic.

'Getting there,' he replied.

I spotted a prone figure reaching up and placing something beneath the belly of one of the Black Hawks.

'You can do it, buddy,' Jack said as he peered through his own scope.

'Just two more to go,' Mike replied.

The next minute felt like an hour as we watched Mike creep towards the second Black Hawk and stick on the second C4 charge. But then, as part of me knew it would, Mike's luck ran out.

Someone shouted a ceasefire order and the shooting immediately stopped. One of the soldiers heading back towards the Black Hawks froze, and it was easy to see why – he pointed his weapon towards the guy on his belly beneath a Black Hawk.

'Fuck!' Jack hissed.

I aimed and fired before I'd even had a chance to think about it. The soldier's head sprayed with blood and he crumpled to the ground.

I swung my scope back to Mike. He was on his feet and running back to us.

Everything slowed down as I saw the other soldiers swarming around the helicopters. They'd spotted Mike too and started to shoot at him as he ducked and weaved, running back to us at a full sprint.

'We've got to help him,' Jack said.

'Cover me!' I lowered my visor and leapt on to my Zero. I twisted the throttle right back and raced out of the jungle with a surge of instant torque. I sped towards Mike as Jack's covering fire hissed past me.

Through my visor's night vision, I saw figures sprawling on the ground around the helicopters. I braked hard as I skidded to a stop next to Mike. 'Get on!'

He leapt on to the back. 'Shit, it's good to see you.'

'You too.' I glanced back to see one the soldiers grab hold of the mini-gun in the doorway of the middle Black Hawk. 'Hang on!'

I spun the bike round and raced back to Jack. The ground around the bike exploded with enemy bullets. I ducked down over the motorbike's handlebars as Mike clung to me.

A bullet struck me and a white-hot needle of pain pierced my thigh. I jammed my jaw shut, trying to ignore the pain and keep control of the bike.

'Mike, blow the charges!' I shouted into my headset.

'I can't! All those people.'

'You have to do this! Otherwise we're going to die!'

'Oh god...' His hand holding the trigger rose into view.

I clamped my hand over his. 'Together.'

'Together...'

We squeezed the trigger and an orange ball of light lit up the plateau. Heat blazed across our backs as three explosions rocked the mountain. I glanced in my mirrors to see huge fireballs rolling into the sky as the Black Hawks were lifted up by the power of the blast, bodies flying through the air. A moment later burning metal started showering down. I skidded among the lumps as they hit the ground around us.

God only knew how the maelstrom of death missed us, but somehow I found a path through the metal meteor storm and we reached the jungle. We raced between the trees as ammo rounds began to detonate like hundreds of fireworks being let off at once. We slid the bike to a stop right next to Jack and Mike's Zeros. Jack was already on his, shouldering his carbine, ready to ride out.

'Holy crap, guys, that was close,' Jack said.

'Too close.' Mike jumped off the back of my Zero and on to his own.

'Now we need to get down off this mountain and contact Niki,' I said.

Jack pointed upwards. 'Don't forget there's still a Reaper up there looking for us. It'll be safer if just one of us goes.'

I nodded. A spasm of pain passed through my leg and I clutched it.

Mike stared at my thigh. 'Shit, you've been hit.'

'A flesh wound. I'll live. I'm going. This is my call.'

'The hell you are,' Mike said. 'You need to get Jack to check your leg out. I'll go instead.'

Jack stared past us down the mountain as he tore a medical pack out of his bag. 'Seriously. Give us a break already.'

Mike and I followed Jack's gaze – to a procession of head-lights working their way up the mountain opposite.

I raised the night scope of the carbine to my visor. Four Overseers SUVs were parking up at the beginning of the trail.

'Oh, great, just what we bloody needed, more reinforcements,' I said. 'This changes things.'

Mike shook his head. 'The plan still stands. I'll have to be extra careful. You stay up here and do what you can to hassle Alvarez and his mercs. Meanwhile, I'll do everything I can to get past the new arrivals.'

'But, Mike—'

'Please trust me, Lauren.'

Before I could respond, Mike opened up the throttle on his Zero and raced away into the jungle.

Worry twisted my gut. 'What the hell are you doing, Mike?' I said over the intercom.

'What needs to be done,' Mike replied. 'Anyway, please keep quiet. I'm trying to concentrate.'

Over the shouts of the mercs recovering boxes from the blazing Black Hawks, we heard the slap of leaves as Mike sped away from us. But he wasn't making for the trail – a moment later I saw his motorbike reappear at the top of an impossible slope.

'Mike, what are you doing? It's too risky,' I said.

'I have to, Lauren. Just wish me luck.'

'We have everything crossed here, buddy,' Jack said.

And then his motorbike disappeared over the almost sheer edge with Mike skidding the bike sideways to control his rapid descent.

'Shit, you have some serious guts,' Jack said.

'As long as you don't see them spread across the mountain,' Mike replied, his voice starting to break up with static.

Jack laughed but my heart was in my mouth as the minutes stretched on. I tracked Mike's progress through my carbine's scope. At least it helped distract me as Jack worked on my leg. He stabbed me with a shot of adrenaline, which took most of the edge off the pain. When he spread superglue over the flap of skin that had been opened up by the bullet and then pinched it together, I surprised even myself with the creativity of my swearing.

'What is it with you and getting yourself shot?'

'Must be my magnetic personality or something.'

Despite the odds against him, Mike was now a third of the way down the mountain.

But in a moment everything changed.

A pulse of light came from the sky and something hurtled towards him. The Reaper drone!

'Incoming missile, Mike!' I shouted.

Only crackles and pops came back through my speakers as the projectile streaked down. My heart rose to my throat, sheer horror rolling through me. Mike's bike burst with light as the missile hit. A plume of earth and stone erupted from the side of the mountain, obliterating the view. A slap of wind reached us, then a loud boom a split second later.

'Mike, are you there?' I whispered into my mic.

There was only silence as the rising pillar of light faded away. Just a smouldering crater in the mountainside remained. I looked towards Jack who shook his head.

And like that, Mike was gone, scrubbed out of existence. It was on me for letting him go.

Tears splintered my vision and a sob broke through my lips. A sense of utter emptiness rushed up and threatened to drown me.

CHAPTER TWENTY-TWO

MIKE WAS GONE. Dead. Snuffed out in less than a second.

'Lauren,' Jack said, his tone gentle as he pulled off his helmet.

If he hadn't been so damned brave, he'd still be here...

'Lauren,' Jack repeated, gazing into my eyes.

And now we're going to have to tell his family that he's dead. Did he even have any family? I looked past Jack down at the fire. It spread out in a ring from the explosion through the dried grass.

Jack gently shook me. 'Wherever you are in your head right now, I need you to return to me, as hard as it is. We need to come up with a new plan and quickly.'

My eyes focused on Jack's for the first time.

'There'll be time to grieve later, but right now we need to make Mike's death count for something.'

I could hear Jack's words, but could barely process them.

The whack of rotor blades grew louder and over the opposite mountain ridge a police helicopter appeared.

'Oh, shit, as if Alvarez needed more reinforcements,' Jack said.

I managed a vague nod, still unable to speak. Even the

abstract concept of saving the world didn't seem important any more compared to the sheer agony of losing Mike.

Jack pulled me into him and I felt myself melt into his embrace, his warmth reaching into me, steadying me as a cyclone of grief spun through me. I took a shuddering breath. It seemed that I wasn't the dispassionate soldier I'd come to think I was. But right now I needed to pull myself together. That was what leaders did when everything went to shit. And, like Jack had said, there would be time to grieve later.

I breathed through my nose as the small helicopter swept up over the hill and came to hover at the far end of the plateau. A squad of soldiers emerged from the jungle and formed a defensive circle round it as it landed as far as it could from the burning Black Hawks.

Watching it helped me to dodge the abyss of pain within about the loss of Mike. The dull sting in my leg from the bullet wound was also a welcome distraction.

I pulled away from Jack and his eyes searched mine. 'Are you OK?'

'I'll have to be...to honour Mike's memory if nothing else.'

'I know this will sound like a cliché, but it's what he would have wanted.'

'You're right...' I felt my resolve harden, a determination to see this through reigniting inside. 'OK, so it looks as if the Overseers will be able to airlift the micro mind out of here after all.'

But Jack was shaking his head. 'They're going to struggle with that craft – it's only a Robinson R44 Raven. It hasn't much in the way of lift. Throw in the thinner air of this altitude and it won't carry the micro mind, since it weighs a good ton or so.'

'OK, that's better news at least.'

'It is, but we're still in the same situation. We're alone without backup and Niki will be flying straight into a firefight. Not to mention the fact we'll be running low on ammo soon. I'm down to my two last smoke grenades.'

'I have one flash bang left.'

'At least that's something.'

The rotors of the helicopter were slowing as I raised the carbine's scope to see who was in it. I felt zero surprise when I saw Villca and the thin policeman who'd helped him abduct Cristina emerge from the cockpit.

'They've arrived late to the party,' Jack said, peering through his own scope.

'Probably fleeing Machu Picchu to avoid being thrown into jail.'

Jack nodded. 'So what's our next play here, Lauren?'

There it was again – the chain of command. I was increasingly feeling out of my depth as leader, especially as I'd just lost someone on my watch.

I clutched my fresh resolve and looked into Jack's eyes, trying to work out what to do. 'Alvarez knows we're out here and will be expecting another attack. And when those Overseers in SUVs get here, things will tip heavily in his favour. Our priority is still to reboot the micro mind. Do that and it can hopefully handle the rest.'

'In that case, I think we have two options,' Jack replied. 'The first is that we take out the Raven too, but they'll be expecting us to try that and it will almost certainly end up being a suicide mission.'

'So what's your second idea?'

'We head back to the micro mind and seize it from Alvarez and the others.'

'Jack, that also sounds like a suicide mission. Plus the micro mind is far too heavy to lift between us and carry off to somewhere safe.'

He scowled at me. 'So we give up and Mike sacrificed his life for nothing?'

'Bloody hell, don't go off at the deep end with me. I'm not saying that. But you have given me an idea. Why don't we let the Overseers do the heavy lifting for us?'

Jack's expression softened. 'How do you mean?'

'Are you're absolutely certain they can't airlift it out?'

'Not with that helicopter. Anything over a ton you'd need at least a Chinook for.'

'So in that case, assuming that Alvarez already has something bigger on the way, how about this? When the helicopter appears, we let them load the micro mind on to it. Then we hijack the craft along with the pilot. We can then call Niki for backup and get as far away from the mountain as we can.'

'Oh, you always make things sound so easy,' Jack said.

'Hey, don't forget I am making this up as I go along.'

'Another Lauren seat-of-your-pants plan in other words.'

'Exactly. It's so insane that it'll be the last thing Alvarez would expect us to do.'

'So how is this hijack going to work exactly?'

'We'll find a way.'

'So there's a liberal sprinkling of blind optimism seasoning on your plan too.'

'With extra Parmesan.' I almost managed to smile, despite my heart still breaking over Mike.

Over the next ten minutes, we watched events unfold down on the plateau.

A group led by Alvarez, with Cristina being escorted by one of the soldiers, soon emerged from the undergrowth. Two Overseers soldiers appeared to be carrying the micro mind easily between them.

'How the hell are they able to do that?' Jack asked.

My anxiety was on a spin cycle as I examined the crystal for any clues. I spotted a glowing circular device of polished steel attached to one of the crystal's faceted sides like a limpet. It had a ring of blue lights round its circumference. There was something strangely familiar about it...

The memory surfaced from the depths of my mind.

'That thing attached to the micro mind has to be some sort of antigravity device,' I said.

'You mean a scaled-down version of what Alice showed us in her lab?'

'Yes, and you know what that means. They won't have any problem airlifting the micro mind out on the Raven after all.'

'Oh crap!'

The group had already reached the police helicopter and were connecting the micro mind to a harness.

'It looks like we're too late to stop this,' I said.

Jack loaded his last magazine into his carbine. 'Over my dead body we're not.'

I grabbed his arm. 'I'm not losing you too, Jack. Mike was bad enough.'

'And I'm not going to just watch them spirit the micro mind away after everything we've been through. The fate of the whole world is too big a price to pay.'

'OK, but we still need to be smart here. Are you thinking that you'll disable the Raven with a bullet through its engine?'

'Not at this range. It would be a difficult shot even with a high-powered sniper rifle. But when the Raven takes off, it will have to fly more or less directly over us to avoid flying higher where the air is even thinner.'

'So we'll bring it down once it's airborne?'

'Yes. It'll need one hell of a shot.'

'What was all that firing-range training for if not for a moment like this?'

'You're right,' Jack replied.

I peered through my binoculars again to see Alvarez boarding the helicopter alongside the pilot. My heart sank as Villca shoved Cristina into the rear passenger seat and sat next to her. 'Shit, scrub that plan. We can't risk shooting the Raven out of the sky with Cristina on board.'

'But we haven't got any other choice,' Jack said.

I stared at him. 'But she's an innocent civilian. She didn't ask for any of this.'

'I know, but you need some perspective here. The fate of the whole world is hanging in the balance based on what we decide to do in the next sixty seconds.'

The helicopter's engine whined as the rotors whirred up to speed.

My mind locked up. Could I really shoot the helicopter out of the sky and kill Cristina? The memory of the missile strike taking out Mike flashed through my mind. No, I couldn't risk Cristina's life in this. There had to be another way.

I scanned the helicopter through my binoculars, desperately searching for an option. I was about to give up when the metal disc attached to the micro mind snagged my gaze.

'That's it!' I said.

'What is?'

'We shoot the antigravity device and the pilot will be forced to land because of the sudden extra weight.'

'But that's an even smaller target than the engine bay. It's a big ask, especially with a fast-moving target.'

'I know it is, but we have to try.'

'Yeah, I guess we do.' A smile filled Jack's face.

'We should wait until we see the whites of their eyes.' I unslung my carbine and rested it in the crook of a tree.

Jack did the same. The roar of the helicopter grew louder as it wound itself up for take-off.

'Let's just hope Lady Luck is with us when we take the shot,' Jack said.

'You are doing nothing for my confidence here,' I complained.

'Yeah, sorry, my bad.'

My jaw tightened as the Raven lifted from the ground. As it rose into the air, it took in the slack connecting it to the micro mind's harness. Soon that was airborne too, slowly spinning beneath the helicopter as it was lifted from the ground.

'Damn it, the crystal gyrating like that will make it even friggin' harder to hit,' Jack muttered.

'Tell me about it.'

The Raven turned on its axis, dipped its nose and headed over the jungle – straight towards us.

As I was down to my last ten bullets, I flicked my carbine's selector to single-shot mode. Through its scope I could see the antigravity pad gyrating as the Raven raced towards us.

Jack took the first shot, his suppressor doing its job to minimise the muzzle flash as well as the sound of his bullet. He grimaced. 'Damn it, nowhere near.'

I did my best to steady my breathing. I waited, anticipating where the antigravity pad was going to be rather than where it currently was. I breathed out as I squeezed the trigger and fired. At the same moment the Raven moved a fraction to the right and I lost sight of the crystal in the scope. When I reacquired it, there was no sign of any damage to the metal device.

Then the helicopter was on top of us, beginning to race away. We had seconds left at most.

Jack flicked his carbine's selector to automatic mode and grimaced as his shots went wide again.

The Raven had already reached the next ridge and was climbing to clear it.

Desperation blazed through me as I braced my legs. Through the scope the ring of lights on the device was barely visible as it gyrated back into view.

Please, god, let me pull this off...

I channelled all my concentration, ignoring the wound in my leg, everything, and fired...

Sparks blazed out from the antigravity plate and its lights blinked out. The micro mind lurched downwards and the Raven's engine screamed as it battled to maintain height against the sudden dead weight of the crystal dragging it down towards the jungle canopy.

Jack stared at me. 'How the hell did you pull that shot off?'

'Lady Luck obviously adores me,' I replied.

The helicopter bucked and weaved, snaking its way through the air towards the SUVs in the car park at the bottom of the trail.

'Crap, it looks as if the pilot might be able to make it to those vehicles,' Jack said.

'Let's get a move on then,' I told him. I stowed my weapon and raced towards my bike, pulling my helmet back on.

'You mean we're going after them?' Jack asked.

'Of course we bloody are.'

'You do remember what just happened to Mike when he tried to get down the mountain on a motorbike?'

'Let's just pray that Lady Luck hasn't gone for a tea break then.'

Jack shook his head at me as he leapt on his bike, fastening his helmet on. Together we sped away through the jungle and out on to the trail.

Luckily, no bullets hissed passed us as we sped away. I would take any break that came our way right now, but what about that damned Reaper drone still up in the sky?

Without even discussing it, we dived off the track at the first opportunity, exactly as we'd seen Mike do.

Skidding down the steep mountain had to be the most frightening thing I'd ever done in my life. Not only was the slope almost vertical, but our Zero bikes were so steeply angled downwards that we were both in danger of being pitched over the handlebars. The only thing that kept me going was the threat pressing down on us from that unseen eye in the sky.

We drew closer to the blackened patch of ground where Mike had been taken out, wisps of smoke still rising from it. There was no sign of the wreckage from his Zero motorbike and my heart lifted for a moment. But then I spotted burnt lumps of blackened flesh scattered across the mountain and bile filled my mouth. The bike must have pitched over the nearby cliff and was lying in a mangled heap at the bottom of the mountain. A searing pain far worse than my bullet wound swirled inside me.

'Jesus, the poor guy,' Jack muttered over the intercom.

The stench of burnt flesh filled my nose as we passed the impact crater. I tried to ignore it as our motorbikes slid over loose shale and we continued our breakneck journey downwards.

I managed to glance up to see what was happening with the Raven. Across the other side of the valley, smoke billowed from the police helicopter's engine and was dropping rapidly towards the treeline.

'Shit, they are going in harder than I expected,' Jack said.

'But what about Cristina?'

'Just pray that Lady Luck is looking after her too.'

I couldn't imagine her terror right now. However I tried to justify it in my mind, this was my doing.

Hope surged in me as the pilot somehow found something left in the dying helicopter. We heard a final scream from the Raven's engine as it made a slow, spiralling descent and disappeared into the jungle about a mile away from the parked SUVs. A moment later a distant thud reached us and black smoke billowed from the crash site.

Please be OK, Cristina—

'Watch out, Lauren!' Jack's voice came through my helmet's speakers.

I snapped back just in time to see another cliff edge rushing up towards me. I gripped the brakes so hard I was surprised the handles didn't come off in my hands. With a stomach-churning judder, my Zero came to a stop right at the lip of the cliff, a sheer drop of at least a hundred metres beyond it, jagged boulders below. Jack just avoided cannonballing into me as he skidded to a stop to my right.

He peered over the edge. 'Holy fuck!'

'Yeah, that.' Before my brain had a chance to catch up with the fact we'd both just nearly plummeted to our death, I opened up the throttle and sped away along the edge of the cliff.

We were once more hurtling down the mountain on a small goat track towards a thicket of jungle dead ahead of us.

A sixth sense kicked in that something was wrong. I glanced over my shoulder to see the thing I'd been dreading – a white flash of light in the sky.

'Missile launch!' I shouted into my mic. 'Make for the tree-line – it's our only chance!'

I opened the throttle wide, ducked my head down over the handlebars and raced towards the jungle below us. Jack became a blur next to me as he kept pace, both our Zeros bouncing hard over the uneven ground. Stones flew up from our wheels as we sped across the scrub-covered mountainside, the safety of the trees' shadows just ahead.

I didn't even attempt to brake as we hurtled into them at full speed, hitting several low branches that bounced off my helmet and bruised my arms and chest.

A shape blurred overhead.

'Get down!' Jack shouted through the intercom. He reached out and grabbed hold of my Zero. We both toppled sideways, our bikes skidding away from us as we slid to a stop.

A heartbeat later a wave blast smashed into us with a roar. Overloaded by the deafening noise, my ears hummed into silence as the explosion roared over us with a wall of heat. With a stutter of static, my night vision failed and darkness clamped in around me. I struggled to breathe as the blast rolled away through the jungle. Between the cracks spidering my visor, I saw trees on fire around us.

Jack's face, silhouetted against the flames, loomed into view over me, his mouth moving silently. Gradually the silence was replaced by a ringing noise, which then became a muffled version of his voice.

'We have to get out of here,' I heard him saying at last through my helmet's intercom.

I managed a nod as my night vision stuttered back into life.

My body felt as if I'd been run over by a rampaging elephant as I managed to stand, my leg wound stinging like a bitch. Nearby, our Zeros were partly covered with earth, but otherwise looked intact.

We worked together as quickly as we could to dig them out, my body trembling as a trickle of blood ran down inside my helmet from my right ear. We climbed back on to the bikes. I was going to need a lot of plasters when this was all over.

Then, impossibly, we were heading down the mountain again, through the jungle, leaving the burning trees far behind.

It might have been minutes or even hours; I wasn't aware of much else until the slope began to level out as the river came into view.

We crossed the bridge and saw smoke rising from the jungle where the Raven had gone down. As we set off on the trail back into the jungle, the gloom began to give way to the copper tones of the building sunrise starting to tint the mountain peaks in the distance.

I barely registered any of this. All I could picture was Cristina's twisted body in the wreckage. I knew right then that if I saw her dead, especially after what had happened to Mike, it would be the end of me.

CHAPTER TWENTY-THREE

I COLLECTED no end of additional bruises as we rode through the jungle, thanks to being body-slammed by countless more branches as we sped between them. The occasional one caught at my leg wound, making spots dance in front of my eyes. We weren't the only things being battered. Both Zero motorbikes were looking pretty dented too, but to their credit neither bike had missed a beat. It wasn't my physical injuries that were the problem, more the utter mess my head was in. Losing Mike had tipped me into a dark place and Cristina's fate was weighing heavily on my soul. I had their blood on my hands.

Ahead of us the rising column of smoke was only a few hundred metres away.

'Time to get ready for whatever is waiting for us,' I said into my mic as my insides hollowed out.

'Be ready for anything,' Jack replied.

That was exactly the problem. My imagination had conjured up a terrible nightmare. I unclipped the strap holding my LRS in its holster, ready to draw it quickly if necessary.

We both slowed to a crawl and nausea crept up the back of my throat as I prepared myself to see Cristina's mangled body.

Just ahead through the trees, I saw flames licking around the canopy of the crashed Raven. It hung from the branches of a tree, its metal fuselage bent like a deflated balloon. My gaze swept to the cockpit. The pilot and Villca had been thrown through the canopy and their bodies lay still on the ground. I felt nothing at seeing the police commandant dead. He'd had everything coming to him. But there was no sign of Cristina's body, nor Alvarez's – and no sign of the micro mind either.

Jack pointed at the ground as we stopped next to Villca. 'Look, there are footprints heading out from the wreckage. So the good news is that Cristina may have survived the crash. The bad news is it's likely so did Alvarez.'

'But Cristina could still be badly injured.'

'Yes, I realise that, but at least she's probably alive.'

In the dim light of the growing sunrise I could make out tyre marks leading away through the jungle with a large groove between them.

Jack was gazing at the indentations in the ground too. 'These suggest a search party found them and dragged the micro mind away. Which means they can't be that far ahead of us.'

Fresh determination filled me. 'Come on, we still have a chance to catch them. This one is for Mike.'

We raced away, following the track that had been helpfully cleared for us. Within moments we'd reached the main trail, also chewed up by the dragged micro mind.

As we rode along it, sweat poured down my back, despite the deep chill inside me. It seemed my body had joined my mind in being a bundle of contradictions. I wasn't sure how to feel both physically and emotionally. Hard soldier or grieving civilian who'd lost her friend. I certainly had no idea where my reserves of energy to carry on were coming from.

Thanks to the Zeros' silent motors, we heard voices just ahead above the chatter of the jungle. A moment later we saw the glow of vehicle headlights between the tree trunks.

'Looks as if they've already made it back to the car park,' Jack said.

'So let's do this last bit on foot,' I said into my mic.

'Roger that.'

We pulled up and dismounted, hiding our bikes with leaves. Both armed, and with the Empyrean Key stowed safely in my rucksack, we crept through the trees towards the SUVs, where at least twenty Overseers soldiers had gathered. A big truck at the rear drew my attention.

A harness from a crane mounted on its flatbed was being attached to the now mud-covered micro mind. Alvarez, who I was disappointed to see looked fine apart from a bandage to his head, was directing the loading of the micro mind on to the truck. My whole being lifted as Cristina appeared from behind another vehicle, her arm in a sling. She headed up to Alvarez. I was expecting her to lash out, or at least shout at the man. I wasn't prepared for what happened next.

Alvarez reached out for her gently and squeezed her shoulder with the tenderness of someone greeting an old friend. Cristina nodded and smiled back at him.

'What the hell? She should be spitting in his face,' Jack said.

'God knows how, but he seems to have her wrapped round his little finger. We'll just have to put her straight when we rescue her.'

'Damned right,' Jack replied.

I looked at the micro mind as it was slowly raised by the crane on to the back of the truck. 'OK, have you got any smoke grenades or flash bangs left? I'm out.'

'Two smoke grenades, one flash bang. Why, what are you thinking?'

'You set them off back on the trail to draw the attention of Alvarez and his mercs. Then I'll try to hijack that truck – right after I rescue Cristina.'

'There are so many holes in that plan it's not even funny. And even if we manage to pull this off, what's to stop the Overseers firing another Reaper missile right up our tailpipe?'

'They won't risk destroying the micro mind.'

Jack pulled off his helmet and gazed at me. 'Right, you're the boss.'

I couldn't help but notice the lack of conviction in his voice. But I already knew what I would have to do if it came to it.

'I'll circle back and help you the moment I have their attention,' Jack said.

His eyes slid away from mine and he headed off into the jungle towards the trail. Whatever was going on with him, I had to ignore it. I didn't have the head space for that right now.

I checked the last magazine for my carbine. Only three rounds left. My LRS wasn't much better – just a few bullets. But if this went to plan, I wouldn't need either weapon.

I watched the micro mind being lowered on to the truck and detached from its harness. Then a flash of light came from the trail, followed by several rounds of bullets that pinged off the vehicles.

Alvarez began shouting orders and the Overseers raced forward to return fire into the smoke billowing across the track. But Alvarez himself wasn't going anywhere and he ushered Cristina into the safety of an SUV. He grabbed a merc hurrying past him and pointed to the vehicle she was sitting in. The guy nodded and he and his two colleagues took up defensive positions round the SUV. Alvarez drew his pistol and began scanning the treeline around him.

Fuck. The guy was a mind reader, or more likely that we'd used this stunt one too many times on his soldiers.

OK, so I needed an instant plan B. I made sure I had the carbine set to single-shot mode and fired my remaining rounds straight at Alvarez.

Maybe it was instinct that made him duck, and my bullets hissed harmlessly over his head. A split second later, his mercs returned fire and I threw myself sideways as bullets sliced the air. I discarded the carbine and grabbed my LRS from its holster as the guards moved forward, shooting as they came. But then two small black shapes arced towards them from the jungle.

'Grenade!' the guy at the head of the mercs shouted.

I aimed my LRS and winged one of three soldiers. He wheeled away, clutching his shoulder.

The other two threw themselves flat as the grenades struck the ground and billowed smoke over them.

Jack burst out of the jungle and sprinted towards me. 'Time to get the hell out of here.'

'But Cristina—'

'Take them out!' Alvarez shouted, cutting me off.

Bullets whistled out of the pall of smoke that obscured the Overseers and their vehicles.

'But we still have to grab that truck with the micro mind.'

'Then let's do exactly that.'

Together, at a run, we circled round towards the front of the vehicle as gunfire crackled, the mercs shooting up the surrounding jungle.

Jack and I kept low as we darted across the road beneath the level of the cab.

The driver was peering into his rear-view mirror at the smoke billowing over the rest of the vehicles.

I tightened my grip on my LRS, aiming it at the door, as Jack grabbed hold of the handle and yanked it open.

The female soldier in the driver's seat stared first at me and then at my gun pointed straight at her head.

I started to pull the trigger when I thought of Mike and stopped. No, I had to be better than this. Instead, I put my finger to my lips and gestured for her to get out of the cab. She quickly nodded and climbed down. I waited until she had her back to me and aimed a sharp hand chop at the pressure point on the back of her neck – a move that Tom had shown us. The woman crumpled to the ground unconscious.

Jack raised his eyebrows at me, but without a word dragged her into the undergrowth. He helped himself to her peaked cap as I jumped into the cab and pulled off my crash helmet.

He got into the passenger seat and handed me the hat. 'A disguise.'

I pulled it down over my ears and relief swept through me as I spotted the keys in the ignition. 'You think we might actually pull this off?'

'Oh, we've got a long way to go yet.'

As if in answer, the SUV with Alvarez driving, Cristina in the back, roared out of the smoke and screeched to a stop in front of the truck.

I glanced in my rear-view mirror. An Overseers soldier was running along the side of the truck, waving his arms. 'Quick, get down, Jack,' I whispered. 'Someone's coming.'

He ducked down into the footwell as I gripped my LRS. Just one bullet left. The soldier banged on the door and with my heart hammering, pistol ready, I lowered the window.

'We're moving out before we get caught in another guerilla attack,' the soldier said.

Without catching his eye, I nodded and turned the ignition. The truck roared into life and two other Overseers leapt up on to the back of the truck, carbines in hand. The guy who had spoken to me ran back to one of the other SUVs parked behind us.

Alvarez drove off.

I selected first gear and the truck rattled as we followed Alvarez's SUV, the other vehicles behind us in convoy.

'So much for stealing the truck and making a rapid getaway,' I said. 'Any suggestions, Jack?'

'You mean you're actually interested in what I think?'

'What do you mean? I ask you your opinion all the time.'

'Do you?'

I glanced down at him. 'What's that meant to mean?'

'It means a good leader is also a good listener. I could have told you that rescuing Cristina wasn't a viable option from the get-go. If we'd done it my way, we could have made a clean getaway.'

'If that's what you thought, you should have bloody well said something.'

'Maybe, but you should have asked, Lauren. Being in charge isn't about being an autocrat.'

'Have I really been as bad as that?'

'On a few occasions. But I'll cut you some slack – you've also had to make some tough calls.'

I picked over his words as I drove, replaying the last few days. I'd been so busy thinking on my feet about what to do, I may not have asked for the opinions of Jack and Mike enough. And maybe if I had, a different course of events might have taken place. Maybe Mike would still be alive.

A lump filled my throat and I swallowed it down. This wasn't the moment for losing the plot.

I pulled myself together. 'OK, you may have a point. Seems I have a lot to learn in my new role.'

Jack's face softened as he saw my expression. 'Sorry, that came out more harsh than I intended. Lack of sleep, getting shot at and almost blown up several times has that sort of effect on me. And coming off my meds at the same time is just the icing on the friggin' cake.'

I smiled as I grabbed on to his lifeline of humour. 'Tell me about it.' I peered down at him as he hid in the footwell. 'So what do you suggest we do?'

'Just trust me.'

'Jack, I'd trust you with my life and frequently have.'

'Then hang on to that thought and maybe your ass too. I suggest you ram Alvarez's SUV and drive him off the road. It's the only way – he's between us and our escape route.'

'What about Cristina in the back?'

'Just pray the vehicle's crumple zones do their job.'

'But, Jack...'

'Remember that "trust me" bit.'

I slowly nodded. 'Yeah, OK...' I pushed the accelerator down hard. The engine roared as the truck sped forward. With a sickening crunch, we smashed into the back of the SUV, sending the soldiers in the back of our truck sprawling. Alvarez's SUV spun sideways with a squeal of tyres and toppled on to its roof into a ditch.

There was no time to check the fate of the occupants as shouts and cries came from the soldiers behind us as they hauled themselves to their feet.

'And now brake hard!' Jack shouted, pulling himself up into the seat.

I stamped my foot on the brake and the truck skidded to a stop. With a crunch of flesh into metal, the two mercs slammed into the back of the cab. The SUV behind us smashed into the rear of the truck and smoke billowed from beneath its bonnet as the mercs inside staggered out of the vehicle.

I didn't need to wait for Jack to tell me what to do next.

I pressed the accelerator all the way to the floor. One of the mercs on the back tipped over the side and tumbled away. But the other soldier, blood streaming from his broken nose, hung on to one of the straps tying the micro mind to the flatbed. To make matters worse, the remaining SUVs had scraped past the other totalled vehicle and were catching us up again.

In my mirror, I saw our hitchhiker raising his carbine. 'Fuck!'

Jack lifted his Glock and fired through the rear window. I ducked instinctively as glass showered down in the cab.

'All clear,' Jack said.

I sat up and glanced backwards to see the soldier was gone.

My attention snapped to the road ahead. It was widening out as it ran along the edge of a sheer cliff.

The SUV behind us grabbed its opportunity and accelerated alongside us. An Uzi barrel appeared in the car's open window and flashed with fire. We both ducked as bullets sprayed the side of the truck.

Jack leant across me and fired his carbine over me at the vehicle, bullets sparking off the vehicle's roof. Then he clicked on empty.

'I'm out!' he shouted.

'Oh, let me deal with these bastards,' I said.

I hauled the wheel hard over and swerved our truck into the SUV. With a bang of metal on metal, the SUV's wheels tipped over the edge of the cliff. Almost in slow motion, it toppled into the abyss, the soldiers inside screaming as they disappeared from view.

Automatic fire raked the back of the truck, snapping my attention back. A soldier was hanging out of the window of the last remaining SUV.

'Grab the wheel, Jack.'

All credit to the guy, he didn't even ask me what I was going to do as he took control.

I leant out and fired my LRS at the SUV, forcing it to brake hard to avoid being hit.

'Lauren!' Jack shouted.

I turned back round to see a tight left-hand bend coming up. I grabbed the wheel from Jack and braked. With a sickening screech of tyres, the truck started to slide sideways. The flatbed holding the micro mind hung out over the edge of the cliff for a nausea-inducing second. But then the tyres grabbed purchase again and we shot forward along the road and into a steep-sided narrow ravine.

In that split second I had a new plan.

I braked again and we slewed to a dead stop.

'Lauren, what the hell?' Jack said.

'Your turn to trust me.' I slammed the truck into reverse and we gathered speed as we shot back to the entrance of the ravine. The final SUV came skidding round the bend. I saw the driver's eyes widen in horror as he saw the large truck barrelling towards him in reverse. Unable to stop in time, his SUV slammed hard into our truck, making us lurch against our seat belts.

'Hang on!' I shouted. I gunned our engine and more automatic fire peppered the back of the cab. Dust kicked up from our tyres as the truck began pushing the SUV out of the ravine towards the cliff edge. At the final moment the soldiers inside jumped clear of their vehicle as it tipped over the edge and tumbled away down the side of the mountain.

I didn't wait for the pretty fireball. With a graunch of gears, I selected first and we surged forward. I glanced in my mirror to see the Overseers soldiers haul themselves to their feet, hands on their heads as they watched us speed away.

'Nicely done, Lauren.'

'Sorry I didn't consult you on my plan, but there wasn't exactly a lot of time.'

He held up his hands. 'We're all good, trust me.'

'So now let's get as much distance as we can between us and Alvarez. I don't think we're out of the woods by a long way yet. Can you take the wheel again? There's something else I need to do.'

'Sure.' He leant across and took hold of it.

I fished the Empyrean Key out of my rucksack and struck it with the tuning fork. The circular icon with concentric lines radiating out hovered over it.

'Exactly what we suspected,' I said. 'Cristina managed to turn off the self-repair mode and shut the micro mind back down.'

'Will that be a problem to sort out?'

'It should be as easy as this...' I selected the icon and four arrows pointing inwards appeared as it turned red. I glanced over my shoulder and saw a faint blue light glowing within the crystal again. 'Self-repair mode re-engaged.'

He grinned at me. 'Way to go. Now let's get off this damned mountain. I'm sick to death of it already.'

'You and me both,' I said. I grabbed control of the wheel back from Jack, pressed the accelerator and we raced away down the road.

As we continued to carve along the switchback road, I kept glancing back towards the top of the mountain. Fires from the crashed SUVs blazed like beacons on the slopes in the growing dawn like funeral pyres. And from the top of the peak a column of smoke drifted up that had to be coming from the wreckage of the Black Hawks.

Jack glanced up at them too. 'Quite the night's work.'

'It will certainly put up the Overseers' insurance premiums.' I peered over my shoulder at the large crystal on the back of our truck. The light within was growing stronger. 'Hopefully not long now until the micro mind finishes rebooting.'

'But what happens then? Do you think Lucy will put in a house call?'

'That's what I'm praying for,' I replied. 'At the very least this is another piece of the puzzle in the missing parts of her memory. It'll hopefully help her to remember what her mission was.'

'And specifically how we can neutralise the threat from the Kimprak, as ultimately that's what's driving everything we're doing right now. And of course you'll get to see Lucy again.'

I raised my eyebrows a fraction. 'And?'

Jack glanced across at me and smiled. 'Oh, come on, Lauren, tell me you're not dying to see her?'

'Of course I am. She may not have been my biological parent, but in every other sense she was my mum, a mentor and also my best friend. I've missed her every single day since she died.'

'Even if you're talking to an AI facsimile?'

'Even then. I guess it's a bit like looking back through an old photo album.'

'An album that can talk back to you,' Jack said.

'Pretty much. And anything that helps to fill the hole in my soul, even a fraction, I'll welcome with both arms.'

'Now that I understand.' He fell silent and looked ahead at the road, lost in his own thoughts for a moment.

Of course he understood. He'd lost his wife after all... There was still so much that we both skated over with each other, memories too painful to keep pulling out into the light of day. Maybe he would open up to me one day. I hoped so.

Ahead of us the valley opened out as we left the mountain behind. With every passing minute, I felt my adrenaline ebb away, replaced by a bottomless pit of exhaustion.

Jack looked at his Sky Wire and frowned. 'Still no damned reception.'

'Just how big do you think the Overseers' jamming zone is?'

'Big enough to give us a serious issue. But from memory there's just one more bend to go and then it's a straight run all the way back to Cachora. We can hide out there and, if our Sky Wires still aren't working, use a landline to call Niki.'

'Sounds good. I'll need a big brew of tea the moment we get to town.'

'You Brits and your tea,' Jack said.

'Hey, I'm agnostic. Coffee is great and everything, but sometimes only tea will hit the spot.'

'Especially when you've almost been killed countless times over the last two days.'

'Now you're really starting to understand me, Jack.'

He snorted. 'I'm trying.'

I caught a glint of light from the corner of my eye. I turned and I saw a point of light through the shattered window – growing bigger fast.

'No fucking way – they just fired another bloody missile at us.'

'But you said they wouldn't risk destroying the micro mind.'

'I was obviously wrong.' I slammed the brakes on, a fresh plan already in my mind. 'We've no other choice. We need to get out now.'

Jack nodded, opened his door and leapt from the truck. As soon as he was clear, I slammed my foot down on the accelerator.

He spun round. 'Goddammit!' He sprinted alongside the truck as I began to accelerate away. 'What the hell do you think you're doing, Lauren?'

'What I have to, to protect the micro mind and you,' I called back. I selected second gear and the truck surged forward.

In the wing mirror, I saw Jack running, but already falling away. More pressingly, the missile was gathering speed fast and streaking towards me like a bat out of hell. I ground the accelerator into the floor of the truck.

I had a sketch of a plan, a last desperate roll of the dice, quite possibly downright stupid. But what other choice did I have if these were my last few seconds alive?

I turned the truck towards the steep embankment on the right of the road, fighting every instinct to veer away from it.

The suspension lurched as tarmac turned to rocky ground. I braced myself as the truck raced towards the edge. Through the right-hand window, I saw the point of light growing fast as it hurtled straight for the truck.

This was going to be close.

I caught a blur of movement behind me. In the pre-dawn gloom, the silhouette of a motorbike was closing in on the truck and then its rider threw a small object on the road.

What?

My thought was swept away as the truck crashed through a low stone wall and flew out into open air. It started to tip towards the trees lining the steep slope beneath.

In the next second everything seemed to happen at once: the truck slammed into the tops of the pine trees, throwing me forward; my ribs cracked sharply against the wheel; the branches slammed past the cab as a pulse of fear rose up in my throat.

Real time rushed back in with a bone-jarring crash as the truck's nose crashed into the ground. With a grinding of metal, the vehicle tipped forward and the flatbed holding the micro mind came to rest against the broad trunk of a tree. Just for a moment I hung at a crazy angle. Then, with a lurch and a splintering of branches, the truck toppled sideways. The windscreen exploded as the vehicle landed hard on its tyres at a steep angle across the slope.

Sudden white light blazed from the road above me. A split second later it was followed by a much brighter flash that lit up the mountain. The thunder of an explosion shook the truck and rolled away across the valley.

There was the sound of expanding metal creaking and then flames burst from beneath the twisted bonnet.

I took a breath and registered the agonising pain coming from my stomach. I glanced down to see a long shard of windscreen glass sticking out of my abdomen. I stared at it in disbelief as icy numbness quickly spread through me.

The motorbike rider was now racing down the impossible slope and skidded to a stop next to the cab. He jumped off and sprinted towards me.

I stared at the man's face as he yanked the driver's door open.

Mike looked in at me, his face pale.

'You're alive...' I whispered.

Mike didn't answer. He was staring at the blood bubbling up round the slab of glass buried in my stomach.

With a shout, Jack came skidding down the embankment. As Mike stepped aside, I caught the look of confusion in Jack's face to see his friend alive. Then his eyes locked on to my wound and something flickered through his expression. A look of utter dread.

He ripped his jacket off and pressed it round the glass projectile. 'It's going to be OK, Lauren.'

But I could hear the lie behind his words and see the fear building in Mike's expression.

I groaned. 'We both know there'll be no happy ending for me this time. You and Mike have to get away while you can.'

Jack just stared at me. 'Lauren, I can't lose you too.'

Too? The thought evaporated as I looked into his shining eyes. 'It's already too late for that. Seems that Lady Luck has turned her back on me.'

Blue light began to flare around me. Was this my end? The fabled tunnel of light? But no, it was coming from the flatbed.

I saw Mike staring at the source of the light, and his eyes widened. He grabbed my rucksack and fished out the Empyrean Key.

'You need to try to contact Lucy.'

I tried to focus on his face that had started to blur. 'But she's not here.'

'If this micro mind has restored enough of its functions, you may be able to transport us over to E8 and Lucy might be able to help.'

A chill ran through my body, rapidly icy cold. I felt the weight of the Empyrean Key as Mike pressed it gently into my hand.

Jack leant in, looming over me. 'Please, Lauren, you have to try.'

Their faces blurred further as Mike struck the tuning fork against the orb. A point of fuzzy light flared into existence above and I tried to focus on it. But I couldn't make it out. Darkness was creeping into my mind.

'Lauren, keep your eyes open,' Jack said from a very long way away.

With every last scrap of energy, I rolled my wrist forward. Then the world went dark.

CHAPTER TWENTY-FOUR

A COMPLETE AND utter darkness closed in around me. It felt like ice had encased my body. The rational part of my brain, the part that wasn't freaking out, was trying to process what was happening.

This is probably just my mind shutting down as I slide towards death.

But then the darkness became tinged with grey. Slowly, so slowly, the grey started to turn to a dark, pulsating red. And then sounds began to reach me: the bleeping of electronic equipment and muffled voices. I tried to grasp them with my mind, like a swimmer hanging on to driftwood in a vast ocean of numbness. One of the voices became louder...

'Clear!' Jack shouted from the darkness.

A burning jolt of pain shot through my body.

What the fuck?

I felt a dull pressing sensation in my chest as a single tone hummed out.

'Clear!' Jack yelled again.

Another burning blaze of pain surged through my body and the single tone was replaced by a beeping noise.

'Oh, thank Christ,' Mike said from somewhere nearby.

'Lauren, can you hear me?' Jack asked.

Of course I can...

But grogginess pulled at my thoughts like the strands of a web. I couldn't open my mouth to speak. I started to slip away again from the pain, back into oblivion.

'Lauren, you need to open your eyes.'

What?

'Don't you dare die on me!'

Then, like a dam wall had broken, a memory came rushing back in.

I'd deliberately driven the truck off the road...seen Mike driving past me...had hit those trees...the missile had struck the mountain road...then I'd crashed.

It was like stone scratching over my eyes as I opened them. I could see a bright cluster of lights straight above me. The tang of disinfectant filled my nose. Either side of the table I was lying on, three figures stood. Jack and Mike on one side, both wearing surgical masks. On the other was a young-looking Aunt Lucy, her pretty brown eyes pinched with concern as she gazed at me, no mask covering her mouth.

As my senses slowly rebooted, I took in the white room. It was filled with displays that showed my vital stats, including my heart rate. I was in an operating theatre.

'How...' I coughed, the rest of my words stuck in my throat.

Jack leant in close to me and I could see the tears in his eyes.

I swallowed and tried again. 'How did you manage to get me to a hospital in time? And how come Lucy is here?'

'You managed to transport all of us here,' Jack said.

My gaze travelled to my aunt. 'You mean this is actually E8?'

She nodded and gestured at the room. 'You can thank Jack

for all of this. Little sunflower, you were dying when you got here. But Jack told me exactly what he needed to save you. I conjured up this kitted-out operating theatre according to his specification.'

'I was dying?' I asked.

'Actually, your heart had stopped, so technically you did die there for a moment,' Jack said. 'Luckily, and no small thanks to Lucy magicking up all the right kit here, I was able to bring you back. It was touch and go, though.'

So I'd been dead... My gaze shot down to my stomach, expecting to see the large slab of glass sticking out of it. Instead, there was only a large bandage covering the wound.

I looked back at Jack. 'You operated on me?'

He nodded. 'With Lucy and Mike's help. I wouldn't have been able to manage it alone – it was too big a procedure.'

'I'm not sure I did much to help,' Mike said. 'I nearly passed out several times. Lucy did all the heavy lifting alongside Jack.'

Lucy beamed down at me.

'Thank you so much, all of you,' I said. 'But, Lucy, how come you're here if the micro mind hasn't fully rebooted?'

'That's a good point. You're right – my other micro mind still has some time to run. However, some of its low-level AI matrix systems had already come online, including the one that links it to me. Through that link and utilising the waking micro mind sensors, I was able to detect what was happening to you. I bootstrapped my systems into the micro mind with a temporary coding patch. Through that, you were able to activate it with the Empyrean Key before you lost consciousness. You didn't exactly give me a lot of time to work with, but I managed to create a communications bridgehead through which I was able to transport you here.'

'To be honest, I'm surprised to be alive,' I said.

Jack nodded. 'I think anyone in your situation would be. But

I'll warn you now that it will take several months for you to make a full recovery. You've suffered a serious abdominal trauma.'

I tried to sit up. 'But we need to get back to the micro mind before Alvarez seizes it again.'

Jack pushed me back to the table gently and shook his head.

'You can relax about rushing back to the micro mind,' Mike said. 'Remember that Lucy can control how much time passes back in our world whilst we're here. Isn't that right, Lucy?'

'Absolutely. I can more or less return you within a matter of seconds from the moment you left it. Certainly you can stay here as long as you need to fully recover without endangering my other micro mind.'

Despite Lucy's reassurance, my mind instantly filled with a dozen objections. 'But I'll go stir-crazy just lying here for months. I'll have way too much time to think about the future of our world that's hanging in the balance.'

'Actually, I can help you with that too,' Lucy said. 'I can also control how time passes in E8. All I need to do is this...' She snapped her fingers and a bright light pulsed around the operating theatre.

The next moment, I found myself lying on a sunlounger on a tropical beach. Blue sea gently lapped the shore and palm trees stretched away either side of me. And I felt fantastic, not an ache anywhere. My brain struggled to process the transformation in my physical condition. The hospital gown I'd been wearing was gone and I had on a white T-shirt and shorts. My legs even had a slight tan to them. Mike and Jack sat opposite me holding cocktail glasses with umbrellas poking out. The shocked looks on their faces reflected how I was feeling. Beyond them, I could see Lucy in a swimsuit walking out of the surf. She strode up the beach towards us like that famous scene from the James Bond movie *Dr. No*.

What the hell? I pulled up my T-shirt. There was no vast hole in my stomach – only a faint scar line that had almost faded.

Jack and Mike stared at it too. 'But that's impossible,' Jack said.

Lucy neared us, drying her hair with a towel that had just appeared out of thin air. She looked great, maybe too great – Mike's eyes were all over her like a horny teenager. She grinned at him as she dropped into the empty lounger beside me.

Oh, she so knew what she was doing, pushing Mike's buttons.

With a shimmer in the air, another umbrella cocktail materialised before her on the table.

Jack gestured to my stomach. 'How, Lucy?'

She gave him a grin. 'I put you all into what your species think of as suspended animation. However, your bodies were still functioning, albeit at a greatly reduced rate, and I made sure you were maintained with nutrients and the rest. That allowed Lauren's body to heal. So what seemed like a mere second for you was actually six months of R & R.'

My gaze tightened on her. 'Please tell me that "the rest" didn't involve bedpans?'

Lucy laughed, took a sip of her cocktail and pulled a face. 'Less limes next time. The less you know, the better. Let's just say a few tubes were involved.'

'Oh, that paints such a lovely mental image,' Mike said.

'You might not like that part of it, but this is seriously incredible,' Jack said. 'The number of patients I could have saved if we had this tech in our world.'

Mike rubbed the back of his neck. 'All I know is I feel as though I've just had the best night's sleep ever.'

Lucy nodded. 'In a sense you have – a very deep six-month nap.'

This was quite the mental leap. One moment I'd died and now I was alive. Just as I'd thought had happened to Mike.

I raised my chin at him. 'Now we get to you being alive. We thought you'd been wiped out by that bloody missile strike.'

'I nearly was,' he replied. 'If I hadn't thrown a flash bang, I would have been a smouldering hole in the ground.'

'Oh, fast thinking, buddy,' Jack said. 'It blinded the Reaper's laser-guidance system?'

'Exactly.'

'But we saw charred flesh!'

'I think that was a mountain goat that wasn't quite so lucky.'

A laugh bubbled up in my throat. 'Oh, the poor thing.'

'I know, just minding its own business and then, bam, good-night.' Mike shook his head. 'Without radio contact, I had no way of letting you know I was alive. So I kept to the jungle, pursuing my original mission and managed to slip past Alvarez's mercs. I managed to make contact with Niki, who is on his way with a full security team to support us. I was slowly working my way down the mountain when you screamed past in your truck, the missile closing in on you. I took off in pursuit and used my last flash bang to confuse the missile.'

'I thought I saw a smaller flash before the explosion – your flash bang, right?'

Mike nodded. 'It was just as well. A moment later it would have taken you and the truck out for sure.'

'So much for my stupid plan then. It seems I owe you my life, Mike.'

He shrugged. 'Hey, it's part of the job description and what we do for each other.'

'Yes, it is.' I reached across and squeezed his wrist. Then I swung my legs off the lounger and stood on the warm sand. I breathed in a deep breath of sea air. I felt great, fantastic even. Along with everything else, the utter exhaustion of a few moments ago was completely gone. It was as if I'd been on the best spa weekend ever – without any of the dodgy green juices they try to force-feed you.

I turned to face the others. 'I don't know how I'll repay any of you for what you did.'

'Hey, you thanked us enough already by not dying,' Jack said.

I smiled at him and looked at the gently rolling surf. 'Hey, what's the water like, Lucy?'

'Do you really need to ask? It's utterly perfect of course.'

'I wouldn't expect anything less from you.' I padded over the sand towards the sea as a warm breeze sighed over my skin. I breathed in the rich scent of ozone and let the sea gently lap over my feet as I reached the shoreline. A seagull skimmed over the water, sunlight dancing in diamonds across the spray.

My thoughts started to untangle as I let the moment soak into my soul. Seconds ago, which had really been months, I'd crashed a truck. But I'd been transported to this. It was quite the mind-melt.

The seagull turned on its wingtip and soared overhead, silhouetted against the sun.

Jack came over to join me.

'This is like an impossible dream,' he said.

'A slice of heaven, that's for sure. But as wonderful as this is, we need to get back to our own reality to finish our mission.'

'Cut our vacation short in other words.'

'Hey, we have been here six months already.'

'Yes, I guess we have.' He tilted his head to the side as he looked at me, but didn't say anything.

'What?'

'You look good, real good. The beach lifestyle suits you.'

'It does most people, although just sunbathing bores me rigid. A good hike or snorkelling is more my thing.'

'Yeah, mine too.' He turned towards the sea to watch the seagull as it wheeled back.

My gaze wandered over to him. The blond Viking here in paradise with Lauren Stelleck. A chick-flick fantasy right there. But this was all an illusion, and Jack had already made his feelings clear to me, pulling back whenever we got anywhere close to real intimacy.

I pushed away the knot of sadness inside. No, saving our world was where my focus needed to be. 'Come on, we have work to do.'

He sighed. 'Tell me about it.'

Together we headed back over to the sunloungers where Mike was chatting to Lucy. We were too far away to hear their conversation, but their laughter drifted over to us.

'They look like they get on well,' Jack said to me.

'Don't they just? I'm not sure what Jodie would say if she could see them together right now.'

'That's Mike's business, and it's probably better she doesn't hear about it from us. But will you look at her pulling him in? The guy doesn't stand a chance.'

'OK, now you're starting to weird me out. The idea of Mike and my aunt... I mean, yuck.'

'Keep telling yourself she's just an AI and not your real aunt.'

'I know, but even so...'

Jack nodded. 'Yeah, I get it. Weird and a bit creepy too.'

'You're not wrong.'

Lucy and Mike stood up and came over to us. A touch of nausea rose in me as Lucy looped her arm through his. I was going to need some serious counselling if they got it on.

'Cute,' Jack said, trying to suppress a smile.

'Oh, just shut up already,' I said.

Mike gazed at us both with a questioning expression. 'Something up?'

I quickly shook my head. 'No, just talking about getting back and finishing the mission.'

Lucy unhooked her arm from Mike's. 'In that case, I need to brief you about a developing situation back in your world. My core micro mind is currently situated in orbit directly over your position at Choquequirao. Even though I've not been able to help directly, I've been keeping an eye on you.'

'You have?' I asked.

'Think of me as your friend in the sky – the opposite of the Reaper drone that's been stalking you.'

'Shame you haven't been able to do anything about that,' I said.

'My systems are too degraded to launch the sort of sophisticated computer attack that the Sentinel AI you encountered, Lauren, could have managed. However, what I can do is give you information that might prove just as useful. It's not only the Overseers who have been keeping an eye on you.'

'Who else? A foreign government?' I asked.

'No. It's actually a UFO I've detected in the immediate vicinity. It appears to have been monitoring the situation too.'

'You're shitting me?' Jack said.

'Not at all.'

I stared at her.

'It's a class of vehicle that has been referred to as a Tic Tac craft.'

'Yes, I know about them from the UFO boards,' I said. 'It's the craft made famous by the US *Nimitz* encounter.' I nodded to Jack, remembering our conversation about them back at Eden.

'The very same,' Lucy replied.

A thought struck me. 'That might explain the flash of light I saw when we first arrived at Choquequirao. Jack said it couldn't have been the Reaper as they usually fly too high to be spotted.'

'I love how matter of fact you are about dropping an alien UFO into the conversation, Lucy,' Mike said.

'Oh, that's so me,' she replied with an elfin grin.

She was so playing him. I tightened my gaze on Lucy. 'But why has it turned up here? To help us? If so, it's done a big fat lot of nothing so far.'

'All I know about these shepherd species, as the Angelus referred to them, is that they come to observe your world, but have a policy of non-interference.'

'How very *Star Trek* of them,' I replied.

Jack clicked his fingers. 'But maybe if we made contact with them we could persuade them to protect us against the Kimprak?'

'Now that's a hell of an idea,' I said. 'Lucy, is that something you could help us with?'

'Not with my current limited abilities, although it's a possibility as I begin to recover the rest of my systems.'

'That sounds promising,' Mike said.

'So have you any other bombshells to hit us with?' Jack asked Lucy.

'In the few minutes we've been away in our world's time, Alvarez has made radio contact with his people and more reinforcements are on the way.'

'OK, ideas, guys. What should we do when get back?' I made a point of looking at Jack, who gave me a small smile. Yes, I would make sure I really listened to his and Mike's ideas from now on.

'I still think we should hide out somewhere and guard the micro mind until it has been repaired,' Jack said.

'Unfortunately, the Reaper is still monitoring your position,' Lucy told us. 'If I could disable it, I would have done so already. But its flight-control systems have been hardened against any sort of hacking attempt.'

I was staring at her. A huge express train of an idea had just taken hold of me. 'What if there was another way for you to help us?'

'Such as?'

'You know you created a perfect copy of my Swiss army knife that I was able to take back with me into our world?'

'Yes, what about it?'

'And you can create anything we can imagine in E8, right?'

'Pretty much, within certain constraints.'

Jack stared at me. 'Oh, I see where you're going with this. You want Lucy to conjure up some sort of hard-core sci-fi weapon for us to take out the Reaper drone when we return.'

Lucy shook her head. 'My programming prevents me from giving your species more advanced weaponry than you currently have. Once again, it's the Angelus version of that show that you mentioned, *Star Trek*, which I made a point of watching. They have something similar to its prime directive about not interfering with the natural development of other species except in extreme cases.'

'But could you conjure up a missile we could use to take it down?' I asked.

'Nothing bigger than a shoulder-launched variety because of the limitations I mentioned. It can be no bigger than something that you are able to carry out of here, as creating a physical object takes a considerable amount of energy. To use a *Star Trek* analogy again, think of the *Enterprise*'s teleporters and how they were limited to objects not much larger than a person.'

'But you could conjure up some weapons, right?' Jack asked.

Lucy beamed at us. 'Oh goodness, yes.' She clicked her fingers and the beach vanished. Now we were standing in a large glass room hanging in space. A nebula that I was certain was M42 hung beyond the glass. Thankfully we somehow had gravity and we were all standing on a solid floor rather than floating around like astronauts. But although the setting was extraordinary, it was what was inside that stole my breath away. Racks of shelves arranged like the inside of a supermarket ran the length of the room. The only thing missing was food and the checkouts. Instead of produce, the shelves were filled with weapons of every sort and size.

Jack whistled as he turned round to take it all in. 'All right, now we're talking.' He picked up a large rifle with a wide barrel. It looked as if it could have taken out a charging rhino – maybe even a battle tank. He caressed it with his hand. 'Nice.'

'There might be something more suitable for dealing with the Reaper,' Lucy said. 'If you'd like to follow me...'

We followed her to an adjacent aisle stacked with a selection of black tubular devices a couple of metres long.

Jack picked up one. 'A Stinger missile?'

'Indeed they are,' Lucy replied.

'I do love your weapons toyshop, but a Stinger only has a range of about fifteen thousand feet. The Reaper is flying way above that altitude.'

'True, but there is something I can do to help you there. I've been monitoring its systems and I believe there is a way for me to bring the drone within the range of a Stinger. Unfortunately, because of my current limited functionality, I can't get past the encryption protecting the Reaper's critical flight systems. However, its non-critical systems are another matter. I can spoof the GPS signal it's receiving to make the Reaper think it's flying at a different altitude. Ideally, I would then just fly it into the mountain, but unfortunately its radar systems would stop that from happening. However, I can fool it to fly at a low enough height to put it within range of a Stinger missile.'

I gestured towards one of the tubes. 'So you're saying we could shoot it down with one of these?'

Lucy shrugged. 'I believe so.'

'OK, so say we bring down the Reaper, then what?' Mike asked. 'As far as I remember, that truck was totalled. And there is no way we can just carry off the micro mind between us. It weighs at least a ton.'

'If we had the Overseers antigravity device, we could easily move it,' Jack said.

'A what?' Mike asked.

'Oh, you mean this.' Lucy snapped her fingers and a smooth metal disc appeared in her hand, the lights round its edge unlit.

'Hang on, that one doesn't look shot up,' Jack said.

'That's because I recreated it from the one clamped to the side of the micro mind. You can take this working version back with you.'

'But what about your Angelus prime directive and all that?' Mike asked.

'It doesn't apply in this instance,' I said. 'Humans have already built this – we saw it in Alice's lab. Right, Lucy?'

'Absolutely. Granted the Overseers only have this technology because they reverse-engineered downed alien craft, but they have it nonetheless. So you are free to take this back to your world and use it at your own discretion.'

'So we can move the micro mind with this device, but where to? We don't know when Niki and the security team will arrive.'

'Ah, don't worry,' Lucy said. 'I've been able to monitor traffic in the immediate area and located a pickup truck that will be driving on a road just below the crashed truck in the next ten minutes.'

'The first of those Overseers reinforcements you mentioned?' Mike asked.

Lucy shook her head. 'No, just a local farmer heading towards Cachora.'

'That's where we wanted to get to,' Mike said.

'Perfect. In that case, once I return you to your world, you'll have plenty of time to reach the road on foot with the micro mind and intercept the truck.'

I peered at others. 'So to summarise our plan... We head back there, take out the bloody drone and temporarily blind the Overseers to our location. We hitch a lift with that local to the town with the micro mind on the pickup. How does that sound?'

'Good to me,' Jack replied.

'But what if this farmer dude doesn't want to help us?' Mike asked.

Jack raised his eyebrows a fraction and gestured at the aisles lined with weapons.

Mike pulled a face at him. 'We're not holding up some poor local at gunpoint.'

'If that's what it takes to get his attention,' Jack said.

'Guys, that won't be necessary, just leave it to me,' I said. 'I'm an expert when it comes to hitching lifts. Who can ignore a woman stranded after her vehicle has broken down? I'll hit him with a sob story and if necessary we can also throw some cold hard cash at the guy for his troubles.'

Now Jack raised his eyebrows at me. 'Just remind me, is this the same stranded woman who's packing a LRS?'

'What he doesn't know won't hurt him,' I replied with a grin.

'In that case it sounds as if you're all set,' Lucy said. 'I'll transport you back once you've helped yourself to whatever you need from the armoury.'

Jack grinned at her. 'Oh, trust me, we will.'

Mike blew his cheeks out and shook his head.

CHAPTER TWENTY-FIVE

BACK AT THE base of the mountain, Jack aimed the Stinger missile launch tube to the sky, his brow furrowing as he peered into the sight. 'How can I shoot down what I can't even see?'

'You must have missed Lucy's briefing on that whilst you were drooling over those guns,' Mike said.

'How many times must I tell you, never call them guns. Rifles, pistols, carbines, machine guns, but never just *guns*.'

I shook my head. 'For a medical guy you do seem a bit fond of weapons.'

Jack shrugged. 'Hey, everybody needs a hobby.'

'I expect Jack is one of those guys who watches those dodgy YouTube videos where people get all sweaty over shooting *guns*,' Mike said.

Jack glowered at him before returning his attention to the Stinger's scope.

'OK, chill, you two, we've got a job to do,' I said.

A blinking white light appeared in the dawn sky. Through my binoculars I could see the Reaper was flying in a circular path, slowly descending towards us.

'Nicely played, Lucy,' I said.

Mike peered up at it. 'Bonus points for a direct hit, Jack.'

'I'd settle for a beer at the Rock Garden.'

'That too.'

Jack stiffened his stance as he angled the Stinger towards the Reaper and squeezed the trigger.

There was a cracking sound like a large calibre bullet being fired and a thin missile burst out of the tube. A second later a flame lit the rear of the projectile and it hurtled away, almost straight up, trailing black smoke.

'Fly, you beauty, fly,' Jack whispered as he lowered the launcher to the ground.

We all watched as the Stinger ascended rapidly until it became a dwindling spec in the sky. The Reaper banked steeply to one side and veered away.

'It looks as if the drone's operator has just spotted the present we sent for him,' Mike said.

'Come on, come on...' I said. I held my breath as the two points of lights converged.

A flash of light was followed by a billowing smoky explosion. A rumbling sound reached us as flaming specks of debris started to fall from the sky.

'Splash one bird,' Jack said.

'Nice shooting, Tex,' Mike told him. 'I owe you that beer.'

'I'm not from Texas.'

'Yeah, Oklahoma, whatever.'

'You're going to have to make it two beers at this rate.'

'Look, I hate to get in the way of your big bro romance here, but we need to shake a leg if we're going to catch that lift Lucy mentioned,' I said. 'Let's get the antigravity plate attached to the micro mind and then we'll cut down through the jungle straight to the other road.'

Mike and Jack nodded and ducked into the trees, heading back towards the crashed truck with its all-important load.

I hung back and glanced up just in time to see a wing section of the Reaper crash down on the side of a mountain in the distance.

Take that, you bastard... I turned and followed the others into the jungle.

A short while later, we were rolling along a tarmac road in Stefano's battered truck. The local farmer looked almost biblical with his giant white bushy beard. If they ever needed somebody to be god in a movie – if Morgan Freeman couldn't make it – I'd recommend they checked this guy out. Stefano had allowed us to load the micro mind on to his truck. Thanks to the antigravity plate, it only weighed about fifty kilos now. I say *allow*, but my powers of persuasion hadn't had quite the effect I was hoping, so I'd had to pull my LRS on him. Thanks to that little stunt, the poor guy kept glowering at me and Jack riding up front with him. Who could blame him? At least it meant Stefano hadn't asked too many questions about the 'geological sample' the westerners had dug up.

Mike was riding in the back, fighting a losing battle with a goat who seemed intent on eating the tarp that we'd covered the micro mind with. He had two holdalls of weapons and ammo back there that Jack had brought back to our world from Lucy's all-you-can-eat armoury buffet.

With every mile we put between us and Choquequirao, I felt myself relax a bit more.

I turned in my seat towards Stefano, who was giving me a look like I was a particularly rancid bit of cheese. 'We need to make things right with you.'

His eyes became slits. 'Says the *señora* with a gun pointed at me.'

'Sorry, we can do without that now.' I slid my LRS back into my holster. 'I only pulled that on you because you just wouldn't listen. And as a sign of our gratitude...' I dug into my rucksack. As I pulled out the wad of thirty thousand dollars, Stefano's eyes widened. 'This is for you – to apologise for any misunderstanding between us.'

He glanced at me and then back at the roll of hundred-dollar bills. 'So what are you, smugglers?'

'Yes, but not in the way you mean,' Jack said.

I nodded. 'It might not seem like it right now, but we really are the good guys.'

Stefano scratched his epic beard. 'I suppose you didn't leave me back on the roadside with a bullet in my head.'

I pulled a face at him. 'We are so not those people.'

'Maybe you're not.' More beard scratching.

I held the roll of money out to Stefano again. 'Please, for your trouble.'

He took the money from me and it was like the sun coming out from behind a cloud as he smiled at me. 'Maybe I was a bit hasty to judge you.'

'No, I think I would have thought the same too. So let's start over. What do you say?'

Stefano gave me a toothy grin. 'Deal.' He reached out and shook first my hand and then Jack's.

'Now that's more like it,' Jack said. 'Sorry about before.'

'Already forgotten. So what are your plans when you get to town?'

'We have some friends coming to meet us, but we'll need to be outside town to do that,' I said, not adding the reason: because we didn't want anyone to see the XA101 coming in to land. It would cause way too many questions. I nodded at the roll of money. 'I don't suppose you can take us out somewhere?'

'I have some errands to run in town first, but after that, sure. Meanwhile, you should try some tamales for breakfast.'

'Tamales?' I asked.

'A corn dough filled with peppers, cheese, raisins, peanuts and olives.' Stefano kissed his fingertips. 'They are delicious, señora.'

'Sound great. We'll buy you breakfast too, of course.'

The sun was well and truly up when the town of Cachora appeared in the distance, nestling between the mountains. So far I'd managed to resist the temptation to check the Empyrean Key to see whether the micro mind had fully repaired itself. If it decided to fly up into the sky like Lucy had, it'd be tricky to explain that to Stefano.

The warmth of the morning bathed my face through the windshield and I felt a sense of lightness with it. If it wasn't for the others, I wouldn't have even seen this new sunrise. It was certainly hard not to see this new day for what it was – an enormous gift – in no small part thanks to the medical skills of the guy sitting next to me. If romance was off the cards between us, that didn't mean he couldn't be a damned good friend.

Jack chose that same moment to look my way and caught me staring at him.

'What?' he asked.

'I'll tell you later,' I replied with a small smile. *Like never*, I thought to myself.

As we drew closer to Cachora, I started to make out white-stucco-walled buildings with terracotta-tiled roofs.

Other vehicles had appeared on the road too, all headed towards the town. Each was loaded up with an assortment of vegetables, cages of chickens or a few goats like Stefano's vehicle. Thankfully there was no sign of any of the flash black pickups or SUVs that the Overseers seemed to favour. By contrast the vehicles the locals drove into town were battered and ancient. I didn't need the life stories of the owners to know that these people weren't particularly well off.

Jack looked at the clock on the dash. 'There's a lot of traffic for seven a.m.'

'It's market day, so it's much busier than usual,' Stefano replied.

'Oh, right.'

I glanced over my shoulder at Mike, who was trying to pull a corner of tarp out of the goat's mouth. He rolled his eyes at me.

We reached the outskirts of Cachora and joined the growing line of vehicles filing their way through the main cobbled street. It was already crowded with stalls with blue polythene roofs, selling everything from potatoes to pneumatic drills.

Stefano drove slowly through the packed pedestrians crowding the stalls and pulled up outside a small bar.

We were soon tucking into the famed tamales, Stefano too. I realised right away why he was so enthusiastic about them – they were hitting all the right taste buds. Even the black tea was great, despite Jack's efforts to get me to try his coffee, which he told me was 'a home run when it came to full-bodied flavour'.

After the excitement of downing the Reaper, I almost felt like a normal tourist in a bar, just eating breakfast and chilling out. The chart-topping pop song from some ancient boy band playing on the radio was briefly drowned out as a warble came from my bag.

I exchanged glances with Jack and Mike as I took out my Sky Wire. Niki's name was displayed on the screen.

I took the call. 'Hey, how's it going, Niki?' I said, trying to sound as casual as possible for Stefano's benefit.

'All good. I can see from your GPS marker that you're in Cachora now. Is that correct? What happened?'

I glanced at the faces of the locals around me. Now wasn't the time to give him a proper briefing. 'Yeah, we have that geological sample we were after. A really kind local guy helped us out. We're in a cafe eating breakfast with him right now.'

Stefano beamed across at me.

'In other words, you can't talk freely?' Niki asked.

'That's right.'

'OK, I just wanted to let you know we'll be there within thirty minutes. I'll send the coordinates of a suitable rendezvous point to your Sky Wire.'

I gazed at Jack and Mike. 'That sounds great.'

'Good. I look forward to seeing you,' Niki said. The line clicked off.

'Everything OK?' Mike asked.

'Yes, it seems our friend is going to be here quite soon.' A message popped up on my screen containing a map link. I turned to Stefano. 'Any chance you could run us out to meet them now?'

Stefano gave me a wolfish look and dropped his voice to a whisper. 'Away from prying eyes?'

'Something like that.'

Stefano wiped his mouth and gestured at his empty plate. 'After this feast, it will be my pleasure. I'll just use the restroom and then we shall go.' He pushed his plate away, stood up and headed off to the loo.

Mike gestured with his chin towards the truck through the window. 'The sooner we get out of town the better. If that micro mind reboots whilst we're still here...' His eyes flicked to the locals gathered round us.

'The last time I checked it was OK, but I could do so again.' Below the counter I quietly took the Empyrean Key out of my bag and nestled it on my lap. The radio station had moved on to a Queen song, and when I struck the stone with my tuning fork, no one noticed the gentle chime ringing out.

I could still see only the reboot option; the other icons remained missing.

I shook my head. 'It's not there yet, but it can't be much longer now.'

'Good to hear,' Jack said.

As the note from my tuning fork started to fade, a strobing multipointed star icon appeared. I stared at it.

'Problem?' Mike asked, reading my expression.

'Not sure. Lucy's E8 icon has appeared and it's blinking.'

'Maybe she needs to talk to you.'

'OK, but not in here. If I suddenly disappear, that'll draw attention for sure. I'll just pop to the ladies and see what this is about.'

The other two nodded.

I hid the Empyrean Key back in my bag and headed for the loo, almost running into Stefano as he emerged from the solitary toilet. He gave me a guilty look as I passed him. When I entered the cubicle, I realised why – it smelled as if something had crawled out of someone's bum and died in there. I flapped my hand in front of my face, trying to clear the stench, breathing through my nose as I slammed the loo seat shut.

Bloody men!

I sat on the seat and placed the stone orb in my lap again. With a fresh strike of the tuning fork, the starburst icon reappeared, still pulsing. I flicked my wrist forward. At once my surroundings faded, replaced by the glass room with the M42 nebula outside. It was now empty of shelves, but Lucy was standing before me.

'Thank goodness you saw my message,' she said.

'Why, what's the problem?'

'The Overseers have sent in another Reaper drone and this one has been programmed to use just radar and its altimeter, rather than rely on GPS. They must have got wise to what I did to their last one. They've been able to track your position to Cachora. Within the next three minutes, a convoy of Overseers vehicles will be arriving in town.'

'But what about all the people here?'

'That's why you need to get out of there as quickly as possible. You can guarantee Alvarez won't mind shooting civilians if it means he can get to you.'

'Oh god, you're right. We'll leave right now.'

'Good luck,' Lucy replied.

The glass room vanished and I was back in the toilet. I stuffed the Empyrean Key back into my bag and rushed out into the bar. I hadn't said a word, but both Jack and Mike were already staring at me.

'What's wrong?' Jack asked as I reached them.

'We need to make ourselves scarce, and quickly.' I turned to Stefano. 'Something bad is about to go down and we need to leave town straight away.'

'Then I will drive you,' he said.

'No, it's safer that you stay here.'

'Safer?'

I traded a desperate look with the others. 'Look, I haven't got time to explain it, but can we buy your truck off you?'

'But...'

Jack reached into his backpack and slipped him the container of gold sovereigns. 'This should more than cover it.'

Stefano handed the keys to me.

'Thank you, Stefano. Thank you for everything.'

'No problem, my friends. May god protect you.'

I shook his hand.

Outside, we heard the honking of car horns in the distance, getting louder.

Jack jumped on to the back of the truck and began unzipping

the holdall bags, as I leapt into the driver's seat with Mike riding shotgun.

Jack grabbed a pair of binoculars from his pack and peered through them. Then he spun round. 'There's a whole line of black SUVs headed into town. Get us out of here, Lauren.'

I turned the ignition and the engine coughed into life. I clenched the wheel as we began to edge forward, squeezing the truck between the people packing out the street. In my wing mirror I could see Jack with his hand on a carbine, ready to snatch it from the holdall if the moment came.

Slowly, too bloody slowly, we crept along the street and rounded a corner. Behind us, somewhere out of sight, the sound of honking vehicles was now accompanied by angry shouts and cries.

I quickly scanned the GPS marker on the Sky Wire's map. There was a small track heading out towards it on the far side of Cachora. We'd make for there and hide out until Niki arrived.

We were crossing a junction when shots and cries came from behind us. I glanced in my mirror to see four black SUVs racing along the street, sending people scattering.

'Fuck, their Reaper must have eyes on us,' I said.

Mike gawped at me. 'They've got another one of those bastard things up there?'

I nodded.

'Shit!'

I pressed the accelerator and leant on the horn to alert Jack. He grabbed the carbine and pointed it at the lead SUV behind us. People jumped aside, cursing us as we sped between them. At the next junction, another SUV raced into view and stopped, blocking the road.

My heart thundered as several soldiers leapt out, their Uzis aimed at us despite all the people in the way.

I slammed on the brakes and the truck slid to a stop. The

convoy behind us pulled up too and soldiers disembarked, Alvarez among them.

'Damn it, that bastard survived the car crash,' I said. I scanned his vehicle, but couldn't see any sign of Cristina. What had become of her? Had my little stunt cost Cristina her life? My heart scrunched up into a tiny ball.

Mike stared at me. 'All these people are going to be caught in the middle of a firefight.'

'Don't I know it.'

I jumped out of the truck and Jack chucked a carbine to me. The locals stared at us with wide eyes and started to back away.

Alvarez held up a hand to his soldiers. He walked towards us, pistol in hand, eyes narrowed on us. He stopped about thirty metres from our truck.

'I don't know about you, but I have no wish to see innocent people get hurt. I suggest you lower your weapons.'

Mike climbed out of the truck with his dart gun in his hand.

Jack shook his head. 'Yeah, right. That's a pile of horse shit and you know it. They're witnesses to what's about go down and you won't want any of them left alive, will you?'

The people in the street stared between us and Alvarez and his soldiers dressed in black.

Alvarez raised his hands. 'My friends, these people are nothing but antiquity robbers. They have on their truck a precious artefact that they stole from your precious Choque-quirao. They are attempting to smuggle it out of Peru.'

Immediately the crowd's eyes locked on to us, their expressions hostile.

'Don't listen to him!' I shouted.

But I was only answered with boos and whistles. Three burly Peruvian guys started moving towards us.

'Oh, fuckity fuck!' Mike whispered, raising his dart gun towards them.

My gaze tore to Jack. 'There's only one play left to us here.'

He nodded. 'Do whatever you have to.'

I pointed my carbine into the air and squeezed the trigger. With no suppressor attached, it crackled with muzzle flashes and spat bullets into the sky. People screamed and dived into doorways. Within a matter of moments the street was deserted.

Jack nodded again. 'Nicely done.'

I aimed my carbine at Alvarez as he plunged behind a stall for cover.

And then the world exploded with bullets.

CHAPTER TWENTY-SIX

It was as if we'd been dropped into a western movie where we were the good guys and the outlaws, the Overseers, had ridden into town. Of course the locals saw it the opposite way, thanks to Alvarez's little speech. But now, whether they realised it or not, it was down to us to stop Alvarez bringing a whole world of hurt down on the heads of the citizens of Cachora.

As incoming rounds exploded around us, Jack returned a steady stream of fire from his position on the back of the truck. The slab of battered metal and bags of gravel that Stefano had picked up when we'd got into town were thankfully giving Jack and the micro mind some much needed cover.

I hunkered beneath another parked truck as I tried to think our way out of this. Tactically our situation was beyond awful. We were surrounded front and back and pinned in on both sides by buildings packed with innocent people. Alvarez and his mercs could afford to take their time. However skilled we were with our weapons, this would still be the equivalent of shooting fish in a barrel for the Overseers. No, we needed to get out of here, whatever it took.

As bullets sparked off our truck, Mike stared at me through the open door as he ducked down in the passenger seat.

'We're not going to get out of this, are we?' he said. But then his eyes widened and he pointed past me. 'Hey, look, Lauren.'

I glanced round to see a street stall selling earthenware pots just beyond the nose of the vehicle. At first I didn't understand what Mike meant. But then I spotted the shadows of people running away down a narrow alleyway just behind the stand. Narrow, but still just about wide enough to squeeze a truck through.

'What do you reckon?' Mike said.

'Only one way to find out.' Red laser dots danced over the wall just above my head and the render exploded with bullet holes. 'Jack, can you cover me from the soldiers at the rear?' I called.

'Sure, but what are you going to do?'

'Oh, you'll see. Just get ready to lay down some suppressing fire on my order.'

'Understood.' Jack took a huge machine-gun with a large round bullet belt magazine attached out of his bag.

I vaguely remembered him telling me it was a Rheinmetall MG 3 when he'd helped himself to it from Lucy's weapons supermarket.

I slung the carbine over my shoulder and swapped it for my LRS. 'Fire!' I sprang forward towards the open passenger door, whilst firing at the two SUVs ahead of us. Meanwhile, Jack blazed bullets from his MG 3 at the Overseers' vehicles at the rear, quickly peppering them with holes.

I crawled across past Mike and dropped down into the driver's seat. As the MG 3 gave its staccato bark of a hailstorm of death, I swung the wheel over to the right and accelerated. Return fire ricocheted off the truck. I aimed the vehicle straight at the stall and couldn't help but grimace as we ploughed straight through the trestle table, shattering the pots as we went. The woodwork smashed apart on the truck's bull bars and then we were through into the alley beyond the stall. A scraping bang came from each side as the wing mirrors snapped off on the alley's walls.

I glimpsed a young girl staring at us, frozen, just ahead. Before I could react, a woman grabbed hold of her and yanked her into a doorway. I threw a silent prayer of thanks to her guardian angel.

Just a few more seconds...

In the rear-view mirror, I saw Alvarez appear, gesturing down the alley to his mercs.

'Watch out!' Mike shouted, pointing forward.

We raced out of the alley into another street filled with vehicles. I leant hard on the horn. With a squeal of brakes, two battered old trucks swerved to avoid slamming into us. I yanked the wheel hard to the left and almost threw Jack from the back in the process. We slid sideways as I centred the wheel to correct the skid. As the wheels regained traction, the truck surged forward and we sped away along the road.

My mouth was dryer than a desert as I kept blasting the horn. More vehicles scattered in front of us as we tore between them. I pulled out my Sky Wire and checked the map. The lane leading out to the east side of the town was the next turning on the right.

It seemed to appear out of nowhere. Almost too late I skidded our truck round the bend and we slammed hard into a bin, sending it flying and Jack nearly pitched off again. I saw him glowering at me in my rear-view mirror.

But Mike was grinning. 'Holy shit, you can drive, lady.'

'I guess I can.'

The buildings started to thin on either side of us and we reached some corrugated metal buildings on the outskirts of town.

'Stop!' Jack shouted from the back.

I scanned my mirrors and couldn't see anything, but I trusted Jack. I slammed on the brakes.

Jack pivoted his MG 3 towards the sky and started firing.

Mike peered up and paled. 'He hasn't a rat's chance of hitting that.'

I turned to see a point of light rushing towards us. My stomach clenched into a ball as I realised it was a missile about to wipe us out of existence. But Jack didn't so much as flinch as he kept firing tracer rounds straight at it, as the missile ate up the distance between us.

Impossibly, I saw bullets sparking off the nose of the streaking missile as it flew into the cone of tracer Jack was firing. With a huge flash and a roar of explosion, the shock wave from the blast smashed into the truck and the buildings nearby, shaking us like an earthquake had just hit. Tiles from the roofs around us came crashing down into the street. The shuddering slowly subsided and the truck settled on its shock absorbers as it stopped bouncing. The wail of car alarms echoed between the buildings.

Mike whooped and leant out of his window. 'Good shooting, Tex.'

'How many friggin' times...' Jack said, waving a hand dismissively at Mike. He laughed. 'That sucker had to be a five-hundred pound laser-guided missile going by the sheer power of that blast wave.'

'Shit!' Mike said. 'And they were happy to drop that over a populated town.'

'Yep, absolute bastards. The good news is that a Reaper can only carry two munitions of that size – alongside four Hellfires.'

'So the bad news is that it has one big missile left?' I said.

'Exactly, so let's shift our asses before we bring more bombs down on this town.'

I stamped my foot on the accelerator and we roared off. A large corrugated metal building appeared as I sped round a bend.

'Another incoming!' Jack shouted from the back as he opened fire with the MG 3 again.

As amazing as he'd just been at shooting down a guided missile, I was doubtful he'd be able to pull off the same stunt twice in a row.

I swerved in behind the building, throwing Jack sideways and forcing him to halt his firing.

'What the hell, Lauren?'

'Your turn to trust me,' I called back.

I counted down in my head. *Five, four... Please let this work.* I turned the wheel into the opposite lock. The truck bounced over the ground as its rear fishtailed. I steered into the skid and then straightened the wheel. Our truck shot away from the building at a right angle.

One!

The whole building exploded behind us, engulfed in a massive roaring fireball. I fought to control the truck as the blast wave lifted it into the air and slammed us down hard. The truck ploughed into the earth, the wheels sheering off and flying away. The nose dug in and we skidded round until we were facing the mushroom cloud rising into the sky.

'I hope to god nobody was in that building,' Mike muttered under his breath, not looking at me as he threw his door open and stumbled out of the cab.

I felt a surge of guilt as I climbed out too. I hadn't had a chance to even think about that.

Jack jumped to the ground, clutching his MG 3. 'How's the crystal doing?'

I glanced at the micro mind. It was now strobing with bright blue light. 'This looks like Lucy did just before she took off.'

'So we just have to buy the micro mind a few more critical moments and it can do the rest,' Mike said.

'Exactly.' I grabbed my Sky Wire phone from my bag and dialled Niki, putting it on speaker.

He picked up almost immediately.

'We need immediate evac,' I said.

'OK...' Niki's voice was icy calm. 'We're about five minutes out. I'm locking in your current coordinates. Hang in there.' The phone clicked off.

I turned to the others. 'We need to guard the micro mind until it reboots. Time to make a last stand.'

Jack nodded. 'Damned right. Let's set a crossfire situation to make things as difficult as possible for Alvarez and his mercs.'

'Good call.' I scanned the terrain around us, assessing our tactical situation as if I'd been a soldier all my life.

The blazing fire engulfing the buckled remains of the metal building billowed thick smoke, covering us with choking vapours. At least it was making it hard for us to be seen. To our right stood a rusting old tractor that looked as if it would offer good protection for one of us, a large pile of empty oil drums just next to it. Farther away on our left, there was a tumbling down building with metal struts sticking out and a large pile of bricks at the front.

After Mike's sharp reminder about the building that had just been demolished, I was glad there weren't any civilians around here to get hurt.

'We need to set up an ambush,' I said. 'Jack, if you take the MG 3 to that old building, it will give you a lot of cover. I'll use the tractor.'

'And what about me?' Mike asked.

'Don't worry, I won't ask you to do anything you're not comfortable with. But how about stocking up with flash-bang grenades and hiding out among those barrels?'

'Yeah, I can live with that.'

Jack grabbed one of the holdalls and the MG 3 and headed off to the ruined building whilst Mike helped himself to the flash bangs and sprinted over to the barrels. I loaded my carbine with a magazine of ammo, stuffing spares magazines into my rucksack, and squeezed under the tractor. Once in position, I rested my carbine on a rusting wheel beneath it. It wasn't exactly a pillbox, but it would have to do.

The polluted air scratched the back of my throat as smoke swirled past. Fire crackled in the twisted remains of the corrugated metal building. Was this the place we were going to die?

But as well as fear, determination was also kicking in. This was what all my training had been about, not to mention what our recent experiences had prepared me for. Alvarez and his soldiers were dangerous, but we'd proved more than once that so were we.

Through the hazy smoke, I sighted the carbine's scope on the track. The minutes stretched on.

Will you get a move on already...?

I almost felt relief when I heard the rising note of vehicle engines. A few seconds later, the silhouettes of three SUVs barrelling along the track appeared through the smoke.

The calmness deepened inside me as I put the carbine's crosshairs on the lead vehicle and flicked the selector to semi-automatic.

You've got this, Lauren...

I aimed at the windscreen and squeezed the trigger. The carbine kicked into my shoulder as bullet holes peppered the SUV. I tracked the vehicle, firing bullets as it swerved violently and smashed into the stack of bricks. I kept my carbine trained on the vehicle as it crashed, but no one clambered out.

Splash one bogey...

The bark of Jack's MG 3 snagged my attention and I turned

to see his rounds puncturing the front tyres of the second vehicle. It skidded into an earth embankment, flew into the air and began to tip. It hit hard and flipped over – one, two, three times – before coming to rest on its roof.

Like me, Jack didn't pause and continued to blaze bullets into the vehicle, shredding the metalwork until it burst into flames. Whoever was inside didn't stand a chance.

Splash two bogeys...

But then any surge of confidence that we might easily win this vanished. The final vehicle had stopped and five soldiers, led by Alvarez, were out and split into two combat groups.

Bullets pinged off the tractor as one of the Overseers squads opened fire on my position. The other group was heading for Jack's building. These guys were bringing the fight to us – and spreading out so as not to present a single target.

Pinned down by a barrage of fire, I was unable to do anything as the other squad surrounded Jack's building. One of them lobbed a grenade through an open window and it detonated with a bang.

Cold hard dread churned through me until flashes of light came from another window. Jack was returning fire.

I caught a movement in the corner of my eye. One guy was moving fast to my far right, no doubt an attempt to outflank me. I fired several rounds at the soldier, but he ducked and my shots skimmed over his head. He'd almost reached the barrels when Mike, god bless him, popped up and lobbed a flash bang straight at the guy, quickly ducking back down.

I just had time to turn away from the flash as the grenade exploded. The soldier stumbled to his knees, spraying bullets from his carbine wildly into the air.

I blinked, clearing my vision, aimed and shot a single round. The guy slumped to the ground, clutching his throat where my bullet had found his flesh.

I was in full-blown autopilot combat mode now, not feeling, just doing whatever was necessary to keep us alive.

Bullets ricocheted round the tractor. Straight ahead I spotted Alvarez and one of his mercs behind a mound of earth, a carbine aimed towards me. I managed to duck just as the colonel emptied a magazine that ricocheted off the metalwork above me.

Fucking bastard!

By the time I'd lined up my sight on his hiding position, he'd already dropped back down behind the mound.

I needed to time my shot.

I slowed my breathing and my hunter's patience was soon rewarded. His face reappeared and my crosshairs were already on his forehead. I pulled the trigger. A clicking sound came from my carbine.

Shit!

Another barrage of rounds slammed into the tractor as I loaded a fresh magazine. It was then that I noticed a loud buzzing coming from behind me, like a transformer about to overload.

I glanced back and saw blue light blazing from beneath the tarp on the truck. The micro mind had rebooted!

Flames licked through the ropes holding the micro mind. They snapped as the crystal began to rise into the air.

Immediately, the mercs started shooting at the strobing crystal.

We had to stop them.

Adrenaline blazed through my body as Jack's machine-gun fire rattled out of the building, forcing the soldiers to duck again. Suddenly the situation wasn't about winning, only buying the micro mind a last few precious seconds to get airborne and do its stuff. I sprayed bullets at the Overseers soldiers as Mike did his bit by lobbing another flash bang towards them.

The light in the crystal began to strobe faster until it was almost continuous.

Any moment now it would be out of here. Hope had started to rise through me when I spotted a large white winged drone hurtling from the sky. The Reaper, but there were no missiles under its weapon pylons. So what the hell was the pilot flying this thing remotely trying to do?

I caught sight of Alvarez as he peered over his mound and talked rapidly into his radio. He tracked the Reaper with his eyes, as it dived straight at the crystal.

Shit, Alvarez had ordered the pilot to ram the micro mind with the drone.

I shimmied out from beneath the tractor, no longer caring about my own safety. I shot wildly up into the sky at the incoming drone as it closed to less than a kilometre. I was dimly aware of the merc next to Alvarez turning his carbine towards me.

We'd lost and I didn't care what happened to me any more.

But then a whirring sound came from above.

I glanced up just in time to see a small missile racing up towards the Reaper as it kamikaze-dived towards the micro mind. The missile slammed straight into the drone and an explosion ripped through the craft, sheering one of its wings off. Streaming smoke corkscrewed as the Reaper plummeted to the ground and crashed into scrubland just beyond the border of the town with a loud explosion.

Just for a moment everyone stopped shooting, all stunned by the sudden turn of events.

Then the air rippled as a craft appeared out of thin air. It was like an XA101 in design, but easily twice its size and with overlapping armoured plating on its surface – along with a mini-gun mounted under its nose. The weapon swivelled towards Alvarez and his men.

Recognising the threat, the Overseers colonel was already

shouting orders. His soldiers' fire converged on the craft but bounced harmlessly off it.

With a fury of fire, the newly arrived craft returned the compliment and tracer rounds blazed from its gun. In a scything sweep of death, its bullets sliced the nearest mercs in two, splattering their blood over the ground.

Alvarez was still screaming orders as he and his mercs began to fall back, shooting at the craft as they went. Their bullets continued to spark harmlessly off the fuselage as the craft rotated its wings and came rapidly in to land. With a swirl of rotor wash, it settled on the ground, its rear ramp already dropping.

Niki and his security team exploded out of the craft, weapons already raised to fire at the retreating Overseers.

A woman with a blonde crew cut dropped flat to the ground with a large sniper rifle in her hand. She peered through the rifle's scope and fired once. One of the fleeing soldiers, at least a hundred metres away, was flung backwards as her bullet found its mark. The woman calmly swivelled her gun towards Alvarez. But any hope of mine that he was about to get what was coming to him was dashed as he disappeared behind a pile of burning rubble. I raced towards Niki and the others.

'Permission to pursue, Captain?' the woman asked Niki.

'Permission denied. We have more pressing priorities,' Niki replied.

I reached him at the same time as Jack and Mike.

'I tried to contact you as we were coming in to land, but got no response,' Niki said.

'Sorry, but we were just a bit preoccupied, as you probably guessed,' I replied.

'Yes, that was quite the firefight.'

A buzzing sound grew louder overhead. We looked up to see the micro mind now hovering a few hundred metres above us.

Static washed over my skin as a huge lance of blue light burst from its tip and shot up into the sky.

Mike pointed upwards. 'I think that's some sort of homing beacon...'

Elation surged through me as I spotted another tetrahedron come rushing down the beam of light towards its crystal twin.

'Lucy?' Niki asked.

I smiled. 'It has to be.'

Any sense of euphoria was swept away as I realised Lucy was about to slam straight into the other micro mind. But then, with not so much as a sigh of wind, her micro mind came to a dead stop, just a few metres above the other one.

'That just broke all the laws of physics,' the woman who'd fired the sniper rifle said.

Jack raised his shoulders at her. 'You get used to the madness eventually.'

The two craft started to move slowly towards each other again as if they were being drawn magnetically together. As they finally touched tip to tip, arcs of energy leapt between them.

After the sheer spectacle of what we'd seen so far, I didn't think any of us expected what happened next. Rather than stopping, Lucy's micro mind carried on sliding into the other crystal. The two merging micro minds only slowed to a stop when they had reached the halfway point. Now their combined form resembled a three-dimensional six-pointed star. The crystals began to rotate to reveal a seventh star point that had been out of view to us, pointing downwards.

'Any ideas what's happening, Mike?'

'I wish I did, but knowing Lucy I can guarantee it's going to be interesting.'

He wasn't wrong.

With a crack of thunder, lightning blazed from the tip of the combined crystals, shooting straight into the ground. The earth began to vibrate beneath our feet. Around us, shimmers of light danced through the air as the electric smell of ozone burned my nose hairs. Then a single harp-like note grew louder until we all had to clamp our hands over our ears. It felt as if every molecule of my body was vibrating to it. The sound started to change, splitting into two, reminding me of the haunting melody of whales singing to each other. The two voices rose and fell in a duet until they gradually became one voice again. It was one of the most beautiful things I'd ever heard and I had tears in my eyes as it began to fade away.

With a shudder, the newly combined micro minds raced up into the sky until they disappeared from view.

We all watched the spot in stunned silence. When a Sky Wire clipped to Niki's webbing burst into life, we all jumped.

'We have a new radar contact detected at three hundred miles per hour and closing fast,' Delphi's voice said.

Niki stuck his finger into the air and made a circling gesture. 'Everyone, time to evacuate – we have an incoming bogey.'

We ran into the belly of their craft. Niki's security team dropped into bucket seats lining the walls as he escorted us into a sectioned-off cabin at the front. Much like an XA101, screens lined the walls, currently relaying a live view of the outskirts of the town outside. Seats had been mounted aft and forward that Niki gestured to us to sit in. But there was one major difference between this and an XA101. In the middle of the cabin was a single seat with control panels built into its arm.

'What's this aircraft, Niki?' Jack asked as he sat down.

'It's officially known as an X102C, the C standing for a larger combat variant of the XA101. However, it's been nicknamed the Flying Armadillo due to its layered-armour hull design.'

'It certainly seemed to shrug off those incoming rounds,' I said.

'Which is particularly impressive considering it's just a proto-type. This is its first live mission test.'

'Now you tell us,' Mike said.

I gestured towards the seat in the middle. 'So what's that, the captain's chair?'

'No, it's actually the equivalent of a CIC in a battleship.' Niki sat down opposite me.

'A what?' Mike asked.

'A combat information centre,' the woman said with a clear Australian twang as she entered the cabin. She headed for the central chair, dropped down and flipped a switch. Automatic harnesses swivelled over us. With a gentle whine and swirl of dust, the Flying Armadillo took off.

'Delphi, hand over combat control to the weapons officer, Ruby Jones,' Niki said.

'Handing over,' the AI system replied.

Niki glanced at us. 'It was Ruby who took down that Reaper drone and laid down suppressing fire as we came in to land. Although the automated systems on the Flying Armadillo are good, Ruby is far better.'

'Thank Christ you turned up when you did,' Jack said. 'It was looking dicey out there for a moment.'

Ruby shrugged. 'All part of our premium-service package. Air fresheners are extra.'

She punched a button in the arm of her chair and a glass tube descended around her on which a cluster of HUD information was overlaid. Ruby moved a joystick to the side that made her whole chair rotate to face the now closed rear ramp and the view of the town beyond the burning pall of smoke.

'Bogey is now one hundred and fifty miles out,' Delphi said.

'Extreme evac procedure, priority Alpha,' Niki said.

'Understood,' Delphi replied from the cabin's speakers.

My stomach dropped into my seat as our rate of ascent accelerated. In less than ten seconds Cachora was just a sprawl of buildings in the far distance.

The wings began to rotate back to horizontal and we surged forward.

'Enemy craft at one seventy-five miles,' Delphi announced.

'Just how fast is that damned thing moving?' Mike said.

'Mach eight,' Niki replied with a grim face.

'What the hell flies that fast?' I asked.

'A threat I was worried about but didn't think the Overseers would dare to deploy.'

'Delphi, engage self-defence mode,' Ruby said, in a voice way too calm for the situation.

'Affirmative,' the AI replied.

On the screens, the armoured skin of the Flying Armadillo turned the exact cobalt blue as the sky around us.

Ruby moved a joystick in the other arm of her chair. The floor and ceiling monitors switched on as Mike grasped his harness and squeezed his eyes shut. We were now immersed in a 360-degree view of the surrounding landscape. The mini-gun in the nose rotated in its mount to point backwards.

Ruby peered at her HUD. 'Get ready, everyone, we're about to have company.'

'Five miles out...' Delphi announced. 'Three...two...one...'

On the rear screens, bordered by a red diamond-shaped HUD marker, a black metallic triangle, like a starship coming out of warp, came to a dead stop less than five miles above the town. From our position slightly below its altitude, we could see three discs of blue light at each corner of the triangular craft.

This was something I'd dreamt about since first coming across it on the UFO forums. To read about it was one thing, but to see it with my own eyes exceeded my wildest expectations.

Mike gawped openly. 'Is that a bloody UFO?'

'In a sense, but that's actually one of ours,' I replied. 'It's a TR-3B Astra, right, Niki?'

He nodded. 'Yep. You've obviously really stirred the hornet's nest, for the Overseers to risk sending one after you in the middle of the day with so many potential eyewitnesses.'

'But they can't see us now you've engaged stealth mode, right?' Jack asked.

Ruby nodded. 'Let's hope it stays that way. The US military have been experimenting with rail guns on their Astra fleet. It we get hit by one of those rounds, it will slice straight through our armour like a hot knife through butter. So just in case...' She flipped a switch and I saw a *missiles armed* message flash up on her HUD.

'Oh, fucking hell – out of the frying pan, into the fire,' Mike said, looking pale with his eyes still closed.

'I'm detecting a full-spectrum sensor sweep,' Delphi announced.

An intense column of light flashed out from the TR-3B, zooming through the sky like a lighthouse beam. Within moments it locked on to the region of sky we were flying through.

'That can't be good,' Jack said.

'Looks as if they are searching for the air vortexes our electric motors are carving through the air,' Ruby replied.

'Delphi, initiate silent running,' Niki said.

At once I felt the craft slowing. 'Shouldn't we be going faster, not slower?'

Niki shook his head. 'Easing back on the power reduces our aircraft's wake vortex, which they can detect with a Doppler radar. Now it will be much more difficult for them to locate us.'

Just when I thought I might be able to relax, the Astra did its warp thing again. Suddenly it was less than a few hundred metres to our starboard. Its sensor beam began to sweep through the air.

I held my breath as though that might help, then almost jumped out of my skin when Delphi's voice broke the tense silence.

'Second contact detected.'

'As though one Astra isn't enough to friggin' finish us off,' Jack muttered under his breath.

Ruby stared at her HUD display. 'No, I don't think it's another TR-3B. This craft is moving at Mach twelve.'

Niki gave her a surprised look. 'But that's considerably quicker than the current generation of Astras.'

Before anyone had a chance to respond, a tubular craft about the size of a fighter jet blurred into existence directly between us and the Astra with not so much as a shudder of a shock wave. The Overseers craft started to bank towards it.

I gawped at the new craft. 'The Tic Tac I briefly spotted over Choquequirao. Lucy said it had been monitoring us.'

'In other words, a real-deal UFO has joined the party,' Niki replied. 'As incredible as that is, why?'

As if in answer, the Tic Tac jinked round the Astra at incredible speeds, flitting to either side of it like a dragonfly. It kept changing its flight path at impossible right angles that would have smeared any pilot's brains all over the cockpit in a conventional aircraft. But the Astra was no slouch either and tried to rotate towards the craft.

Something lanced from the TR-3B and a boom rattled the Armadillo's cabin, making me think they'd spotted us and opened fire. But then the aircraft settled and I spotted a bright-burning orange scar had opened up across the surface of the gleaming white UFO. It ducked sideways and zoomed towards the horizon at a mind-bending speed. A split second later, the Astra blurred away after it.

'Can someone tell me what the hell just happened?' Jack asked.

'I think our alien friends just saved our butts,' Ruby said. 'The way the TR-3B was flying around the Astra was like it was trying to deliberately draw attention away from us and lure it away.'

'Will the Tic Tac be OK?' I asked, thinking we almost certainly owed it our lives.

'Going by the fact it's already hit Mach twelve and the Astra can't keep up, I'd say that it's more than holding its own.'

'Oh, thank god.'

Alice's voice came over the cabin speakers. 'I wouldn't have believed that encounter if I hadn't just seen it for myself on the live feed from the Armadillo's cameras.'

'I take it you've been monitoring our situation, Alice?' Niki said.

'I dialled in a minute ago through the remote uplink when Delphi reported back to me you'd ordered an emergency evacuation,' she replied.

A large pop-up window opened over the view of surrounding sky. Within it appeared a video feed of Alice sitting in her wheelchair at the desk in her office.

She looked around the cabin as if physically sitting among us. 'Thank goodness that you're all OK. You had me worried there for a while.'

'You and us both,' Jack replied with a smile.

Alice leant forward in her chair, her hands clasped together. 'So tell me everything.'

'You'd better get the coffee on then, because there's a lot to get through,' I said.

She smiled. 'I'll get a large pot. But you won't be left out. If you check the compartments under your chairs, you'll find a thermos for each of you with coffee or tea prepared according to your preferred poison.'

I quickly found an insulated pot of tea, some milk and Earl Grey teabags. 'You, Alice, are a flipping saint,' I said.

I noticed from the monitors that we had just crossed over the Peruvian coastline. The Flying Armadillo began to bank gently on a new heading to run parallel to it. A short while later, tea now brewing, I settled back into my seat and started to relax for the first time in what felt like a lifetime, and we began to brief Alice about everything that had happened.

CHAPTER TWENTY-SEVEN

It had taken a good couple of hours to get Alice up to speed, from the discovery of the underworld temple at Machu Picchu to the battle with the Overseers up on Choquequirao and then outside Cachora.

Alice, via her video feed, had listened intently throughout, asking a few questions here and there. What had got the biggest reaction was when I'd shown her the faint white scar on my stomach. I'd explained how Lucy had given me six months of healing time in E8, but how that had been the equivalent of just a couple of heartbeats in our world. She had shaken her head with a combined expression of shock and amazement.

'So much for this being a stealth mission,' she said as she leant back in her wheelchair and sipped her third mug of coffee.

'I have to take responsibility for that,' I said. 'I was the one in charge.'

Jack shook his head. 'Responsibility may go with the role, but what happened certainly isn't on you. The important thing is that you kept it together when things went off the rails, as I knew you would.'

Mike nodded. 'None of us would be sitting here now without your leadership, Lauren. Your quick thinking got us out of some tight corners.'

'But I felt out of my depth almost all of the time.'

'That's an entirely normal aspect of being in charge,' Alice said. 'A good leader is one who knows how to adapt to a situation and when to take risks to get things done.'

'I guess, but I can't help think about Ricardo getting killed.'

Niki shook his head. 'Hey, don't be so hard on yourself. Any blood spilt is either on the hands of Alvarez or Villca.'

'I know you're right in my head, but it just doesn't feel that way in my heart.'

Jack patted my arm. 'Give it time and it will start to.'

I gave him a grateful smile.

'And one thing you really mustn't lose sight of is all the good you've done,' Alice said. 'The rumours about the discovery of a hidden temple covered with gold beneath Machu Picchu have spread like wildfire across the internet. They're already saying it's the archaeological discovery of the century and it will transform the local economy. I will personally ensure that any local people who have been affected by what happened are duly compensated via one of my charitable organisations.'

I thought of all the guides living in Cristina's apartment block. At least that was something. 'It's just a shame that Jack can't take any credit for finding that underworld temple.'

He shrugged. 'No, I'm good. Just being there was enough for me. But please tell me that the authorities have got their hands on Evelyn Fischer?'

'I'm afraid there's been no mention of her in any of the reports, so it's likely she's already fled the country,' Niki replied.

'With the Overseers backing her, I think you can take that as a given,' Alice said.

'And what about Cristina being taken hostage?' I asked. 'Is there anything we can do to help her?'

'We'll spread the word around our contacts, but I suspect Alvarez will keep her close. With Cristina they now have the same edge that you have given us with the Angelus micro minds.'

'But surely she wouldn't work willingly for Alvarez,' Mike said. 'After all, they abducted her from her husband and child.'

Jack scowled. 'But she wasn't exactly behaving like a hostage around Alvarez.'

'We don't know what he did to her, Jack,' I said. 'Maybe she's just playing along until she finds the opportunity to escape.'

'Maybe...' He pulled a face at me.

I couldn't help but feel he had a point, though. But if that was true, I had no idea what Cristina's motivation could be.

'One thing is for sure, this mission became far more dangerous than any of us realised,' Alice said. 'We'll need to rethink any further missions for your group.'

'What do you mean?' Jack asked.

'We're going to make a change to your team, for your own safety.'

I thinned my lips at Alice. 'If you're considering getting rid of any of us, you can think again.'

Alice held up her hands. 'No, you misunderstand me, Lauren. I mean, you need an additional military specialist on your team to deal with the combat situations you seem to keep finding yourselves in.'

I gestured towards Jack. 'But we already have him.'

'With all due respect, and I'm sure you'll be the first to agree, Jack, he might be a trained soldier, but his speciality is field trauma.'

'Absolutely,' Jack said.

Alice sat back and gazed at us. 'Before you think I'm taking anything away from any of you in being able to look after yourselves, I'm really not. You have shown yourselves more than capable. However, Tom had already been thinking that adding a highly trained military expert to your team wouldn't hurt.'

I turned the thought over in my head. 'I'd be the first to admit that some of the tough calls I've had to make in combat situations haven't always sat easily with me.'

Mike nodded. 'And you know my thoughts on the matter of taking anyone's life.'

'Look, before you paint me as a crazed killing machine, I only did what had to be done because I had to,' Jack said. 'If someone wants to take that load off, I'd be more than happy.'

'So you're open to the idea of introducing somebody who could add to what your team can do in the field?' Niki asked.

I glanced at Mike and Jack, who both nodded. 'That's a yes from the three of us. Have you got someone in mind?'

Alice's gaze turned to Ruby. 'How about it, Ruby?'

Ruby stared at her. 'Seriously, Alice?'

'If the group are happy for you to join them, I certainly am too. You are a highly skilled soldier who could help keep this team alive.'

'I'd be happy to – if Lauren, Mike and Jack are OK with it?'

I glanced at Jack and Mike. 'That's a big fat yes from us, especially after what we've seen you can do.'

'Then count me in,' Ruby said.

'We're going to need a name for our group at this rate,' Mike said.

'The misfits?' I suggested.

Mike snorted. 'Works for me.'

Jack shook his head. 'You Brits are just so weird, but fine, let's go with that.'

'I rather like it,' Ruby said with a grin.

'All right, now that's sorted out, I need to brief you on the recent major development I hinted at earlier,' Alice said.

The cockpit display next to Alice's video window showed a point of light growing fast.

Ruby was already revolving her chair towards it. 'Delphi, have you got a lock on the incoming bogey?'

'Negative – the object has no radar signature,' the AI replied.

'Crap, so it could be a stealth missile.' Ruby grabbed the joystick in the left arm of her chair. 'Delphi, magnify object.'

A pop-up screen appeared and zoomed in over the object.

The tension flowed from me. 'Ruby, you can relax. It looks as if Lucy's about to make a house call in her newly combined ship.'

Ruby nodded and breathed out loudly.

The combined tetrahedrons raced towards us. At the last moment the craft switched direction to fly parallel to the Armadillo.

Alice stared to the side of the camera, presumably at what we were seeing. 'Very impressive. Lucy must be using a similar anti-gravity drive to the one the TR-3B uses. I wonder if she would share the specs of the drive with us.'

'That's an interesting question. I'll put it to her. Normally her programming would prevent her from giving us tech we don't already have, but she already replicated an antigravity device that the Overseers used to transport her.'

Alice sat up straighter. 'You mean she could give us the key to developing a workable drive for my experimental craft, *Ariel*?'

'Since the Overseers already have it, I don't see why not. Anyway, I doubt Lucy is out for a joyride, so I'd better check in with her. I'll ask her as soon as I get a chance.'

'If she agreed, our efforts would be greatly propelled. It would open up all sorts of possibilities.'

'Then leave it with me.' I took the Empyrean Key out of my rucksack and struck it with the tuning fork. At once the multi-pointed star icon appeared, already pulsing. 'Good news – it looks as if Lucy wants us to pop over to E8 to see her.'

Niki sat up. 'Whilst we fly at high speed?'

'Knowing Lucy, that won't be any problem.' I looked back to Alice. 'Please don't freak when we cross over to the other dimension and vanish.'

'Thank you for the heads-up. I'll put some more coffee on and will be waiting for your update.'

'Does that mean everyone else on the Armadillo will travel over as well?' Ruby asked.

'No idea. Maybe it'd be best to put the craft on autopilot just in case.'

'You got it,' Niki said. 'Delphi, you heard Lauren. Engage autopilot.'

'Engaged,' Delphi replied.

'OK, get ready for the rush,' I said. I selected the E8 icon and flicked my wrist forward.

The cabin vanished around us and, like a cut edit in a film, we were back in Lucy's tropical paradise. Now there was a dining table set out on the sand with seats for six people. Niki and Ruby were with us, but the rest of the security team in the rear compartment were nowhere to be seen. This was obviously invite only.

Niki gasped as he took in our new situation. 'But this is incredible.'

'That is the understatement of the century, Captain,' Ruby said, shaking her head.

In a semi-transparent silky dress that Mike was having a hard time not to goggle at, Lucy approached us holding a silver bucket filled with ice and a bottle of champagne. She placed it down in the middle of the table, turned to Niki and Ruby and shook their hands.

'Welcome to my own little slice of heaven in E8.'

Niki stared at her. 'You're really an AI?'

'The last time I checked. Do please call me Lucy.'

'Right...' He scraped his hand through his hair.

I had a pretty good idea how they were feeling right now – I'd been there.

Lucy beamed at Jack, Mike and me, giving us each a tight hug in turn. 'You guys are simply the best. Huge congratulations on what you just pulled off.' She gestured to the bucket and pulled out the champagne from the ice. 'I for one think we need to celebrate.'

'A big fat yes to that,' Mike replied.

She grinned at him and popped the cork. A moment later the six champagne flutes on the table had been filled and Lucy was handing them to us.

I took a sip and let the bubbles tingle over my tongue. 'Oh, the good stuff.'

'The very best, Dom Pérignon, which I believe humans highly rate.'

'Well, it's a lot better than my usual bottle of Prosecco for a fiver from the local Co-op.'

'Oh, you're worth such a lot more than that to me,' Lucy replied, smiling.

'You're pretty special yourself,' Mike said, looping his arm round Lucy's waist and squeezing her.

I was fighting the urge to be sick in my mouth when I caught Niki giving Mike a look set to kill, almost as if Mike was propositioning his daughter. Mike, however, had let his arm fall away, hadn't noticed anything. Bless him and his thick skin. But why was Niki reacting like that anyway? It wasn't like it was his business really.

'I need to update you with what I've learnt since merging with the other micro mind,' Lucy said.

'Which is?' Jack asked.

'I now know where that virus came from that attacked the systems of my linked micro minds. The Kimprak were behind it.'

A cold feeling of dread worked its way up through me. 'You mean they've already been here to Earth, like the Angelus?'

Lucy shook her head. 'Thankfully no. If that were the case, there wouldn't be life of any kind left. The virus that attacked the systems actually originated in the Tau Ceti system.'

'How did it get from there to here?' Ruby asked.

'An Angelus probe, part of a network left behind by them to monitor the development of life across millions of systems, was monitoring an M-class planet in the system, waiting for sentient life to develop. It had been carrying out this mission for half a million years when the Kimprak asteroid ship arrived in the Tau Ceti system. With no way to intervene, since the probe was simply a monitoring device, the AI could only stand by and witness the atrocities the Kimprak carried out as they mined the world and destroyed all life on the M-class planet. But that probe waited for the Kimprak to depart Tau Ceti and then was able to extrapolate the flight path to predict the next destination of the Kimprak ship.'

'Which we now know was Earth,' Mike said.

Lucy nodded. 'When the probe's AI realised the destination, it followed its programming and transmitted an emergency warning of the coming threat to my micro minds. Unfortunately, during that broadcast, it made itself visible across a wide spectrum of frequencies. The Kimprak attacked the probe and managed to embed a virus into its data signal. And that's when the advanced Angelus technology made the situation far worse.'

'How exactly?' I asked.

'That probe and my micro minds were linked together by a quantum-entanglement system that allowed instant communication however great the distance between the Angelus and the AIs. Thanks to this, the Kimprak virus was simultaneously transmitted to every one of my micro minds hidden here on Earth. There was only time for a single emergency protocol to be triggered, meaning many higher-level functions were wiped out, preventing them from falling under the control of the Kimprak. Although the attack was almost simultaneous across my entire network on Earth, my core micro mind was the last link in the communications relay by two billionths of a second. In that tiny window of time I was able to put my own high-level systems into a deep sleep state. All this happened nearly four years ago. It was that hibernation mode that you woke me from when you found me.'

'Can the damage to the other micro minds be repaired?' Mike asked.

'Thankfully, yes. The reintegration of the second micro mind has already demonstrated this. There is no reason for the rest of the micro minds not to wake now too.'

'So now we know who attacked you, but why?' Niki asked.

'I presume they saw me as a threat, but in what way I don't know. The only clue I've learnt from the second micro mind is the existence of a common algorithm very deep within our code.'

'Which does what?' I asked.

'That's the problem – there is no usual help file with it. All I can gather is that it's also something to do with defending this planet from the Kimprak threat.'

'But we still don't know how exactly?' Mike said.

Lucy shook her head. 'Unfortunately not, and it's so frustrating. I can sense the fingerprints of the code of that algorithm throughout my systems. And every instinct, as you humans would say, tells me that it's something incredible waiting to be unlocked. However, for reasons best known to my Angelus creators, they have made it very difficult for a single micro mind to access and activate it directly. By my estimate, I will need to have integrated at least seven micro minds in order to activate this secret protocol buried within me.'

'It sounds as if it's something designed to be used in extreme situations,' Mike said.

'But if that's true, why make it so difficult to get at?' I replied.

'Could it be the equivalent of an Armageddon weapon, something that could destroy an entire world?' Niki asked.

'Whatever it is, it's locked away behind multiple firewalls,' Lucy said. 'Think of a long corridor with a sequence of doors across it, each one being a firewall. We've just unlocked the first door.'

'And the prize is at the end behind the final door, right?' Jack asked.

'Just so,' Lucy replied. 'But maybe we have one clue. Did you happen to hear something when our micro minds merged?'

'Yes, it sounded like the whale song we heard back at Choquequirao,' Jack said.

'That was actually a harmonic broadcast triggered by the algorithm. And even though I can't directly analyse it, I can see its effect. Like striking your tuning fork against the Empyrean Key, Lauren, that sound vibrated through this entire planet's core. It also subtly changed the Earth Song of this planet, just as I did when I was first activated.'

'And what's the significance of this?' I asked.

Lucy gave me a helpless look and shook her head. 'I don't know. But if we discover any further micro minds, we will hopefully find the answer to that question.'

'There can be no *hopefully* about it,' Jack said. 'We *have* to find them. I don't even want to think about the alternative.'

Ruby nodded. 'Absolutely.'

'Lucy, there's something you may be able to help Alice with,' I said. 'Think of it as a plan B. You know you replicated that anti-gravity drive plate of the Overseers? Would it be possible for you to help Alice develop her own drive for the *Ariel* craft she's been working on?'

'Well, as the Overseers already have ships with it, I don't see why not. My core programming should accept that as a valid reason. And now I have a certain level of control over my flight systems, I can make regular contact with you, if that would help?'

'Of course it would. That would be amazing.' My heart lifted. Of everything, this was almost the biggest deal to me. No longer would I be wondering where Lucy was. From now on, if we really needed her, she would be by our side – mine specifically.

'Alice will be delighted,' Niki said. 'You working directly with us will be a huge asset. Especially now the Overseers seem prepared to deploy their Astras against us, which could be a major issue in future missions.'

'*Future missions* is about the last thing on my mind right now,' Mike said. 'All I want to do is get back and have a beer or three in the Rock Garden.'

Lucy clicked her fingers and Mike's champagne glass was replaced with a bottle of beer. 'Well, part of that can start right now.'

Jack gave Lucy a guilty look. 'Hey, I don't suppose you have one of those for me? I've always been more a beer man.'

Ruby widened her eyes just a fraction. 'And me...?'

'Of course,' Lucy replied. She snapped her fingers and beer bottles appeared in Jack and Ruby's hands.

Lucy raised her glass of champagne. 'Before we discuss anything else, I'd like to propose a toast. Here's to saving your planet.'

'To saving our planet,' we all echoed. I took a sip of champagne and clinked my glass on Jack's beer bottle. Over his shoulder I noticed a lone seagull wheel over the ocean. As it rose into the sky, my heart soared with it. It was starting to feel as if we really might have a chance against the Kimprak after all.

LINKS

Do please leave that all important review for **Earth Cry** here: https://geni.us/EarthCry

So now you've finished **Earth Cry** are you ready for the next book in the series?

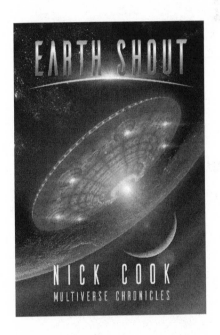

On the eve of launching a network of CubeSats, Tom is still missing in the field. What happened to him and why is Alice, president of the Sky Dreamer Corp, so evasive whenever his name is brought up? Back at Eden, Ariel is nearing completion – Sky Dreamer Corp's own secret antigravity prototype craft that promises to give them the edge they so badly need in their fight against the Overseers. But with tensions within the team at an all-time high, can Lauren find her feet as the true leader she needs to become to guide the others through their greatest challenge yet?

Earth Cry is available now on Kindle, in paperback and free within KU Unlimited. You can buy Earth Shout here: https://geni.us/EarthShout

OTHER BOOKS BY NICK COOK

Prequel to the Multiverse Chronicles

The Earth Song Series (The Multiverse Chronicles)

The Fractured Light Trilogy (The Multiverse Chronicles)

AFTERWORD

So here we are again at the end of another book, one that has been incredibly interesting to write.

I probably had far too much fun coming up with the concept of Eden. It was an idea that just seemed to grow and grow with each edit. As well as SPECTRE's volcano lair from the James Bond movie *You Only Live Twice*, I was also influenced by the Krell's hidden city in one of my all-time favourite sci-fi movies *Forbidden Planet*. But there was also a third influence at work – and a real-life one – Biosphere 2, an attempt to recreate Earth's natural biological systems within a closed environment. This certainly needs to be cracked if we are to have self-sustaining space colonies on planets such as Mars in the future. The intention with Biosphere 2 was to create an environment where water, food and oxygen were all generated within the habitation. It didn't exactly go to plan, but a lot was learnt from the experiment. I recreated this project on a far smaller scale in the Mars simulation chamber within Eden. If you're interested in learning more about Biosphere 2, I recommend you watch this documentary: https://www.youtube.com/watch?v=-yAcD3wuY2Q.

Another area that I briefly touch upon in *Earth Cry* is research into technologies that might be able to help reverse global warming. Again, this is based on real and ongoing experimental work. The brilliant Joe Scott discusses some of the current possibilities in this excellent documentary: https://www.youtube.com/watch?v=GfRo8_RfefA. It's well worth subscribing to his channel if you're interested in this topic.

The vectoring rocket engine is also a real rocket design by NASA, but abandoned for cost reasons despite promising results. Curious Droid, another great YouTube channel, gives a fascinating insight into aerospike engines here: https://www.youtube.com/watch?v=K4zFefh5T-8.

Away from the technology, Machu Picchu is the main setting in the book. I visited the site a few years ago and I could honestly have spent chapters just describing how jaw-dropping it really is. But there's another reason why Machu Picchu is close to my heart...it's where I proposed to my wife, Karen. Thankfully she said yes – whilst the llamas looked on slightly mystified. There's a good reason why it's on many people's bucket lists and all I can say is that it lives up to the hype. If you ever get a chance, do go. This video will give you a feel for what Machu Picchu is all about: https://www.youtube.com/watch?v=lNIEZ61PyGo.

Thank you for reading *Earth Cry*. If you're reading on a Kindle, please take two minutes before you go to click to the next page and leave an Amazon review. Or if you're reading a paperback, hop over to the Amazon or Goodreads website and leave your thoughts there. Each review really does help to spread the word.

Finally, to get exclusive cover reveals, writing and sneak peeks of my new books, you can subscribe to my newsletter here: www.subscribepage.com/b4n4n4.

Lauren and the team will return in *Earth Shout* in the not-so-distant future. I will be back!

Nick Cook, July 2019

Made in the USA
Columbia, SC
14 October 2021

47172018R00183